## WATER TOO LONG.

His head was pounding, and his heart was hammering. There was a bad pain in his chest, and he felt like something was going to burst any minute.

Something was holding down the eight-year-old, preventing him from rising to the surface. He bent over double to claw at the thing that was wrapped around his legs. He touched it, grabbed it, and felt it move in his hand.

He pried at the thing, and tried to loosen its grip on his legs. Finally, he felt the thing let go. As he kicked off the bottom, he looked back to see what awful sea monster had been holding him underwater.

It was a girl, or what was left of a girl. Jess knew instinctively that she was dead, although he had never seen a dead person before. She had grayish white skin that hung loosely on her skeleton and flapped as the lake water lapped around her.

She was the most horrible thing he had ever seen; and, just before he blacked out, he realized that she wasn't alone. There were three of them, three little dead girls with the loose skin of their faces arranged in what might have passed as smiles, their stick-thin arms reaching up for him . . .

**Prepare Yourself for**

# PATRICIA WALLACE

LULLABYE                                        (2917, $3.95/$4.95)
Eight-year-old Bronwyn knew she wasn't like other girls. She didn't
have a mother. At least, not a real one. Her mother had been in a
coma at the hospital for as long as Bronwyn could remember. She
couldn't feel any pain, her father said. But when Bronwyn sat with
her mother, she knew her mother was angry—angry at the nurses and
doctors, and her own helplessness. Soon, she would show them all the
true meaning of suffering . . .

MONDAY'S CHILD                                  (2760, $3.95/$4.95)
Jill Baker was such a pretty little girl, with long, honey-blond hair
and haunting gray-green eyes. Just one look at her angelic features
could dispel all the nasty rumors that had been spreading around
town. There were all those terrible accidents that had begun to plague
the community, too. But the fact that each accident occurred after
little Jill had been angered had to be coincidence . . .

SEE NO EVIL                                     (2429, $3.95/$4.95)
For young Caryn Dearborn, the cornea operation enabled her to see
more than light and shadow for the first time. For Todd Reynolds, it
was his chance to run and play like other little boys. For these two
children, the sudden death of another child had been the miracle they
had been waiting for. But with their eyesight came another kind of
vision—of evil, horror, destruction. They could see into other
people's minds, their worst fears and deepest terrors. And they could
see the gruesome deaths that awaited the unwary . . .

THRILL                                          (3142, $4.50/$5.50)
It was an amusement park like no other in the world. A tri-level mar-
vel of modern technology enhanced by the special effects wizardry of
holograms, lasers, and advanced robotics. Nothing could go wrong—
until it did. As the crowds swarmed through the gates on Opening
Day, they were unprepared for the disaster about to strike. Rich and
poor, young and old would be taken for the ride of their lives, trapped
in a game of epic proportions where only the winners survived . . .

*Available wherever paperbacks are sold, or order direct from the
Publisher. Send cover price plus 50¢ per copy for mailing and
handling to Zebra Books, Dept. 4093, 475 Park Avenue South,
New York, N.Y. 10016. Residents of New York and Tennessee
must include sales tax. DO NOT SEND CASH. For a free Zebra/
Pinnacle catalog please write to the above address.*

# BLACK ICE
## PAT GRAVERSEN

**ZEBRA BOOKS**
**KENSINGTON PUBLISHING CORP.**

ZEBRA BOOKS

are published by

Kensington Publishing Corp.
475 Park Avenue South
New York, NY 10016

First Printing: March, 1993

Printed in the United States of America

*This book is dedicated to Barbara Sarotte, my sister, my friend, my constant source of medical information, and to my sister-under-the-skin, Helen Cavanagh, my fellow travelers through this never-endings circle we call Time.*

"Take what you want," said God, "and pay for it."

Spanish proverb

# *Prologue*

*Winter Falls, Connecticut*
*The summer of 1928*

The three young men met at the public library after dark and strolled toward Jeremy Winter's house on the edge of town.

"Did you get the stuff?" Jeremy asked, after glancing around to assure himself that no one could overhear their conversation.

"Right here." Colin McCall shook the paper sack he carried at his side and rattled its contents. "Are you ready, Johnny?" he asked, grinning mischievously.

"This is a mistake," Johnny Gibson answered. "we don't know what we could be letting ourselves in for." He was the practical one of the three, the one who always played devil's advocate to the schemes of the fun-loving Colin and the innocent Jeremy.

"It's all in fun, Johnny, but if you're scared, just go on home, and Colin and I will do it alone, won't we, Colin?" Jeremy walked backward in front of them, barely able to contain his excitement.

"Sure." Colin grinned again and slapped Johnny Gibson on the back, confident that he wouldn't abandon them. The three had been friends ever since Colin could remember, just he and Johnny, from first grade on, until Jeremy, who was four years

7

younger, had started following them around and, eventually, joined them. Puberty, sexual initiation, their first drunken binge—they had been through all of it together, and Colin didn't plan to go through tonight's ritual without Johnny by his side.

They had been planning this evening for a long time, waiting for all the elements to fall into place. Now they had, and when Jeremy's parents announced that they were taking their 1927 touring Model-T and driving into New York City for the weekend, Colin had quickly assembled the items they would need and enlisted Jeremy to make the necessary preparations at the house.

Jeremy's grandfather had founded the town of Winter Falls and his family still lived in the rambling mansion the old man had built for his family on its northernmost boundary. The house was huge, and Colin had once literally gotten lost wandering through its circuitous corridors while he waited for Jeremy.

Tonight, the three old friends crossed a side porch and entered the house through a door which opened onto the rear staircase, once used by servants. On the second floor, Jeremy led them down a narrow hallway and stopped beneath a piece of rope that dangled from the ceiling. No one said a word as he reached for the rope and jerked it, lowering a set of steps that would allow them access to the attic.

Colin felt a weird sensation in the pit of his stomach, something like the feeling he experienced when he kissed a pretty girl and wondered if he would be able to talk her into bed before the end of the evening. He led the way up the ladder, the brave and fearless leader of his little pack.

It was dark in the attic, which had only one narrow window to admit the light of the pale yellow moon. Jeremy removed a flashlight from his pocket and flicked it on, then waved it around to impress his friends with the preparations he had made. Colin was glad to see that his instructions had been followed. The trunks and boxes had been cleared out of the attic's main room, leaving a large, cavernous expanse in which to mount their experiment. A perfect circle had been drawn on the narrow floorboards with blue chalk, and inside the circle, a pentagram. Jeremy was an artist, and his talent was evident in even this simple design. Colin gave Jeremy a thumbs-up sign, and began to empty the contents of his paper bag inside the circle.

Johnny pulled matches out of his pants pocket and lit the two black candles Colin had purchased through the mail from an occult supply store in New York City. Jeremy lifted the wooden crucifix, stared at it for a minute, then turned it upside down, with the head of Christ pointing toward the floor. He balanced it on an easel set on a small table he had previously placed within the circle. He turned when he became aware of Colin's eyes on him, and at that moment, Colin almost decided to call it off. Maybe Johnny was right, maybe they were taking a chance, playing around with something dangerous, something they didn't understand. Then Jeremy smiled, and Colin smiled back, ashamed of his own cowardice.

"Whatever happens, don't leave the circle of protection," Johnny said, as if he had memorized that line and needed to say it, so that later he could say: "I warned them. They can't say I didn't warn them."

"Are we ready?" Colin asked, and when his two friends nodded, he lifted the upside-down crucifix and spoke in a loud, clear voice: "O Lord of Fire! O Lord of Air! O Lord of the Earth! Satan, come forth and bless us with your presence!"

There was no light in the attic room except from the flickering candle flames and the pale moonlight which had crept in through the room's single window. But the room seemed to be getting darker

9

with every word that Colin spoke. The candle flames sputtered, and their melting wax emitted a bitter smell that made him feel nauseous.

He laid the crucifix aside and forced himself to raise the antique silver bowl he had taken from his mother's china cupboard. He touched it to his lips. He gagged as the warm blood touched his mouth, but he managed to swallow a few drops of it before he passed the bowl to Johnny. Johnny's eyes met Colin's but the question had already been answered once, and Colin refused to answer it again. He had bought a live chicken and cut off its head with an axe; he wouldn't give them any more than that. If he had enjoyed it, if he had wondered what it would be like to take a human life, that was his own business, not theirs.

The three joined hands and, their lips stained with sacrificial blood, they called on Satan to appear in their midst.

"Luficer! Beelzebub! Mephistopheles! Appear to us now!" Jeremy's clear tenor rang out, and Colin incongruously remembered that his young friend had for years been a soloist in the church choir.

"Prince of Darkness! Lord of the Underworld! We are your humble servants." Johnny's voice was deep, gentle, reassuring, cultivated for years to complement his professional bedside manner.

Colin raised his own voice in supplication, calling out the names he had memorized in preparation for this night: "Belial, Meresin, Abaddon, Mammon! Come forth!"

But no one came. The room was getting too warm, up under the eaves on a hot summer night. Jeremy made a motion with his hands to mimic opening the window, and Colin glanced at Johnny before agreeing. Jeremy stepped cautiously out of the circle, stood still for a long, tense moment, then walked rapidly to the window. At first, it seemed as if it wouldn't open, then the wooden sash creaked and it moved upward a few inches. Jeremy returned to the circle of protection and let out a sigh of relief when he was back within its boundaries.

The three men formed their own small circle and remained standing. Colin now held the reverse crucifix at arm's length over his head, offering this symbol of his depravity to the entity they were calling forth from the nether land.

Several long minutes passed, and Colin was about to suggest that they repeat the chant when Jeremy suddenly spoke, his voice loud in the huge, silent house.

"What was that? I heard something."

"Shhh," Johnny hissed. "You'll break the spell."

"Repeat the chant," Colin ordered in a tense whisper, but when neither of the others found their voice, he cleared his throat and spoke into the deepening blackness of the room.

"Lucifer, Beelzebub, Mephistopheles! Prince of Darkness, Lord of the Universe! Belial, Satan, Meresin, Abaddon, Mammon!" The names slipped off his tongue as if they were the language of his childhood.

His voice rose as he repeated the musical chant again: "Lucifer . . . Satan . . . Belial . . ."

A booming clap of thunder shook the house and scared the three friends half out of their minds. Colin could feel Jeremy shaking, and he felt Johnny's hand on his arm, as cold as ice.

The thunder had barely stopped reverberating through the room when Jeremy whispered again: "I hear something," and no one shushed him this time because they heard it, too.

It wouldn't have been a frightening noise to hear in the bright sunlight of a summer's day. But this was the dark of night, the witching hour, and the noise was the most terrible thing Colin had ever heard in his entire life. It was a soft hiss, a gurgle, like the release of steam from a radiator. Like that, but not that.

11

Johnny poked Colin in the ribs, and they both held onto Jeremy, who was swaying back and forth, doing a slow dance step, heel to toe, toe to heel. In the far corner of the room, the corner farthest from the candle light, a thin column of gray smoke rose up from the floor. Jeremy giggled nervously, and Colin put his free hand over his friend's mouth to silence him. The three instinctively moved closer together, and Colin could feel Jeremy trembling violently.

A breeze came in through the open window, and the black candles sputtered but the misty smoke-thing remained the same. It undulated as it moved languidly upward, floor to ceiling, mesmerizing the three friends, who clutched at each other's arms and leaned against each other for support.

"Say something," Colin muttered under his breath, "finish the ceremony."

"Come, Master, visit us and grant our wishes." Johnny Gibson's voice was shaky but it was loud, and maybe that's what put Colin over the edge.

"Cut it out, you assholes, you're both acting like you're scared shitless." He released Jeremy's arm and took a half step backward, separating himself from the fear that left a sickening stench in the air around them.

"And you're not scared?" Johnny whispered, but Colin didn't have a chance to form an answer.

"Look!" Jeremy yelled, and pointed toward the corner where the gray smoke still hung in the air.

"There's something there, Colin, what do we do now?" Johnny had gotten control of himself, but the sound of his voice was still irritating to Colin.

He turned and glanced at the corner, and felt the hair stand up all over his body. There was definitely something in the corner, something taking shape, something forming and moving slowly in their direction. There was also a horrible smell, and it wasn't from the candles or from his friends' fear. It was the odor of sulphur, strong and acrid, and it was coming from the thing in the corner.

Jeremy whimpered and grabbed ahold of Colin's arms.

"It's going to hurt us," he whined, "it's going to hurt us, Colin." He cried and pulled on Colin's arms, stepping dangerously close to the edge of the circle.

"Stop it, damn it!" Colin wrestled his arms out of Jeremy's grip and shoved his friend away from him. It all happened so fast that Colin could never remember the sequence of events clearly. Jeremy tottered, fell backwards, tried to regain his balance, stumbled and landed on his hands and knees outside the circle. Johnny started to go after him, but Colin instinctively held him back, and they watched together as the awful black shadow twisted and seemed to become aware of Jeremy's predicament. It moved toward him, as fast as a lightning flash, before Colin could even begin to think about what he should do next. Jeremy saw it coming and lashed out, flailing his arms and legs, butting at it with his head, but he might just as well have been striking it with a feather. He screamed as the thing moved over him, into him, absorbed him and turned him into itself, making him one with it.

It was over and done with in seconds, but Colin and Johnny were afraid to move out of their protective circle for several minutes. They were both shaking so badly that they could hardly stand, and Johnny was praying out loud, begging God's forgiveness. Jeremy lay on the attic floor in a fetal position, hugging himself and blubbering, while his friends looked on helplessly and shivered from the sudden cold in the room.

After a period of time that neither of them would have been able to identify, Johnny stepped out of the circle and Colin followed. Together, they approached Jeremy with caution. They rolled him over onto his back, and Colin was overcome with a sense of horror and unreality. Jeremy looked up at him, and Colin

13

knew that whatever had made his friend a unique human being was gone. Jeremy was gone; the thing that lay drooling on the attic floor had absolutely no resemblance to Jeremy Winter. Colin would have sworn that it had no soul.

"Go downstairs and call my father." Johnny shouted. "For God's sake hurry!" Colin took one last look at Jeremy and ran from the room. He literally jumped from the attic to the second floor of the house and raced down the hallway, searching for a telephone. He found one in what appeared to be the master bedroom, and grabbed it up, shouting for the operator. In the seconds while he waited for her to answer, Colin McCall saw his future pass before his eyes. In two more years, he planned to graduate from Harvard Law School, the first college graduate in his family. The same year, Johnny Gibson would get his medical degree from Yale, so that he could go into practice with his father. That was supposed to be how it would happen, but it was all over now. Both of their lives would be ruined if they had caused Jeremy Winter irreparable harm. Jeremy's parents were rich and powerful figures in Winter Falls; they owned the bank and at least half of the real estate in the county.

Colin glanced at the telephone receiver he held in his hand, and a plan began to take shape. Maybe it was already too late for Jeremy, maybe nothing could be done for him. If it wasn't too late, well Johnny was halfway through medical school. If anything could be done to save Jeremy, Johnny could do it by himself, without his father's help, without having to inform everybody in town what they had done. Colin slammed the heavy black phone into its cradle and retraced his steps back to the attic, moving much more slowly than he had a few minutes ago, before he discovered that there was a lot more at stake than Jeremy Winter's life.

# Chapter One

*Winter Falls, Connecticut*
*January 1993*

It was fifteen degrees Fahrenheit on the January day that Cassandra McCall and her eight-year-old son, Jess, came back to Winter Falls, Connecticut. Cassie had left town when she was sixteen, and had sworn that she would never return. She had kept her promise to herself for ten years, until the day the telephone call came, and she knew she had no choice. Now here she was, on the porch of her parents' rickety old house, holding on for dear life to her little boy's hand.

"You like it, don't you, Jess?" she asked, but she already knew the answer. The boy was pulling her through the door, his curiosity far outweighing her hesitation. It would be the first house he'd ever lived in, after eight years of rooming houses and low-class apartments in Tucson and Phoenix. Cassie had never felt quite comfortable in her parents' house, and she felt that her presence there now was an intrusion, but how could she explain that to the child?

"Yeah, Mom, I like it fine," the boy answered her. "Are we going to live here for a long time?"

"For a while, we'll see." Her answer was purposely vague but Jess didn't seem to mind.

Cassie edged past the colorless old chair she had sat in as a teenager, legs thrown over one threadbare arm, until her father smacked her and told her to sit up straight, like a lady. Over there, to the left, the stairs that led up to her old bedroom, where she would make up the bed for her son with his own Christmas-new Ninja Turtle sheets, carried on the plane from Phoenix.

She stopped dead in the shabby dining room and looked up at the ceiling; beyond it, she found her childhood room, as if the years had been peeled away. She was sitting on the single bed, her long hair in braids, polishing her nails. Her father was there, too, in baggy brown pants and a grayish white T-shirt, a can of beer in his hand. He lounged in the doorway and stared at her until she looked up, then jumped and spilled the precious red polish on her bedspread.

"You'll pay for that, missy, out of your lunch money."

"But, Daddy—"

"Don't answer me back, girl, or you'll go without your supper tonight."

"I don't care." Then he was unbuckling his belt, smiling evilly, and the mature Cassie cried out for the young Cassie, who had been trapped in that room for sixteen long years.

"What's wrong, Mom?" Jess was tugging on her hand, trying to pull her in the direction of the staircase, but Cassie couldn't go up there yet. Instead, she steered him toward the kitchen, away from the bad memories.

In the room where Cassie felt her mother's presence most powerfully, there was worn linoleum on the countertops and the floor, and one shiny new, totally out-of-place touch: a fancy blender sitting in the middle of the kitchen table, like a centerpiece. She explained it to her son: "Your grandpa loves his milkshakes, chocolate made with real Hershey's syrup and French vanilla ice cream. He drinks one every day for lunch, every day of his life, has ever since I can remember. At least, he did."

"Can I have one for lunch tomorrow, too?" the boy asked.

"Sure you can." Sure you can—if there's ice cream left in the freezer and Hershey's syrup in the cupboard over the stove. Otherwise—

Cassie was broke, she wasn't sure she had enough money left to see them through the week for staples, let alone extras, like ice cream, but that was nothing new. When the private investigator had walked into the bar where she was working days while Jess was in school, she had been broke. When the telephone call came the next day, from Dr. John Gibson, III, she had been forced to accept his offer of one-way plane tickets from Phoenix to Bradley International Airport, just north of Hartford, where he'd had them picked up and brought here, back to the scene of her miserable childhood.

"Are you gonna cook dinner tonight, Mom?" Jess was opening the cupboards he could reach, examining their meager contents, probably looking for peanut butter or Spaghetti-O's.

"Sure, if we can find something to cook," Cassie answered. "There might not be anything you like here, your grandpa is a few years older than you are. He might not have the same taste in food as you do."

The boy giggled at that, as Cassie gave up on her own perusal of the refrigerator and decided to try the freezer. "Nothing much here, either. I don't know, honey—"

The doorbell rang, and Jess took off running through the house, which was laid out like a railroad flat, kitchen in the back, dining room in the middle, living room in front. On the second floor, two bedrooms and a storage room followed the same simple floor plan, with the addition of a narrow hallway that created a little more privacy.

"Jess, don't—" Cassie yelled, but it was too late to

17

stop him. She heard the door scrape across the warped entryway floor, heard it slam shut behind their visitor.

"Who is it, Jess?" She reached the living room in time to see Dr. John Gibson throw his head back and forth, as if he thought he could shake off the cold. He was bundled to the teeth, his cheeks rosy, his nose red as Rudolph the reindeer's, almost as red as his hair.

"With that hair, I'd know you anywhere," Cassie told him as she took one of the brown grocery bags from his arms and carried it back to the kitchen.

"You haven't changed a bit," he returned, "you're still the prettiest girl in town."

Cassie blushed and used her son as an excuse to change the subject. "This is Jess," she said, touching the back of his head, moving him closer. "Say hello to Dr. Gibson, Jess."

"Hello," the boy said obediently before he wiggled out of his mother's grasp. He climbed onto a kitchen chair for a better view of the goodies the young doctor was unloading: a half gallon of French vanilla ice cream and a container of Hershey's syrup, Skippy peanut butter, a box of Cocoa Puffs, and, wonder of wonders, two cans of Spaghetti-O's. Jess lost interest when he saw that the other bag contained cold cuts, a loaf of bread, a tub of whipped butter, and other things that grown-ups thought were necessities.

"What is all this?" Cassie asked.

"I thought you might need a few things to get you through till tomorrow. Here, Jess." The doctor took a lined pencil tablet from the second bag and offered it to the boy. "I thought you might like to keep a record of your adventures in Winter Falls, to take back to Phoenix with you."

Cassie waited until Jess expressed his thanks before she picked up her conversation with this man who had been a boy of eighteen the last time she saw him.

"We don't need charity, doctor."

*"Gibby,* my name is *Gibby.* That's what you called me when we were kids, and that's what I want you to call me now. I know you don't need charity, and this isn't charity. There's plenty of money in the bank, we just have to get your dad to sign a power of attorney in the morning."

When she just stared at him without speaking, Gibby repeated himself. "There's always been plenty of money."

"I don't understand. If there was always plenty of money, why did they live like this?"

"Truth?"

"Truth."

"I don't have a clue." Gibby laughed, then Jess laughed, and it was easy for Cassie to laugh along with them. She allowed herself to think that maybe, just maybe coming home hadn't been such a bad idea after all.

She fed Jess while she and the doctor carried on a forced conversation about old times, skirting around the subjects they couldn't discuss. Finally the doctor left for the night and Jess was sound asleep in the double bed Cassie had decided to share with him until she had enough nerve to open the door to her old bedroom—and her mood changed.

"Why did I come back here?" she wondered aloud, as she prowled through the old house, opening and closing all the doors but one. "What did I think I could do here? Did I really think he'd want me to come back?" She finally sat down on the living-room sofa, another relic from her childhood, and let the long-submerged memories flood into her conscious mind. It wasn't surprising that the first one was about the lake.

Lake Wahelo. She was tempted to open the front door to the freezing cold air and stare out in the direction of the lake. You couldn't see it from the house. It was on the other side of the thick grove of trees called "the woods" by the townspeople. But

Cassie knew it was there; she knew its exact direction through the trees. It was Lake Wahelo that had put Winter Falls on the map in its little corner of the world. Every spring and summer people taking car or bicycle trips wandered into town and asked directions to the lake. Every fall, near Halloween, teenagers came in carloads, hoping to see the ghosts of the three little girls who had drowned there fifty years ago.

It was the last thing Cassie thought about before she fell asleep that night, with her precious Jess curled in her arms in her father's bed: how her three young aunts had died such horrible deaths, and how the town where they lived had immortalized them and thus gained immortality itself.

Across town, on the other side of the woods, a full moon floated in the midnight sky above Lake Wahelo. The smooth black surface of the several inches of ice that covered the lake did not reflect the light of the moon. The old-timers who hung out at Nell's Cafe could have told you that the light of the moon and the stars never reflected off the dull lake water or the ice that covered it. They said it was because the remains of the three small girls were down there, not in the plot marked out for them in Winter Falls Cemetery, that the waters of Lake Wahelo refused the light of the moon and the stars. Lake Wahelo, once called simply Winter Falls Lake, had been renamed for the three little girls who died there, their bodies never recovered to this day: Wanda, Helen and Lorraine McCall.

The next morning, as she prodded Jess to dress in a freezing cold bedroom, Cassie was still despondent. She turned up the heat when they went downstairs, and heard the ancient pipes start to crackle a few minutes later. A blue plastic bowl and a spoon, Cocoa Puffs and milk, and Jess stopped whining. Watching him eat, his blond head bent over the bowl, made Cassie feel better again. Not good, but better. She felt that with any luck at all her father's health

20

would improve, and he would be able to come home and take care of his own affairs again. If he had as much money as Gibby thought he did, he could surely afford a housekeeper, or a nurse to live with him. Then she and Jess could go back to Phoenix. Maybe her dad would even buy them a bus ticket or something. They could look for another tiny apartment, and she could probably get her old job back. Tiny said he always needed good barmaids. Yes, that's what would happen. Getting through the next few days would be the hard part, but she could do that. She'd certainly done worse in her lifetime.

"Come on, Jess," she urged, "let's be ready when Dr. Gibby gets here to pick us up."

"He's here, he's here," Jess yelled before Cassie even had time to put his bowl in the sink and run water into it. She tried to stuff the boy's skinny arms into the sleeves of his windbreaker while he tugged at the front door, but then the door was open and Jess was off and running with one sleeve of the jacket flapping.

Before she reached the car, Cassie heard the doctor's voice, and she had to smile. "Hey, son, this is the northeast, not the desert. Now put your other arm in that jacket and get it zipped up before your mother sees you and starts yelling at both of us."

As Cassie slid into the front seat of the doctor's Mercedes, she stole a glance at Jess, both arms in the sleeves of his thin jacket, which was zipped up to within a quarter inch of cutting off his breath.

"Are you sure he'll be all right with Mrs. Johnson?" she asked the doctor when they were on the road that led to her father's dry goods store.

"It's *Miss* Johnson, and he'll be fine. Marilou said she'd love to have the company. You and I will shoot over to Hartford to see your dad, then pick up Jess and take him out for a hamburger. You don't mind staying with Miss Marilou for a couple of hours, do you, Jess?"

"No sir."

"She's the only employee Daddy has?" Cassie asked, getting more nervous about leaving Jess as they neared the store.

"The only one he ever had, so far as I know. Your mother worked there right up until she got sick, and every time I went in there one or the other of them was behind the counter."

"Then he hired Marilou to take Momma's place?"

"Only behind the counter, Cassie. Whatever you're thinking, just put it out of your head."

The sign needed painting, but even without it everyone in town knew where The Dry Goods Emporium was and what they could buy there, which was a little bit of almost anything.

Inside, the aisles were dark and the display tables nearly empty. Obviously, nobody had bothered to replenish the inventory after the boss had a massive stroke and was carted away to the hospital in Hartford. Maybe they hadn't thought he'd come back, that the old store would just close up when it ran out of merchandise to sell.

"Well, I'm here now," Cassie said aloud, and elicited a strange, smug look from Gibby.

Marilou Johnson was nothing like Cassie had remembered her as, and her appearance was reassuring. The woman was tiny, short and frail, with wispy blond hair and enormous blue eyes. She was quiet and soft-spoken, and Jess took to her right away. Cassie kissed him on the cheek, whispered "love you" in his ear and went back to Gibby's car.

On the way to the hospital, Gibby reached over and held her hands steady to stop her from twisting them.

"I never got along with my father," she confessed when his hand was back on the wheel. What she wanted to say was that her father hated her, that she was afraid to see him again.

"It's going to be okay," was all the doctor said by way of encouragement, but the deep timbre of his voice gave Cassie strength to face the ordeal.

"It's a cold one this morning," Gibby said a few minutes later, as he glanced at Cassie's profile, "Jess will have to have a warm coat."

Cassie nodded. "I know," she answered, mentally balancing the cost of a good winter jacket against the pain of watching Jess suffer from the unfamiliar cold.

"Your dad probably has a few down jackets left in stock. We'll talk to Marilou about giving you what you need now and deducting it from your salary when you're straightened out."

"My salary?" Cassie asked, genuinely confused.

"Sure. You didn't think I dragged you all the way up here to take care of your dad's house and his business for nothing, did you?"

"I didn't think about it at all, I guess."

She took time to think about it now, then turned to search Gibby's face. "He'll resent it, won't he?"

"Your dad? He's in no position to be anything but grateful."

Gibby skillfully fitted the dark blue car into a narrow reserved space in the hospital parking lot.

"Do I have to do this?" Cassie asked, shrinking back when Gibby opened her door and tried to help her out.

"I won't leave you alone for a minute, I promise."

"He used to beat me."

"He's a sick old man, Cassie, he can't hurt you now."

"How old is he, he can't be that old? God, he's my father, and I don't even know how old he is."

"He's only fifty-six, but I want you to be prepared for a shock. He looks much older since the stroke, more like seventy than fifty."

Cassie closed her eyes for a minute, then opened them and fixed them on the young doctor's face. "Okay," she said, "let's get this over with." She swung her legs out of the car, took Gibby's arm, and

23

clung to him as they entered the hospital and made their way through the maze of corridors that would lead her to her father. The hospital was warm, and that was good. Gibby had kept the heat up in the car, but the walk from the parking lot had left Cassie chilled to the bone.

"You'll need a good warm coat, too, if you're going to be here through the winter," Gibby said, reading her mind.

She nodded but didn't answer. Her throat was constricting, and her breath was coming in short, painful gasps. She wasn't sure how much longer she could keep walking, pretending, pushing the fear down and feeling it creep up again.

Gibby stopped abruptly and Cassie tottered, struggling to keep her balance. They were standing outside a door that looked identical to all the other doors on the floor, but she knew that it wasn't the same at all.

"Will you be all right?" Gibby asked.

Cassie couldn't look at him. She was too afraid of what he might see in her eyes, and too afraid that he would hate her if he saw it right. She nodded, and clung to the young doctor's arm as he pushed open the door and ushered her forward to the reunion with her father.

# Chapter Two

The heavy drapes were drawn across the windows, cutting off what little light could have found its way into the room on a dreary January morning. It took time for Cassie's eyes to adjust to the gloom after the artificial brightness of the hallway. When she finally saw the shape silhouetted by the faint light on the far side of the room, she tried to back up, but Gibby's hands were firm on her back.

"Go on," he urged, and she took a step forward, then another, putting one foot down solidly in front of the other. As her eyes got used to the darkness, Cassie could make out the high hospital bed, the water pitcher with its plastic straw, the wheelchair where her father sat, silently waiting for her to approach.

The man she had feared for so many years materialized gradually, as if he were a ghost. A trick of the light filtering through the middle of the drapes where they didn't quite meet made him look insubstantial. If Gibby hadn't been there behind her, urging her on, Cassie would have bolted. When she got close enough to see him clearly, the first thing that struck her was how small he was. She had always thought of him as being a big man, a man who towered over his petite teenage daughter—a man whose hands were huge destructive weapons to be feared and avoided.

He slid sideways in the wheelchair, and Cassie gasped, sure that he was making a move toward her, to grab her, to choke her, to show her who was boss. There must have been good things, why did she remember only the bad things? *I'll show you who's boss, missy.*

"I can't do this," she whispered, but Gibby was insistent. "You can."

The old man's arms were sticks protruding from the sleeves of a blue terry-cloth robe, frayed at the cuffs. His thinning gray hair was carefully combed across his forehead. His skin was parchment thin, so dry that it crackled when his body brushed against the chair. It was too warm in the room, and Cassie felt perspiration break out on her brow and trickle down her temples.

"I've brought someone to see you," Gibby said, and Cassie jumped. His voice was loud in the quiet room, which seemed to be insulated from the ordinary noises of the hospital.

She took one more step forward and leaned down toward the chair, cleared her throat and spoke. "Hello, Daddy."

The man's inert body jerked, his head snapped upward on the thin spindle of his neck, and he looked straight into his daughter's face. His eyes were the strangest Cassie had ever seen and at the time she didn't think about the effects of the medication that was keeping him alive. She only saw his eyes, black and white, inhuman, cold black circles on a field of fierce white. Her father looked at her and although he was unable to speak, Cassie knew that nothing had changed. His look was one of pure hatred, and it drove her from his room. She ran down the hospital corridors, and out into the parking lot, where she stood in the freezing wind and waited for Gibby to find her.

When he did, minutes later, he led her back inside the hospital where emotional outbursts and flights from reality were obviously the day-to-day routine. No one showed any curiosity as they walked past the admissions desk, around the knot of candy stripers gossiping outside the gift shop. Gibby sat her down in the doctors' lounge and brought a cup of black coffee, bitter and strong.

"Drink this," he ordered and she gulped it down without stopping to catch a breath.

"That wasn't medicine, it was coffee," he joked, and she forced a weak smile. "I'm sorry, Gibby, I should have known I couldn't handle it." Then she gagged, and just made it to the metal sink in the corner before she lost the coffee and the piece of toast she'd eaten for breakfast.

"He's always hated me," she told Gibby as they drove across Route 384 toward Winter Falls a half hour later. She was still trembling with fear and nausea, and she couldn't wait to see Jess, to hold his solid little body in her arms.

"Come on, Cassie, we probably scared him half to death. He hasn't had a visitor since he's been there, and he's never seen me in anything but my hospital whites. He probably didn't even recognize you."

"Did you see his eyes?" She had been asking that same question over and over since they left the hospital.

"How many times do I have to tell you that it's the medication? He's on whopping doses of Inderal."

"His eyes were black and white, Gibby. Nobody's eyes are black and white like that."

"Okay, we'll talk about this later." He reached over and squeezed Cassie's hand, never taking his eyes from the road.

"He recognized me all right," she muttered to herself after she had turned away from Gibby's condescending manner, to stare out the window at the frozen landscape.

"I'm not going back," she said as the Mercedes entered the Township of Winter Falls.

"Back where?"

"You know where. Back there, to that hospital, to that room."

"That's your prerogative."

"My what?"

"Your choice."

"Oh." They were driving down Main Street when she spoke again. "Will he send us back to Arizona?"

"After you left the room, I helped him sign the power of attorney. We'll pick up Jess now, get the two of you some warmer clothes, then—"

"Gibby?"

"What is it, Cassie?"

"Is he, I don't know how to put it, but is his mind all right?"

"You mean is he mentally competent to sign the power of attorney? Yes, he is."

"How do you know?"

"Don't worry about it, he's responsible."

"One more thing I have to say before we get Jess. You don't have to do all this, you know."

He shook his head—so she knew that he'd heard her, but he spoke as if he hadn't. "Tomorrow, we'll take the power of attorney to the bank, and see if we can get your father's car started. You drive, don't you?"

"I know how to drive, but I don't have a license."

"Then that's one more thing we have to do, get you a license."

"It isn't that easy, is it, just go and get me a license?"

"Sure it is, if you know the right people, but we'd better start making a list of the things we have to accomplish to get you settled in."

The "list" seemed endless but by the end of the second week, their goals were accomplished, and Cassie felt as if she had never been away from Winter Falls. She liked Gibby, and, more importantly, she trusted him. To her surprise, she enjoyed working in the store, finding ways to make it more profitable, and she and Marilou were starting to become friends. That was a miracle in itself, since Cassie had never had a female friend before, not in her entire life.

Jess was enrolled in the third grade at the Winter Falls Elementary School and although he complained that his classes were harder than they had been in Phoenix, he seemed to like his teacher. His classmates were a different matter. Every afternoon he would come trudging down the street alone, dragging his feet in the remains of last week's snow. Sometimes Cassie, watching from the window, saw other children run past him, in pairs or in groups, ignoring him as if he wasn't there. It was a painful thing for a mother to watch, and she could only hope that Jess would eventually be accepted by the other boys and girls.

In the two weeks she'd spent in Winter Falls, Cassie had given her father's house a superficial cleaning, laid in a supply of Jess's favorite foods, and spent a small amount of her father's money on items needed to make the house more livable. She bought a new toaster when the old one gave out, and some sheets and towels, since the few left in the linen closet weren't much better than rags. She spent her first two weeks' salary paying for down jackets, as well as boots, blue jeans and warm sweaters for herself and Jess. Now she intended to save some money, so that she and the boy could escape to Phoenix when her father decided that he had had enough of them.

Every morning Cassie pulled her father's ten-year-old Chevy out of the garage and drove it to the dry goods store. The sky overhead was always dark

29

and brooding when she left the house. If the sun appeared at all, it did so briefly. By the time she got home in the early afternoon, it was dark again, a kind of joyless dark that never touched the Southwest, where she had lived for the past ten years. It was a dark unique to Winter Falls, which superstitious people attributed to the town's unhappy history.

Cassie spent her time at the store working on the books, ordering new merchandise, and greeting customers. Marilou said business had improved since Cassie had come back, but Cassie knew it was the curiosity of the residents of Winter Falls that brought them out looking for a sweater or a cap at The Emporium, rather than in the larger department stores that were within driving distance.

She discussed plans to improve the store with Marilou, who was enthusiastic, if cautious, about making changes.

"Your daddy never did like change," she told Cassie. "This old store has looked the same since the first time I walked into it with my momma forty years ago. It was your grandpa had it then, and when we were kids, your daddy, Connor, worked here in the afternoons, after school."

"Anything we want to do, we'll have to get Gibby's help," Cassie told the woman, who seemed to think she was Cassie's employee. "All I can do is add up these numbers and say what I think's wrong here. I wouldn't trust myself to spend any money reordering or anything like that."

"You have a good head for business, Cassie," Marilou told her. "I never would have thought of all the things you see that need improving."

Cassie didn't remind the other woman that she hadn't even graduated from high school, that she had left Winter Falls at sixteen, studied for and gotten her G.E.D. in Phoenix when she was twenty. It was kind of nice to have someone think she was smart enough to make a difference in saving her father's business, whether it was true or not.

But that's what Gibby seemed to think, too, that Cassie was capable of running the house and the business for as long as it took to get her dad back on his feet.

There was only one thing missing, one thing needed to keep her happy in her old home town: a man. Cassie wasn't used to being without a man for more than a couple of days at a time. In Phoenix, on the bar scene, there was never a shortage of studs, and Cassie always had her share. She knew that she was attractive—slim, average height, with long dark hair and dark eyes that were kind of exotic-looking. Jess didn't look anything like her, and several times she'd been asked if he was adopted. That always made her angry, for people to think that Jess didn't belong to her. She had loved his father, even though she'd only known him for a few days when he went away without giving her a way to get in touch with him. A three-night stand with a rock-and-roll drummer, that was how she'd gotten Jess, and she wasn't ashamed of it. He had his father's blue eyes and white-blond hair, and maybe he'd grow up to have his father's talent, too. What did she have to be ashamed of?

Anyway, that had been her one brush with love. Now she wasn't looking for love, she was looking for sex, and for that, she needed a man. But where would she go to look for one? The few she had met in Winter Falls were either too old or too married or just not her type. Of course, there was Dr. Gibby, but she had enough sense to realize that he would want to date nurses or even female doctors, not ex-barmaids.

There was a bar downtown, a block over from the store, but it would be the end of her reputation if she set foot in there, and without a baby-sitter for Jess, she was stuck in Winter Falls, horny or not.

After she and Jess had been in town for three weeks,

Cassie's problem was solved for her, as if fate decided to step in and offer her a solution on a silver platter.

On the day that started the events that led up to Cassie's solution, Winter Falls received four inches of rain within a twenty-four-hour period, and the next day it was still raining. The roof of her parents' house began to leak by the second afternoon. By the time Cassie and Jess finished their dinner of frankfurters and beans, water was dripping into seven pots and bowls in the bedrooms.

When Gibby made his daily telephone check on them, Cassie jokingly told him that they could take a shower without turning on the faucet, if you didn't mind your water a little on the chilly side. For some reason, Gibby didn't appreciate her sense of humor. Ten minutes later, he stood in the kitchen talking into the new telephone he had bought and installed for her.

"Stan, this is Gibby here. Fine, fine, how about you? Good. Listen, Stan, I know you're God-awful busy, but I need to ask you for a favor. Well, thanks, Stan. The problem is with the McCall place. Connor's daughter and his little grandson are staying here while he's in the hospital over at Hartford. Oh, well as can be expected, I guess. Yeah, the upstairs is filling up with water. They could take a bath without turning on the faucets, if they didn't mind their water a little on the chilly side."

Gibby winked at Cassie and tousled Jess's hair, while he waited for a response from Stan.

"Tomorrow will be fine, Cassie will be here. Just tell your man to do whatever he thinks is necessary and send me the bill. I'll take care of it. Sure, Stan, and thanks again."

"How can they work on the roof with it raining like this?" Cassie asked when Gibby turned from the phone.

"You're in luck, Cassie. Stan says this is the end of

32

the rain, and the weather report calls for warm, dry weather for the next few days. The next time it rains, you and Jess will be as snug as two bugs in a rug, right, Jess?"

The boy laughed at the doctor's attempt at humor and snuggled into his arms for a hug, which gave Cassie a momentary pang of guilt that she was raising a fatherless child. But by the next morning, she had forgotten her guilt completely, and it would be days before she felt anything but happiness.

# Chapter Three

"Hi, my name's Corey." The young man smiled and extended his hand. "Stan sent me over to look at your roof."

"I'm Cassie McCall. Come on in for a minute before you go up there. I'll make you a cup of coffee or something."

"That would be great, Mrs. McCall."

"It's *Miss* McCall, but I'd rather you just call me Cassie."

Gibby was right, Cassie was in luck. The minute she laid eyes on Corey Hammil, she knew what the future held for them. She always knew when she clicked with a man, it was a gift, like second sight or something.

Within five minutes Cassie had learned that the boy was nineteen years old, and that he was a student at the university, studying something with a fancy name that was just another word for farming. The kid was smart, but he wanted to go back to Ohio and be a farmer after three more years at the university.

After the coffee, which neither of them finished, Cassie followed him back outside and watched him climb the ladder he had brought with him in the pickup truck. It was shiny aluminum, and if she'd had a camera, she would have taken his picture when he stopped halfway up the ladder to smile down at her.

Corey Hammil was one of the prettiest things Cassie had ever seen, and he knew how to make use of God's gifts. The tight jeans and white T-shirt that reminded her of a TV ad, the thick sandy hair that he kept tossing out of his golden brown eyes all drew Cassie in, a moth to his flame. When he peeled off his denim jacket and squatted on the roof, Cassie climbed up the ladder and told him to hurry. Before the roofing job was half finished, she had him in her bed.

Since Jess got out of school at two-thirty, they had to make love in the mornings, if they were going to do it at all. Afternoons, Corey went off to school. Although he begged to come back in the evenings, Cassie said no, and she meant it. She intended to introduce Jess to her new friend, but not until she was ready, and she certainly didn't want Dr. Gibby to walk in on them. Corey didn't have morning classes on Monday, Wednesday, and Friday, but those were the days he worked for Stan-the-Roofer, as he was known in Winter Falls. That schedule didn't leave the lovers much time to see each other during the week, and that was why Cassie planned the weekend picnic when they'd known each other just a few days.

Corey picked them up on Saturday afternoon in a borrowed car that made Cassie's transportation look grand by comparison. He and Jess greeted each other warily, but the fact that Corey had brought the little boy a new blue ball helped cement their friendship. By the time they got to the lake, Jess was hanging on Corey's neck from the back seat, embarrassing Cassie with his desperate need for attention.

It was an unbelievably warm day for January in Connecticut. After the rain stopped, the temperature had shot up into the forties for three or four days. On this Saturday in late January, it was nearly sixty degrees Fahrenheit. Cassie carried a picnic basket and a green-and-white stadium blanket into the woods beyond the lake. She had taken both items from the replenished shelves in her father's store the day before, and marked their retail price in the little notebook she kept beside the cash register. On payday, she would place that amount in the register drawer, and draw a line through the entry in the notebook. She would insist that Marilou stand beside her from beginning to end, to witness the transaction.

Corey and Jess tossed the blue ball back and forth in a clearing in the trees for several minutes. Corey kept glancing in Cassie's direction, and she knew that he was bored playing with Jess. He wanted to be with her on the blanket but she let him wait a few minutes more before she called them to come and eat the chicken-salad sandwiches she'd prepared from last night's leftovers.

When they finished eating, they walked back to the shore of the lake. The three of them held hands and talked, and Jess was as eager as Corey to hear the legend of Lake Wahelo.

"Why does this place always look so dark and brooding?" Corey asked, bringing up the subject.

"You haven't heard the legend of Lake Wahelo?" Cassie returned in her best scary voice.

"Hey, I did hear something—some kids drowned here a long time ago and the town loonies think they're still out there in the lake, trying to lure innocent victims into their watery lair."

"It was three little girls that drowned, and they were my father's half-sisters."

"No kidding."

Cassie nodded and stared out across the lake, to a spot in the middle that never seemed to catch the sun. "My father never met them, they died before he was born, and he had a different mother."

"God, that must have been really hard on your dad."

Cassie shrugged and kept her gaze on the lake's

calm surface. "He never talked about it."

"Well, come on, don't keep us in suspense," Corey prodded, "tell us what really happened."

"Nobody knows for sure. The girls just disappeared one day. It was a day like this, in the middle of a January thaw." Cassie looked around at the trees and shivered. She tugged at the hem of her mother's old sweater, as if she thought she could make it larger, or warmer.

"They lived with their dad, who was my grandad, and he just discovered them missing, all three of them. Everybody in town turned out to search for them, and what they thought was that the girls had wandered out onto the lake and that they just fell through the ice and drowned."

Cassie shivered violently, and Corey laid his leather jacket across her shoulders. "Hey, it was a long time ago, don't let it get to you."

Corey started to rub her arms, but Cassie turned her attention to her son. "I'm sorry. Jess, Mommy's not upset, I just got a chill for a minute."

Jess said, "Okay," and concentrated on throwing his ball at a tree and running to catch it when it bounced back. Cassie made a mental note to talk to him about the legend later on, to make sure that he wasn't upset by what he'd heard today.

"I'm sorry," she said, turning back to Corey, "but when I was a kid, we scared ourselves silly with stories about hands sticking up out of the water, or about seeing three wet little girls walking along the road at night after dark. I guess I just got caught up in my story again."

"Hey, no problem. Come on back to the blanket and let me warm you up."

Cassie let him lead her through the woods, with Jess running along beside them, until they reached the stadium blanket. She lay down, and Corey threw himself down on top of her. She tried to catch Jess's eye, to let him know it would be all right, but he

37

turned away and walked off into the woods.

"Don't you go too far, Jess, and don't you dare take that jacket off. Do you hear me, Jess McCall?"

"I hear you." His answer was muffled, probably by his anger, but she knew that he wouldn't wander too far from her. She tried not to fool around in front of him, but sometimes the guys didn't understand that Jess was her kid, and that they should cool it when he was around.

Cassie scooted over an inch to get away from a sharp stone that was digging into her back through the blanket, and Corey took her wiggling as a sign that she was ready for him. He planted his mouth on hers and raised himself up on his forearms while he slid out of his jeans without breaking lip-to-lip contact. He entered her without further foreplay, and Cassie gritted her teeth. She vowed to spend some time teaching the young man how to treat a lady before they made love again. It did feel good though. She smiled and wiggled her bottom, as he thrust harder and faster. "Make Cassie happy," she purred, and the young man obliged her.

She closed her eyes, put her lips close to the boy's ear and hummed a few bars of "When a Man Loves a Woman." Maybe the boy would tell her that he loved her today. Not that she loved him—she didn't. But it was always nice to learn that someone loved you.

Corey tried to kiss her again, but she swatted him away and tried to sit up. It was too quiet. The woods had grown silent, no chattering of squirrels, no branches cracking as children or small animals ran between the trees. It was eerie, and Cassie didn't like it.

"Where's Jess?" she asked. "Can you see Jess anywhere?"

Corey stopped moving, sighed, and looked around at the woods. Nothing moved, nothing breathed.

"Where in the hell's Jess?" Cassie asked louder, and Corey scrambled to his feet.

"I thought you said he wouldn't wander off."

"I didn't think he would."

"Jesus!"

Corey thrust his legs into his jeans and ran barefoot through the woods in the direction of the lake. It took Cassie a minute to get to her knees, then her feet. The way she was shaking, her legs could barely hold her weight. When she was standing, she willed herself to move, to run in the direction Corey had taken, toward Lake Wahelo.

She broke from the trees in time to see Corey running across the lake, sliding on the ice, then falling through, up to his hips in the frigid water. He was stuck, struggling to free himself, screaming something unintelligible in Cassie's direction.

Then she saw it, the red windbreaker, floating on the water in almost the exact center of the lake. She screamed Jess's name and ran forward, slid when her sneakered feet left the bank and hit the ice.

"Go back," Corey was yelling, "go for help." He was free of the ice, on his knees, waving his arms at Cassie, urging her to get help. She nodded that she would, then screamed again as he dived into the hole his body had created and disappeared under the ice. She watched for a second, then ran back up the bank. At the top, she stopped and looked around at the half dozen or so vehicles parked in the paved area off to the right of the lake from where she stood. She wanted to scream, but she forced herself to keep calm, to look for signs of life. A new-looking pickup truck was noticeable, and she ran toward it, choosing it over the several cars parked in the lot.

"Help!" she screamed, "help me!" but she was out of breath and she knew that her voice wasn't carrying very far. There was a man sitting in the pickup, but he was ignoring her calls for help. She threw herself against the door of the truck and pounded on it with her fists.

"What the hell?" The door swung open and Cassie

fell backwards.

"Please help me, my little boy has fallen in the lake, he's going to drown! Oh God, help me, please!"

The man lifted her into the truck and slid her over to the passenger side. "No," she screamed, "you don't understand, he's under the ice!"

Her rescuer held her firmly in her seat while he lifted a small microphone with his other hand and spoke: "Anybody out there got your ears on? This is The Swede, we got an emergency here."

"This here's The Beaver, what you got, Swede?"

"We got a boy under the ice out here at Lake Wahelo, been under a few minutes already, I guess. Think you can get ahold of the First Aid Squad and send them out here pronto?"

"Hang on, Swede, we're on our way. Just give us your exact location, and all the information you have on the boy in the water." It wasn't The Beaver who had answered The Swede's call for help, it was a First Aid Squad vehicle, probably on its way back from another emergency.

"Thank God," Cassie breathed, and the man who held the CB microphone shook his head in agreement.

She gave him Jess's age and told him what had happened, then shoved down on the door handle and slid from the tall truck before the man could stop her.

There was no sign of either Corey or Jess. Cassie scanned the lakeshore and the edge of the woods, hoping against hope that Corey had found Jess and pulled him from the icy water. She slid down the embankment and started to edge out onto the ice, not sure that it would hold her weight. The unseasonably warm weather had softened the ice and made it treacherous.

"Don't go out there, lady." Cassie looked behind her and saw the guy from the pickup truck hurrying toward her. She turned back to the lake and spotted

40

Corey coming up out of the water, gasping and sputtering. He had something under his arm, something limp and still. He had Jess.

The sirens were loud, almost upon her, when she realized that she had been hearing them in the distance for the past few minutes. When the sirens died, tires squealed, doors slammed, and three men ran down the bank. They seemed to immediately size up the situation, and to agree on a plan of action without verbal communication.

The youngest of the three ran out onto the ice and made his way quickly toward Corey and Jess. He slid along on his stomach and got close enough to toss Corey a rope, which he tied around Jess's waist. Then Corey inched his way closer to the paramedic and handed Jess over without having to drop him back into the water. The paramedic moved slowly backward on the ice, pulling Jess's inert body along with him, until he was within three or four feet of the shore.

The second man from the first-aid vehicle, the heavyset one, had run to the ambulance for a stretcher and a medical kit, while the third man on the scene tried to reach Corey and Jess. The second man arrived back at the lake in time to take Jess from his partner's arms and lay him gently on the ground at the edge of the lake. While he and the first man bent over Jess, the heavyset man dragged Corey from the water and wrapped him in blankets. The boy was coughing up water but he wouldn't lie down or let the man help him.

Cassie wasn't aware that a police car had arrived at the scene until the cop was standing between her and the paramedics, who were bent over Jess.

"What just happened here?" he asked, intentionally blocking her view.

"My little boy," Cassie managed to say, "he fell through the ice."

"What was he doing out on the lake?" the cop

asked, making a notation on the form attached to his clipboard.

"I was in the woods, and I let him go for a walk. I told him not to go near the lake."

"How old is the boy?"

"Eight years old, almost nine."

"Is his father here?"

"I'm a single parent." Cassie didn't turn to look at the cop's face, but she knew that he was watching her closely, and she could sense his disapproval.

She finally managed to edge around him, to get a better view of the men who were still working to revive Jess. From where she stood, her son appeared to be dead. He wasn't breathing or trying to breathe. He looked as if there was no life in him at all. They had laid him down on his side to expel the water from his lungs, and Cassie could see his dear little face. His skin was gray, his lips blue. She was sure he was dead.

"No pulse," she heard the older of the paramedics say. "Looks like he hasn't been breathing for a long time."

"How long do you suppose he was under there?" the younger man asked. "Miss, are you his mother?"

"Yes, I'm his mother," Cassie answered, moving away from the cop, who was again trying to position himself between her and her dead, or dying baby.

"Was this watch running when he fell in?" the young paramedic asked. He held up Jess's wrist, as though she would have to see the Mickey Mouse watch she'd given him for his seventh birthday to be able to identify it.

"Yes," Cassie answered around the growing lump in her throat.

"Was it accurate?"

"I don't know, almost. Why?" she yelled, then felt ashamed when she realized that they were trying to estimate how long Jess had been under water. "He was under a long time, wasn't he?"

"Twenty-two minutes, if the watch was set for the

42

right time, and if it stopped the minute he hit the water."

"Jesus!" the older paramedic exclaimed, then mumbled, "Sorry" when he saw the look on Cassie's face.

"He's dead, isn't he?" She was amazed that her voice didn't sound hysterical, but merely ragged, as though she hadn't slept for a long, long time.

Neither man answered her. They rolled Jess onto his back, and the young paramedic straddled him, applying rhythmic pressure to his chest. A few curious onlookers had wandered over to the water's edge, and were asking questions of the truck driver who had used his CB to call the paramedics. After they learned what had happened, they waited in respectful silence, all eyes on Jess. For long minutes, the two men worked on him, and Cassie felt a scream rising in her throat. If Jess died, she would scream and scream and scream, until her throat closed up, and then she would refuse to breathe ever again.

The older paramedic said something, and Cassie returned to the reality of the minute. She wasn't sure what the man said—something about "movement in his fingers." Then she heard very clearly: "I'm getting a pulse. He's coming around."

She ran around the cop who had been trying to block her and fell on her knees beside Jess. He was coughing and sputtering, spewing out foul-smelling brown water. He was alive, but his eyes were rolled up in his head and he didn't focus on her face when she said his name.

"Let's get moving," one of the men said, and Cassie was again pushed aside. They lifted Jess onto a portable stretcher and carried him to the ambulance. Both of the men who had been working on him climbed in the back with him, leaving no room for Cassie. The driver guided her quickly to the front passenger seat and helped her in, then ran around to the driver's seat. Within seconds, they were flying up

43

the road toward town, siren blaring.

The police car sped in front of them, and the pickup she had seen Corey climb into was right behind them, so obviously he needed medical treatment, too. Cassie knew that she should be concerned about the young man, but she hadn't been able to look him in the eye since he struggled out of the lake. If she hadn't been so hot for him in the first place, her own little boy wouldn't be so close to death.

Cassie knelt and watched through the glass window that connected the cab of the vehicle to the patient area. She couldn't see Jess but she could see the paramedics, and it seemed to her that they were working over him more frantically, as if something had gone wrong since they'd lifted him into the ambulance.

When the ambulance flew past the first-aid station, Cassie turned to the driver. "Where are we going?" she screamed over the siren.

"Hartford."

She didn't ask why. She knew that the huge hospital in Hartford had the modern technology that would be needed to save Jess's life. If he had been underwater for twenty-two minutes, he would probably be brain-damaged if he lived, but that didn't matter. She wanted Jess, she *needed* Jess to live, even if he wasn't the same Jess she had loved the past eight years.

She knelt on the seat again, but this time she didn't try to see what the paramedics were doing to Jess. She bowed her head and prayed.

"Please, Lord, let Jess live. He's only a little boy, he can't die yet. Just you let him live, Lord, and I'll give you something in return, anything you want, I promise."

# Chapter Four

When he saw that his ball had rolled out onto the ice, Jess almost cried. It was the nicest ball he'd ever had, firm and perfectly round and his favorite color, blue. The ball was a gift from his mother's new friend, Corey, but Jess liked it anyway. As for Corey, Jess wasn't worried. He had seen his mother's friends come and go, and he was always happiest when they were gone. Corey wasn't too old, but he didn't even like to spend time with Jess. You could tell, just from the look on his face, that Corey wanted Jess to go away so that he could lie down on the blanket with his mother.

That was no problem. Jess didn't want to be there when they started to roll around on the blanket. One night when he was seven, he had lain in the dark pretending to be asleep while his mother did the bad thing with a man she brought home with her. After a few minutes, Jess was sorry he was there, and he wanted to get up and run out of the room. But he couldn't, not even when his mother cried and he knew that the man was hurting her.

Jess hadn't thrown the ball hard, and he surely hadn't thrown it in the direction of the lake. It seemed like a puff of wind caught the ball and carried it away from him, out onto the ice, where he couldn't follow. He knew he was supposed to stay away from the lake, and he would have, if the ball hadn't been so new. It wasn't fair to get something new and then lose it right away, especially when you didn't have too many things to play with.

Jess put one foot on the ice and let it rest there for a minute before he put his weight on it. He took his other foot off the bank and slid it up beside the first foot. Nothing happened. He was standing on the ice, and he knew that the water was under the ice, and it was kind of exciting just to stand there.

He looked around, being careful not to move his feet when he turned his head. There were cars in the parking lot, and one neat pickup truck, but no people in sight. He wasn't sure he'd ask for help anyway. He was almost nine years old, big enough to take care of himself when he had to.

He started sliding his feet slowly forward, only a couple of inches at a time. The ball was several feet away from him, but he thought he could reach it if he just took it easy. He kept moving forward and everything looked good until he was about a foot away from the ball. Then something happened. Although there didn't seem to be any breeze, that puff of invisible wind came along again and lifted the ball a few inches off the surface of the ice. The ball moved five or six feet before it came to a stop again. Jess swiveled his head and looked back at the shore. It was much farther away than he'd thought it was. How did he get almost to the middle of the lake so fast? The ball hadn't looked like it was out that far.

*Well, I'm almost there now*, he thought, convincing himself that it would be stupid to turn back without the ball when he had come so far. He crept up on the blue sphere, willing it not to move, and it didn't. He stood over it and savored his victory, then reached down to grab it. He was leaning forward, his hands touching the ball, when he heard the ice crack.

46

He felt a wave of panic, and he wanted to cry out for his mom to come and save him, but even if she'd been standing on the shore, he wouldn't have done it. That would have made him look like a baby.

Jess pretended that he was in control of the situation. He tried to slide his feet backward, to reverse the process that had brought him to this precarious position. It didn't work. The piece of ice on which he stood had broken off from the main body of ice. He was standing on a tiny island in the middle of a lake that suddenly appeared to be huge and menacing. While he was still wondering if he could jump back to a more substantial slab of ice, another terrible thing happened. The ice beneath his feet started to crack and splinter, and Jess's feet started to sink into the water.

He waved his arms and tried to get his balance, but there was nothing solid under him. He sank into the icy water up to his chin before his hands fastened onto the edge of the large ice mass. He pulled himself up until he was only in the water up to his waist. He was going to try to pull himself out; he was sure that he could. Then his hands couldn't hold on and he fell, not slowly, but fast and hard, as if whatever had been holding him up suddenly let go of him.

Jess screamed as the water grabbed at him, forgetting that he was eight years old and supposed to be brave. He called for his mother and for Corey, but if he had been able to think at that point, he would have realized that they were too far away to hear his cries, which only lasted for a few seconds.

Putrid brown water filled his mouth and he tried to spit it out, but the water was all around him, forcing its way into his body wherever it could find an opening. The water closed over his head and he sank to the bottom of the lake. Jess knew how to swim, and guided by his instincts, he put his hands down at his sides and pushed with his feet on the muddy bottom.

When that didn't work, he waved his arms wildly and beat at the water, but he still didn't rise to the surface.

Jess had been underwater too long. His head was pounding, and his heart was hammering. There was a bad pain in his chest, and he felt like something was going to burst any minute. He was sure that he was going to die, but for some reason that didn't scare him. The longer he stayed under, the more calm and peaceful he became. His eyes were wide open, and he could see through the water, see things moving and dancing on the bottom of the lake. There was no sound, just a silence that pressed in on him and gave him a kind of freedom he had never experienced before.

Jess missed his mother; otherwise he might have given in to whatever it was in the lake that seemed to be luring him to stay. With the last ounce of his strength, he twisted and turned, kicked and prodded the lake bottom with his sneakered feet. Then he knew what was wrong: something was holding him down, preventing him from rising to the surface.

He bent over double to claw at the thing that was wrapped around his legs. He touched it, grabbed it, and felt it move in his hand. It was an eel, or something with tentacles.

Jess's fear of drowning was multiplied by his fear of the unknown danger, but he didn't give up. He pried at the thing and tried to loosen its grip on his legs. Finally, when it was nearly too late, he felt the thing let go. As he kicked off the bottom, he looked back to see what awful sea monster had been holding him underwater.

It was a girl, or what was left of a girl. Jess knew instinctively that she was dead, although he had never seen a dead person before. She had grayish white skin that hung loosely on her skeleton and flapped as the lake water lapped around her. She was

48

the most horrible thing Jess had ever seen; and, just before he blacked out, he realized that she wasn't alone. There were three of them, three little dead girls with the loose skin of their faces arranged in what might have passed as smiles, their stick-thin arms reaching up for him.

# Chapter Five

The ambulance raced through small towns and down country roads, siren blaring. The hospital in Hartford was a half hour away from Lake Wahelo, but to Cassie the trip seemed endless, a ride through hell. Time passed too slowly, defying the universal order that set the rhythm of the world. Her head was bowed in prayer, she was afraid to open her eyes and look through the window into the back of the ambulance. If she saw that Jess was gone, that they had covered his face and given him over to death, she knew that she would go mad.

Finally, she became aware that the ambulance had slowed and turned, then pulled to a stop. Immediately, there was a flurry of activity around the vehicle. Cassie opened the door and stepped out, only to be shoved aside by a security guard. "Stand back, lady," he said, without more than a glance in her direction. "Let us get the kid inside."

She backed up until she hit the rough brick wall where the words "Emergency Room" were emblazoned in red neon several feet above her head. She stood there, her tear-filled eyes staring at Jess's tiny body on the stretcher, her hands clenching and unclenching, as she willed herself to stay out of the way.

Several white-clad technicians pushed the gurney

up the concrete ramp and through the automatic doors. There were too many of them, a nurse, a doctor, two or three young men who looked like boys playing doctor. They were shouting at each other, giving orders, agreeing and disagreeing on what procedures to follow. As Cassie ran along behind them and finally caught up to them, she saw what they had done to Jess, and her heart almost stopped beating. There was a hole in his throat, a tube stuffed into the hole, with a strip of white tape holding it there. But the tape wasn't really white, it was covered with blood, Jess's blood.

"What have you done to him?" Cassie screamed, completely out of control. She grabbed at the lab coat of one of the young men and he swatted her hand away. She yelled and reached for him again, then a hand closed over hers and she was pulled to the side and held back while the gurney rolled through a set of swinging doors and out of sight.

"Cassie, calm down, try to get control of yourself."

"Doctor Gibby? Oh, thank God you're here." She let herself relax against him, let the fear and the anger dissolve for just a second while she regained her strength. Tears ran down her cheeks but she pulled herself away from the doctor and stood on her own.

"They put a tube in his throat," she said when she could find the words. "They cut my baby, Gibby, they cut his beautiful throat."

"They did an emergency tracheotomy in the ambulance, Cassie. They had to do it to save his life."

"What does that mean? Does that mean they had to cut his throat open?"

"They made an incision and inserted a tube so that he could breathe. He stopped breathing on the way to the hospital, there was an obstruction in his airway. If they hadn't done heart massage and inserted the tracheotomy tube, he would have died. He had complete cardiac arrest."

"That means he stopped breathing, doesn't it?"

"It means that his heart stopped beating, Cassie. Those men saved his life."

Cassie's knees buckled and the room spun around her; she reached out for the doctor's arm, to steady herself. She clung to him and moaned, her head thrown back, her eyes closed, dangerously close to losing it.

Then there were strong arms shaking her, forcing her to come back from the edge of insanity. "Don't do this, Cassie, don't flip out on me. Jess is going to need you, if he's going to get through this. You have to be strong, for his sake."

Cassie nodded and stopped moaning, but the words she spoke were crazy. "It's the lake, Gibby, I shouldn't have taken him to the lake."

"It was an accident, Cassie, you can't blame yourself."

"Oh, no, no, no!" She shook her head wildly, her long hair flew around her shoulders, her eyes flashed. "It's an evil place, the lake is an evil place, and I was being evil. Do you know what I was doing there, Gibby? I was lying on the blanket with that boy, Corey, and you know what we were doing, don't you? We were—"

She finished the sentence but her face was buried in the doctor's shoulder and the awful words were erased. "Shh . . ." he murmured, as he smoothed her hair and held her, calmed her.

When she stopped shaking he moved away from her. "Corey wants to see you, Cassie, he's been asking for you."

"No, I can't."

"Okay, you don't have to. I'll talk to him."

"Tell him that I can't ever see him again." The words were coming fast, tripping over each other, but they couldn't keep up with her thoughts. "I'm going to change, Gibby. If God spares Jess, if He gives my little boy back to me, I'm going to change, I swear I am."

"You're a good person now, Cassie, and you shouldn't be making deals with God. We're doing everything we can to save Jess's life. If it's medically possible, we're going to give him back to you."

"I know," she answered, willing herself to act rationally. "If something like this had to happen, I'm glad it happened here, so that you could help him."

Gibby kissed her forehead, sat her down on a bench, and disappeared through the double doors that had swallowed up the gurney several minutes before. Cassie leaned against the wall and prepared to wait. She wanted to ask if the hospital had a chapel, but she was afraid to leave her post, even for a minute.

She closed her eyes and must have dozed off, because suddenly there was someone leaning over her, repeating her name loudly and monotonously.

"Miss McCall? Miss McCall?"

"Yes, what is it? Is something wrong?" Her head jerked up and a sharp pain shot through her neck and shoulder.

"I need to fill out a report, Miss McCall. I need to know what happened out there."

It was the policeman from the lake, and from the look on his face, it was more obvious than ever that he didn't like Cassie, for whatever reason.

"What do I have to do?" Cassie asked. She thought that maybe if she cooperated and didn't make waves, the man would show some compassion and not dwell on the fact that she had been with Corey when Jess fell through the ice.

"Just answer some routine questions," the man said in a voice that he had probably memorized after watching an old "Dragnet" episode. "I'll need your full name and address, your son's full name and address, and the names and addresses of any other parties who were with you at the time of the incident."

Cassie answered all of the officer's questions,

except the ones she couldn't answer, like the one about Corey's address. The fact that she didn't know where her lover lived brought a sneer to the middle-aged cop's face, as did her answer that she didn't know exactly how many minutes Jess had been missing when she and Corey started to look for him. When the policeman left her, it was clear to Cassie that for some unknown reason, she had made an enemy, and that she would have to steer clear of Officer Tom Barney in the future.

She took a drink of water from the fountain at the end of the hall, then settled down to wait again. It turned out to be hours later that a solemn Gibby emerged from the operating room and shook Cassie awake.

"Was I asleep? I couldn't have fallen asleep. Is he going to live? Oh God, don't tell me he's dead, please don't tell me he's dead."

"He's not dead, Cassie, but the prognosis isn't good. We suctioned all of the water out of his stomach and some of the blood out of—"

"What blood?"

"There are some ruptured vessels in his lungs. We've inserted two tubes into his abdomen, and we're pumping in warm liquid, literally warming him from the inside out. He's breathing in hot oxygen. We're doing everything we can."

Cassie was disoriented, and only part of what Gibby said made any sense to her. "I don't understand why you're doing all these things. He didn't drown, he was breathing, wasn't he?"

"We estimate that Jess was under the water for approximately twenty-two minutes. The water was cold, and his body temperature had dropped to sixty degrees. He came back from absolute death, Cassie, and he's fighting like hell to stay alive. A few years ago, we would have given up on him and just let him die, but now we know that cold water slows the metabolism. This allows the body to survive with less oxygen. The heartbeat slows down, and the body enters a suspended state. Children have been known to survive after more than thirty minutes in icy water.

"Is he awake?" Cassie asked, unable to digest the doctor's explanation. "Can I see him?"

As they talked, Gibby had been leading her down the hallway, away from the room where the doctors were still working on Jess. He opened a door, ushered her into a small lounge, and poured two cups of strong black coffee. Cassie drank hers down, as if she knew she had to before she would be allowed to see Jess.

"Cassie . . ." The way the doctor said her name alerted her and when she looked at his face, she knew.

"What?" she asked, nausea twisting her stomach and threatening to explode from her throat. "Tell me."

"Jess is in a coma. We don't know if he'll ever come out of it. If he does, he might not be the same."

"Don't play games with me, Gibby, just tell me all of it straight out."

"He might have brain damage."

Gibby let out a deep breath, as though saying it was the worst of it, but it wasn't. Now it was hers, buried like an arrow in her heart.

"I had my tubes tied after I had Jess."

"Don't, Cassie."

"You know why? Because I didn't want another kid, because I didn't want to divide my love between Jess and anybody else. I wanted Jess to have it all."

"He has a chance, we can't give up on him yet."

"I want to see him."

"A few more minutes, until they get him into a bed in the trauma unit."

Gibby tried then to prepare her for what Jess would look like when she saw him, but all the words in the world couldn't have made it easy to see him like that. The tube was still in his throat, although the bloody tape had been replaced with a piece of clean white adhesive. They had washed the blood off his neck and sponged the mud and vomit from his face. He would have looked peaceful if it hadn't been for the machines, with their endless beeps and tracings, and for the tubes that ran into his nose and mouth—big tubes filled with yellowish fluids and colorless liquids, tubes too fat and round and foul to be invading her baby's body. His little body had been perfect before the accident, free of flaws or blemishes. Now it was no longer so. If Jess lived, he would always carry on his body the marks of his near-death experience. The scars would heal but they would never go away completely, and he would always be reminded of that day at the lake. How had Gibby said it? He came back from absolute death. When he grew up, would he be sorry or glad that he had come back? And would he grow up to love his mother, or to hate her for bringing him to Winter Falls and taking him to Lake Wahelo?

They let her stay only a few minutes before a nurse dragged her back to the hallway and into a cramped office. "You never signed the release forms," the woman accused, and Cassie was too tired and sick to argue that no one had asked her to sign them until this minute. She scrawled her name where she was told to sign: Cassandra McCall gives you permission to cut up her son, to poke him and prod him and insert tubes into every orifice of his little body. She gives you permission to try to revive him if his heart stops beating, permission to make life-and-death decisions regarding his treatment.

She ran from the office and walked the hospital corridors until she saw a sign with an arrow that pointed toward the chapel. It was a narrow room, cool and dark, with a remnant of old prayers lingering in the air. Cassie sat on a chair and leaned forward, holding her head in her hands while she spoke Jess's name over and over and over, the best prayer, and the only prayer she knew.

56

Over the next two days there was no change in Jess's condition, and his mother alternated her time between his bedside and the chapel. She wouldn't have remembered to eat, if Gibby hadn't brought her sandwiches and milk from the cafeteria and an occasional cup of black coffee to keep her from falling on her face.

After the first forty-eight hours, he started taking her home for two or three hours each day, so that she could shower and change clothes. She looked around the old house then wondered how she and Jess had lived there. It was so dark, so run-down, and it held so many bad memories within its walls. Cassie sat on one of the rickety kitchen chairs and felt the bad times sneaking back. She began to hear voices. They always started low, then escalated until they were shouting, drowning out the sound of her own heartbeat. Her father yelling, demanding, insisting that he was "the boss." Her mother whining, crying, and finally surrendering her will and her soul to the madman she had married. There was one more voice: the child, Cassie, always defiant, never acknowledging the pain.

When the horn sounded, signaling that Gibby had returned for her, Cassie would fly from the house, once forgetting to pick up her coat on the way out the door.

There was no change for four more days. Jess was in a deep sleep, cut off from the living world that surrounded him. Cassie talked to him for hours at a time, patted his hand, kissed his cheek, and helped the nurses turn his little body several times a day. Once she left the room for a short break, at a nurse's insistence, and literally ran into Corey Hammil in the hallway.

"What do you want?" she asked, although she had vowed that she wouldn't speak a single word to him ever again.

"What's wrong, Cassie, why won't you talk to me?"

57

"I don't have anything to say to you."

"Don't be like that, I didn't hurt Jess. I'm the one who saved him."

"You *saved* him?" Cassie's eyes flashed as she turned them on the boy, who was obviously unprepared for her attack. He took a step backward and faltered, then put out his hand and touched the wall for support. "If you hadn't been so hot to get me on that blanket, he wouldn't have fallen into that lake in the first place, did you ever think of that?" she continued with an uncharacteristic lack of sympathy.

"We weren't doing anything wrong," the boy insisted. "We were just making love."

Cassie's lips twisted before she spoke. "You call that making love? Well, that's not what I call it. I call it fuckin'."

"You didn't have to say that, Cassie."

The boy's face was painted white with pain, but Cassie ignored it. "Oh, yes, I did," she answered, then turned on her heel and went back to Jess's bedside, leaving Corey alone in the hallway, too sick in her own soul to offer him any comfort.

On the seventh day after the accident, one of the senior staff physicians stopped in to see Jess. After a cursory reading of the chart that hung over the end of the bed, the doctor motioned for Cassie to follow him into the hallway.

"Why couldn't we talk in there?" Cassie asked when the man stopped and turned to face her.

"We know so little about the state of coma, Miss McCall. It's very possible that Jess can hear conversations being carried on near his bed. What I have to say—"

"He's not dying!"

"No, no, there's been no change in his condition, and there might not be, not for a long time, maybe never."

Cassie stared at the man's kindly face, vainly waiting for some form of reassurance that she knew better than to expect.

"We have no way of knowing how much damage was done while he was under the ice. He may never come out of this coma. If he does—"

"He'll be retarded, I know, Gibby—Dr. Gibson told me."

"I'm afraid you misunderstood, Miss McCall. It's much more complicated than that. But the point I'm trying to make is simply that your son may very likely never be the same again. You should begin to get on with your life. You should go home, and come to visit Jess once or twice a day. You should go back to your job, see your friends, take up your life where you left off."

"And just give up on Jess?" Cassie asked incredulously.

"No, of course not. You won't ever give up on him, I can see that, but you shouldn't neglect your own health and compound the damage."

"Thank you for your advice, Doctor," Cassie answered, and she knew that she sounded as stiff as she felt. She also knew that she would never do what the doctor suggested, although she realized that his suggestions were meant for her own good. She went back to Jess's side and vowed to stay there until he woke up and smiled at her again. She talked to him incessantly, telling him fairy tales and repeating the words of songs she had memorized, crazy old songs they kept on the jukebox where she worked in Phoenix.

The next day Gibby tried to get her to go home for a few hours, but she refused.

"I'm not going home again, Gibby, not without Jess."

"Cassie, don't be stubborn, you have to listen to common sense."

"No, *you* have to listen to *me*. I'm not going to leave this hospital without my baby. If Jess dies here, then I'll die here, too. Or I'll die in that awful lake

59

that snatched him away from me. But I won't live without Jess. I won't."

She had been facing the gray gloomy square of the window while she spoke. Sensing that Gibby was no longer paying attention to her, she swung around to face him, but her words died in her throat. Gibby was staring across the room, his eyes fixed on something in the area of Jess's hospital bed.

Cassie turned, never taking her eyes from Gibby's until her body faced the bed. She dropped her eyes and slowly, very slowly let them follow the direction of Gibby's stare. She let her gaze travel up the bed, the white blanket, the hospital gown, all the way up to Jess's face. He was awake; he was looking around the room, obviously trying to get his bearings, trying to focus on something he recognized. All of the tubes and needles had been removed, with the exception of the thin naso-gastric feeding tube, and he looked like a healthy, normal little boy waking up from a nap. When his blue eyes met his mother's, he smiled, the biggest, widest, most heart-warming smile Cassie had ever seen. She literally ran to his side and gathered him into her arms.

"Hi, Mom," he said in a scratchy, unfamiliar voice. "I'm hungry."

# Chapter Six

Cassie took Jess home from the hospital two days after he awoke from his coma. The doctors called his recovery a miracle but they cautioned Cassie that he wasn't completely out of the woods yet. He was doing fine but there were still things that could happen, things that she had to watch out for, even though he was young and strong.

The only thing that worried Cassie was that Jess didn't seem to be himself. His appearance was the same and he talked the same, but when she looked deep into his eyes, there seemed to be something missing, some light or spark that had always been there before. It was as if Jess had lost something, left some part of himself down there in the dirty lake water. Well, he was alive, and that was all that really mattered. She had promised God that she would change if He found it in His heart to spare Jess, and as soon as she got the little boy settled in, she intended to set about her reform in earnest.

She made up the old couch in the living room with Jess's own sheets and a new blanket from The Emporium. The coffee table was piled high with coloring books and crayons and colored pencils, all get-well gifts from Marilou. Gibby had lent them a nineteen-inch color TV to help keep Jess occupied, since his doctors had suggested that he stay in bed for a few days and only gradually work his way back to his regular schedule. School was out of the question, at least for a couple of weeks.

When Jess became engrossed in an old rerun of "Gilligan's Island," Cassie went upstairs to the storage room and unearthed her mother's trunk. All of her mother's things were exactly as she had left them when she died of pneumonia. Since Cassie hadn't brought many clothes with her from Phoenix, where it was always summer, she had rummaged through her mother's dresser drawers for sweaters and old corduroy slacks to wear. It was amazing to find that her mother's clothes fit her, since Cassie had always thought her mother was the tiniest woman in the world, and she pictured herself as being round and plump, but they did.

The few outfits of clothing her mother had left were in the drawers, but Cassie was looking for something else today. The lid of the trunk was heavy and hard to lift, but she eventually managed to raise it and prop it up against the wall while she went through the trunk's contents. This is all she had, Cassie thought, and if I died today, I wouldn't even have this much to leave for Jess. When he grew up, he wouldn't even know what kind of person I was. The thought made her sad, and she went through her mother's meager belongings gently and lovingly. There was a photograph album, which Cassie couldn't bring herself to open, and a small, locked clothbound book which might have been a diary. She left both of those items for another day, a day when her nerves were not as frayed as the cover of the little book.

With her next discovery, Cassie broke into tears, and it was several minutes before she could get herself under control again. In its original Goldwater's box, wrapped in white tissue paper, was the red velveteen robe she had impulsively sent to her mother for Christmas the year before her death. She had known that her mother would never be allowed to wear the robe, and she had feared that her father might even throw the gift away, but she had wanted to let her mother know that she was remembered. The robe had cost Cassie much more than she could afford to spend, but it hadn't mattered.

She removed it from the gold-and-white box and ran her hand over the soft fabric, then buried her face in its folds. It moved her deeply to think that her mother might have handled the robe in the same way, and that her mother's tears might have dried on the same spot where hers now fell.

Finally, she returned the robe to the box and dug deeper into the trunk. In moments, she found what she was looking for: a small statue of the baby Jesus and two blue votive-candle holders. It wasn't much, but it was enough, and the best part was that the items had belonged to her mother.

Downstairs, Cassie checked on Jess, took him a glass of orange juice, and returned to the kitchen to search for candles. Her mother had always kept odds and ends of candles in the kitchen drawer in case of a power failure, and they were still there. None of them matched, but Cassie chose a blue one and a green one and placed them in the blue holders.

Jess watched her curiously as she dusted a squat, square table and moved it over against the wall opposite the couch. She covered it with a yellowed doily, then arranged the statue and the two candles on it. Satisfied, she turned to smile at Jess, and was surprised that he didn't return her smile.

"Isn't it pretty?" she asked, standing back to admire her handiwork. "It's to thank God for saving you from drowning."

"God didn't save me," Jess replied matter-of-factly, "Corey did."

"Who told you that?"

"Dr. Gibby. He said Corey dived in under the ice and saved my life."

"Well, he's wrong, Corey had nothing to do with it."

"You mean Dr. Gibby lied to me?"

"That's all, Jess, I don't want to hear another word about Corey Hammil. It was God who saved you and gave you back to me, and now we're going to show God that we appreciate what He did for us."

"Are we going to be religious now?"

Cassie hesitated and she thought she saw the shadow of a smile flicker on her son's lips before she answered. "I'm going to change, Jess, I'm going to be a better mother from now on."

"You've always been a good mother, Mom."

"Well, I'll be a better one now."

"Okay," Jess answered, then he turned his attention back to the TV, which was now showing a rerun of "Bonanza."

When Gibby stopped in later in the day to check on Jess, his reaction was almost identical to the boy's.

"You've been a good mother to the boy, Cassie, you can't be faulted in your treatment of Jess. His near drowning was accidental, it had nothing to do with God wanting to punish you for a lack of maternal responsibility."

"I know what I know, Gibby."

"You're so damned stubborn. Okay, okay, have it your way, if it makes you happy. I wanted to talk to you about something else anyway. I just stopped in at the store, and Marilou isn't doing too well without you. I told her I'd talk to you and see when you thought you could go back to work."

Cassie raised wide, frightened eyes to Gibby's face. "I haven't even thought about it. I don't want to leave Jess alone, I can't."

"Of course, you can't leave him alone, but he'll be

going back to school in a couple of weeks. I thought it might make Marilou feel better if we told her you'd be going back a week from next Monday. How does that sound?"

"I know what you're doing, Gibby. You don't want me to get all wrapped up in taking care of Jess and forget that I have an obligation to my daddy."

"I'm not worried about your dad, Cassie, I'm worried about you. Since the day of Jess's accident, you haven't thought of anything else. Now I think it's time you started thinking about yourself again. I know you enjoyed working at the store, and I think it's important that you get your life back to normal as soon as possible."

"You don't know what it's like to be a mother."

"No, I don't, and I probably never will." Gibby rose, smiling, and walked to the door, stopping to ruffle Jess's hair on the way.

"See you guys tomorrow," he said, as he stepped out into the cold Connecticut evening. "Take care of your mother, champ."

As soon as she thought it was safe for Jess to go out of the house, Cassie took him to the store and left him with Marilou, pleading a bad case of cabin fever. The older woman acted as if Cassie were doing her a favor by leaving Jess in her care. They set up chairs behind the counter and were already playing a complicated card game when Cassie left the store. Since her father's car had started stalling out on her every time she drove it, she had borrowed Marilou's car for her trip into Hartford. She promised that she'd be careful and bring the old green Buick back without a scratch. Although it was ten years old, it was in mint condition, with the average mileage of a two-year-old car on its speedometer.

Cassie's hands were trembling on the steering wheel when she turned into the hospital's parking lot and pulled into a visitor's space. She walked around the building until she found the entrance she and Dr. Gibby had used on her first trip to the hospital. His reserved space was unoccupied, the Mercedes nowhere in sight.

The hospital corridors smelled of the familiar strong disinfectant, but they seemed to be shorter than they were the other time Cassie had visited her father. It was a strange feeling to know that for eight days she had kept a vigil in another building of this facility and never once crossed the walkway between buildings to see him. Actually, Gibby had suggested it once, and Cassie had jumped all over him for his unwelcome suggestion.

Now here she was, her low-heeled boots making little squishy sounds on the highly polished tile floors, as she walked alone down the dreaded route. But she had to do it, that was part of her deal with God. "You owe me, Cassandra McCall," God kept whispering in her ear, and she knew that it was true. She had made a promise, and now she had to pay. It wouldn't have been fair to bring Gibby with her, to use him to comfort her and give her strength. That was God's job, if He didn't mind her putting it that way.

It was a lot easier the second time, and not only because Cassie had psyched herself up for the meeting. For one thing, the day was brighter, and the drapes were open to the late-morning sunshine. Her father's wheelchair had been parked beside the bed, and he was sitting in it.

His head was thrown back, and he was sleeping, snoring softly. Cassie had several minutes to watch his face, to be amazed at how different he looked in repose, before he became aware of her presence in the room and slowly opened his eyes. He started and mumbled something unintelligible but if it was a dismissal, Cassie ignored it.

"Hi, Daddy, I came to see you again, even though I

know you weren't too happy to see me the first time." The old man stared, and a thin thread of spittle dribbled from the corner of his mouth. Cassie wanted to wipe it away for him, but she didn't dare.

"I know you don't like me, Daddy, and I don't know why. I only know that you never did love me like you should have. Do you know that I can't remember a time that you ever smiled at me, or acted like you were happy to see me? Momma loved me, she always told me that she did. But you—"

He slid over an inch or so in Cassie's direction, and she took a step backward before she could stop herself. Her father's face twisted, as if he were trying to smile, and she imagined his voice booming into the room: "Hah! Scared you, didn't I, girl? Just wait till you see what else I can do, wait till you see your old man's full bag of tricks, missy."

Cassie forced her lips to form a thin smile, and willed her legs to continue to hold her upright. When she had lived in her father's house, she had had one rule that kept her from going crazy: don't ever let him know when he gets to you, don't ever let him see the depth of your pain. She mentally wiped her face clean of all emotion as she took one small step back toward the wheelchair.

"I have to go now, Daddy, but I came here today to tell you that I'm going to try to find out why you hate me. If I can find the reason, then maybe I can make you change your mind, and even if I can't, then at least I'll understand why. I'll be back, Daddy."

She wanted to bolt from the room, but she walked slowly, with discipline born of her newly discovered responsibility to herself and Jess. Outside the door, she leaned against the wall and sighed deeply. A passing nurse stopped and looked at her with concern. "Are you all right, dear?" she asked, and Cassie's answer clearly confused her: "I should have kissed him. Next time, I'll force myself to kiss him."

By the time she reached Marilou's car, Cassie was calm enough to trust herself behind its wheel. As a matter of fact, the big old car was a pleasure to drive, and she felt herself enjoying the trip back to Winter Falls. She didn't let herself think too much about the visit with her father and its consequences. It was something she knew she had to do, and she intended to take it one day at a time.

She pulled up in front of The Emporium, climbed out of the Buick, and slammed the heavy car door behind her. Then she noticed that she was parked directly behind a blue-and-white patrol car. She hesitated for a moment, tempted to get back in the car and drive around for a few minutes, to avoid the police. If it was the same officer—what was his name, Tom Barney?—who had grilled her in the hospital, he would no doubt suspect her of being up to something vile because she had left Jess alone with Marilou.

Stop it! she ordered herself, you're not a criminal, and it's probably not even the same cop and, even if it is, he's stopped off to pick up a new pair of leather gloves or something. Hadn't Marilou told her that The Emporium had the contract for ordering uniforms for the four full-time Winter Falls officers and the two part-timers?

Cassie pushed the door open and the bell tinkled, calling attention to her entrance. Marilou was standing behind the counter, her pale blue eyes red and teary. Standing over her was Officer Tom Barney, scribbling on his ever-present clipboard. When Marilou saw that it was Cassie who had entered the store, she started around the counter, twisting her handkerchief and sobbing. "Oh, Cassie, I'm sorry, I'm so sorry. I only left him alone for a minute, to go to the ladies' room. I swear I wasn't away more than a minute, and when I got back, he was gone. I looked everywhere, and Gibby wasn't in his office, and I didn't know who else to call. I'm sorry."

The cop looked up, and his expression left no doubt that whatever had happened now was clearly Cassie's fault. "Well," he said, flashing an evil grin that stopped her in her tracks, "if it isn't the famous Miss McCall."

# Chapter Seven

Cassie sat in the front seat of the patrol car with a silent Tom Barney while he cruised up and down the streets and lanes of Winter Falls. She wanted to tell him to drive faster, to use his siren to force slow-moving vehicles out of their way, but she knew that his approach was the right one. He was systematically driving up and down every street and every alleyway, scanning yards, empty lots and playgrounds for a small blond-haired boy wearing blue jeans and a green down-filled jacket. Cassie didn't like the cop's personality, but she had to admit that he was thorough.

"Where were you this afternoon, Miss McCall?" he asked after slowing down to check out a group of small boys playing kickball in the school yard.

"I was visiting my father at the hospital in Hartford."

"Is that so? I seem to recall hearing that you and your daddy don't exactly see eye to eye."

"I guess you could say that."

Cassie half expected Barney to ask if she had a witness who could testify as to where she'd spent the past several hours, but he didn't. He kept his silence as they approached the outskirts of town, and steered the patrol car onto the road that led to Lake Wahelo.

Cassie gasped when she realized where he was

heading, and the cop shot her a questioning glance.

"You don't like this place, do you, Miss McCall?" he asked.

"No, I don't like this lake, I never have."

"I mean this *town*. You don't care much for Winter Falls or the people who live here, do you?"

"That isn't true. I spent sixteen years of my life here."

"And ran away as soon as you were old enough to board a bus."

"Yes, but—" Cassie's thoughts were swept out of her mind when she saw the figure standing alone at the edge of the lake. He looked so small, so thin. His jacket wasn't zipped, and it flapped in the wind, which was also tousling his fair hair. The cop guided the patrol car toward the boy and parked as close to him as he could get. Cassie was out of the car before it was completely stopped, calling out her little boy's name as she ran.

"Jess, honey, what are you doing here? You scared me half to death."

She knelt on the muddy bank and tried to turn the boy into her arms, but he resisted, his gaze intent on the middle of the lake. Without relaxing her grip on him, Cassie turned to see what held his attention, but there was nothing there.

"What is it, Jess?" she asked. "What are you looking at?"

"I was looking for Wanda," he answered in a monotone, "but I can't find her."

"There's nobody out there, honey." He stood still while she zipped his jacket and pulled the hood up over his head. "Come on, let's go home now. It's so cold out here. Aren't you cold?"

Jess shook his head to indicate that he wasn't, although the tears running down Cassie's face were freezing on her cheeks. She took his hand and Jess docilely let himself be led up the bank toward the patrol car.

"Why are the police here?" he asked when he noticed the car. "Are they here for me?"

"You left the store without telling Marilou, Jess. You had us worried nearly to death."

"I'm sorry if I scared you, Mom. I was okay. I just wanted to come out to the lake and see Wanda."

"Shhh. We'll talk about this later, when we get home."

"Don't tell me you and the boy are keeping secrets from me, Miss McCall." Tom Barney smiled at Jess, a big wide shit-eating grin that didn't fool Jess one bit.

"We'd never keep a secret from a policeman, would we, Jess?" Cassie asked in a sugary-sweet voice.

The boy's answer was perfect: "No, ma'am, not from a policeman."

At the house, Tom Barney insisted on filling out a form so that he could file a report, and Cassie wondered what he was doing with all the paperwork. Did he have a file marked "Cassie McCall" where he was noting all his suspicions until he finally tripped her up and caught her at something illegal? That wouldn't have surprised her.

She let Jess run inside the house to get warmed up while she sat in the car and answered the cop's questions to his satisfaction.

It was a shame, she thought, that she had gotten off on the wrong foot with him because if she ever needed the police to stand up for her in an emergency situation, she would hate to have to rely on Officer Barney.

A few minutes later, she was sitting with Jess on the couch, each of them sipping from a mug of hot chocolate, while she tried to make some sense of what he had said at the lake.

"You said you were looking for Wanda, didn't you?" Cassie asked.

"Uh-huh."

"Wanda what? Does she have a last name?"

"I don't know."

"What does she look like?"

The boy shrugged and cut his eyes away so that he was looking over Cassie's shoulder instead of at her face.

"Just where and when did you meet this girl Wanda?"

"I think I met her the day I fell in the lake, I don't remember."

Cassie sighed and placed her half-empty mug on the coffee table, then took Jess's mug from him, so that she could hold his hands while she talked to him.

"Do you remember when I told you and Corey about the legend of Lake Wahelo?"

"I think so."

"Well, the legend is a big thing around here, and everybody talks about it, especially in the wintertime when there isn't much else to do. What I think happened is that you heard somebody talking about the legend, and you heard them say that one of the little girls was named Wanda. Then you fell in the lake, right out in the middle where the three girls disappeared."

"And I dreamed that I met Wanda?" Jess supplied.

"Something like that."

"Okay."

"What do you mean 'Okay'? Is that what happened or not?"

"I guess so."

"Are you okay, Jess?" Cassie had been thinking ever since they came home that his eyes looked dull and lifeless, and she was afraid that he might be getting sick. She put her hand on his forehead and was shocked at the damp, clammy feel of his skin.

She left the living room, using the excuse that she thought they needed some cookies to go with their hot chocolate. In the kitchen, she dialed Dr. Gibby's number, holding the receiver under her chin while she raided the cookie jar and piled peanut-butter bars

73

on a plate. After three rings, Gibby's answering machine fielded the call, and Cassie left a terse message that she needed to talk to him as soon as possible. "It's about Jess," she added just before the machine cut her off. She was on her way back to the living room with the cookies when Gibby pounded on the front door.

"Marilou told me what happened." He burst into the room, followed by a blast of frigid air, then a burst of the warmth that always seemed to follow in his wake. "How are you, Jess? I heard you had yourself a little adventure this afternoon."

"I went to the lake," Jess answered simply. "Can I watch TV now, Mom?"

"I want Dr. Gibby to take a look at you first. Will you, Gibby?"

"Sure thing. Let's see how you're doing here, fella." The doctor sat down on the edge of the couch and opened the black bag he carried with him. Within the next few minutes, he took the boy's temperature, checked his blood pressure and heart rate, examined his throat, eyes and ears, and prodded his neck and chest.

"Fit as a fiddle," he proclaimed, and passed Jess the remote control, which had been lying on the coffee table.

Gibby inclined his head toward the kitchen, and Cassie understood. "Would you like some hot chocolate?" she asked, and the doctor followed her into the kitchen, where the remains of the cocoa she had made for herself and Jess, was a congealed, unappetizing mess.

"Would you rather have coffee?" she asked, and Gibby nodded.

"His blood pressure is a little low," he said, knowing that Cassie was concerned about Jess's condition, "and his temp is slightly below normal, but nothing to worry about. I'll drop by and check him again tomorrow morning. If he's having any problems at all, we'll take him back to the hospital for testing."

"Do you think there's something wrong with him?"

"No, I don't. A little exposure to the elements seems to be the worst scenario of what he experienced today, and he doesn't have any congestion in his chest or any other serious symptoms. Just watch him carefully over the next few days. Don't let him wander off again."

Cassie turned from the counter, where she had just plugged in the ancient percolator. "For your information, I didn't *let him* wander off. I left him with Marilou while I ran some errands, and he left the store while she was in the little girls' room."

"Don't get all steamed up about this, Cassie, I wasn't accusing you of anything. Anyway, I know where you went today, and you don't have to be defensive about it. I have to admit that I was surprised when one of the nurses told me you'd been in to see your father, but it's certainly not a crime."

"Was I supposed to ask you first?"

"No, of course not. Could we talk about Jess for a few minutes now?"

Cassie shrugged, and waited for Gibby to say what was on his mind.

"Did he tell you why he wandered out to the lake on a cold day like this?"

"He said he went out there looking for a girl."

"Jess said that? That he was looking for a girl?"

"Don't make light of it, Gibby. He said the girl's name was 'Wanda.'"

"Hey, don't look so serious. He couldn't live here for two weeks without hearing the story about his great-aunts, drowning in the lake. He's probably working through the fear that something like that could have happened to him."

"I don't know, he seemed to be confused, like he wasn't really sure what he was doing there."

"Don't forget that he's only eight years old, and he's been through a very traumatic experience. This is one of the things that his doctors warned you about, the possibility that Jess could start experiencing psychological side effects of the accident."

"Don't use that fancy doctor talk on me, Gibby." Cassie set a steaming mug of strong coffee on the table in front of him and went to the refrigerator for milk.

"The near drowning was a very bad thing to happen to a little boy, Cassie. The memories of what happened that day could affect Jess's mind. He could have nightmares about it, and bad memories even when he's awake."

"What if that happens to him, what can we do?"

"We can get a good doctor to talk to him, to try to help him get past it."

"You're talking about a shrink, aren't you? You're sayng Jess might have to see a shrink?"

Gibby nodded, took a big sip of his coffee, and looked as if he might spit it back into the cup. "I guess I don't know how to make very good coffee in that old pot," Cassie apologized.

"It's fine." He took another, smaller sip and set the cup down on the table. He looked surprised to see that Cassie had seated herself across from him and was watching his face carefully.

"What is it?" he asked. "Is something wrong?"

"Now that we've talked about Jess," Cassie answered, "I want to talk about my father."

"Okay."

Cassie sighed and looked down at her hands for a minute before she raised her eyes to Gibby's. "I want to know why he's like he is, Gibby. I want to find out why he doesn't like me, and why he's never been happy. This is important to me, and you're the only person I know who might be able to help me figure it out."

Gibby reached across the table and touched

Cassie's cheek gently. "All I know for sure is that it isn't your fault. You're a good person, Cassie, and a good mother to Jess."

She was tempted to cover his hand with her own, but she resisted the temptation. Her need for human contact was strong, and she almost wished that she hadn't made that promise to God. But even if she hadn't, she knew that she couldn't have treated Dr. Gibby as if he was just like any other man. If he was, she could have risen and moved around the table, her eyes never leaving his. She could have pressed her body against his, and kissed his full, sexy lips until he lifted her onto his lap. But Gibby was a doctor, and he was a special man, a special friend. Cassie lowered her eyes to the vinyl tablecloth and kept them there until Gibby removed his hand from her face and started to talk.

"You're right, Cassie, your father has never been a happy man. Sometimes I think he was born unhappy because of what happened to his own father."

"You mean his daughters' drowning?" Cassie asked.

"Among other things, yes. You know, your grandfather, Colin, had two best friends, my grandfather and Jeremy Winter, the grandson of the founder of Winter Falls. The three of them were spoiled rotten, used to getting everything they wanted and never having to pay for anything. Jeremy was the worst of the three: ridiculously handsome, intelligent, an only child adored by his parents. They were all good boys, but they were extremely curious, and one of the things they were curious about was Satan."

Cassie gasped, and Gibby looked at her with an odd expression on his face, as if he had forgotten that she was there.

"You're not making this up, are you?" she asked.

"Of course not."

"Then tell me how you just happen to know so

77

much about our grandfathers and Jeremy Winter."

"My dad told me, his father had told him. There's a lot more, do you want to hear it?"

Cassie nodded and Gibby looked away, as if he could see the three young men outside the kitchen window of Connor McCall's old house. "One night when John and Colin were in their early twenties and Jeremy was around nineteen, the three of them went up into the attic of the Winter house and tried to perform a satanic ritual. They called on Satan to join them, and as the story goes, he did."

"What happened?"

"Jeremy fell, or was pushed out of their circle of protection and something attacked him."

"This isn't true!"

"My dad said it was true. Jeremy was never the same after that."

"What do you mean 'never the same'?"

"He lost his mind that night. For the rest of his life, Jeremy Winter was little more than a vegetable."

"And you really think Satan came and did that to him?"

"What do you think?"

"I don't know what to think, but I don't want to talk about it any more tonight. Anyway, I have to turn off the TV and get Jess up to bed now."

They walked back to the living room and found Jess asleep on the couch, the TV blaring, the remote control clutched in his hand.

Gibby offered to carry Jess upstairs but Cassie refused to let him. She walked him to the door, so that she could lock it behind him, and told him good night as he went out. He was halfway to his car when she opened the door again and yelled out to him.

"Gibby, what's a circle of protection?"

"It's a circle painted on the floor, or in this case, drawn on the floor with chalk. If you stand inside of it, you're supposed to be protected from the Devil, but if you move over the line, he can grab you."

78

"The way he grabbed Jeremy Winter?"

If Gibby made an answer, she didn't hear it over the rush of the wind and the other sound. She stood quiet for several minutes, door open, letting the cold creep inside the house, while she tried to identify the sound. Finally, she did. It was the sound of water rushing under a thick sheet of ice, water churning in a frantic effort to crack the ice and topple Jess into Lake Wahelo.

# Chapter Eight

Cassie found herself looking forward to the week ahead, and the extra time she'd have to spend with Jess. Ever since he was a baby, she'd had to leave him in the care of sitters while she worked to put food on the table. It had been years since they'd had a whole week to spend together.

The first few days flew by, and she knelt in front of the baby Jesus every day and thanked Him for letting her keep Jess, and for giving her this time with him. Of course, she had to admit that it would be nicer if Jess wasn't so moody, if he didn't just sit in front of the TV screen for hours and hours on end.

By the middle of the week, she started to wonder if there was something wrong with him. She would have asked Dr. Gibby to take a look at him again, but the doctor was in New York City for some kind of a medical seminar until the end of the week. One afternoon, she sat down beside Jess on the couch, took one of his hands in hers and squeezed it. It was so cold that a shock of pain shot through her hand, as if she had wrapped it around an icicle.

"You're so cold, honey." She pulled the folded afghan off the back of the couch and tucked it around Jess's shoulders.

He shrugged it off and hit a button on the remote control. An old "Sea Hunt" episode was just beginning, and that seemed to satisfy the child. The background was a tropical setting, so the water was supposed to be warm, at least on the surface. There was a diver in the water, and a pretty young girl sitting on the boat's ladder with her feet in the water. As the girl swung her legs back and forth, Cassie felt the chill of the water, felt it grow colder and colder by the second. She wondered if this was part of the show's plot and, if it was, how they were conveying this feeling of cold water to the viewer.

She leaned over to hug her knees and almost went into shock. Her legs were as cold as ice, as cold as Jess's hands had been a few minutes earlier. She leaned closer to the little boy and rearranged the afghan so that it covered both of them.

"I'm not cold, Mom," Jess protested, but he was, cold and clammy. She clicked off the TV and forced Jess to turn and look at her. His eyes had that weird vacant look again, and they were shiny, which she knew sometimes to be an indication of the onset of an illness.

"If you're still like this when Dr. Gibby comes home, I'm going to take you into his office for a good examination," she said, eliciting the child's scorn. "I'm not sick, Mom," he said, as if she ought to be smart enough to know that.

Jess went to bed early that night, but Cassie sat up hours past her bedtime worrying and praying.

On Saturday morning, she borrowed Marilou's Buick again, and drove Jess into Hartford for a previously scheduled checkup. When she asked for Dr. Gibson, one of the doctors told her that he was still out of town, and that he would probably be back in his office on Monday morning. She was disappointed that Gibby wouldn't be one of the doctors looking at Jess, because she couldn't confide her groundless fears to these city doctors. With Gibby, it was different. It would seem perfectly all right to tell him that she was worried, but that she didn't know exactly why. She could even tell him about "Sea Hunt," if she wanted to.

The team of doctors examined Jess thoroughly, and gave him a clean bill of health. He was released from their care with permission to return to school on Monday, and to resume his normal activities. On the drive home, Cassie tried to get Jess to show some enthusiasm about his progress and his return to school, but he didn't seem to care much, one way or the other.

She delivered the Buick to Marilou at The Emporium, thinking that she and Jess would walk home, with a quick detour to Burger King for lunch. She was surprised when Jess begged off, saying that he had a stomachache, probably caused by all the doctors poking at his stomach.

When they got home, Cassie knelt before her shrine and asked God's forgiveness for her cowardice. She had decided the night before that she would sneak Jess in to see his grandfather today, just for a couple of minutes. Then this morning she had completely lost her nerve. She hadn't even told Jess that his grandfather was in the same hospital where he had spent eight days in a coma.

When she got up from her knees, the boy was standing in the doorway that led to the kitchen, watching her curiously.

"What do you want, Jess?" she snapped, disconcerted by the intensity of his stare.

"I want to go for a walk," he answered, but he was still looking at her intently, as if he were trying to understand what she was doing, praying to a God that he had never heard her mention before his accident.

"I guess it would be all right. Just zip up your jacket and don't be gone too long. I'll fix us something to eat in a couple of hours."

"Okay. Thanks, Mom."

She stood at the front window and watched him

walk slowly down the street. "Don't go near the lake," she whispered, and he turned and waved, as if he had heard her warning.

Cassie went to the kitchen and looked in the freezer, wondering what she could throw together for dinner that would whet Jess's appetite. It was hard cooking for just herself and a child who was never hungry, and at times like this, she wished she had a microwave. Maybe if they were to stay in Winter Falls for a while, she'd check into buying one on time from The Emporium.

She finally removed a package of hamburger patties from the freezer and laid them out on the counter to thaw. She was sitting at the kitchen table, making a grocery list of all the things Jess liked to eat—when the phone rang. Thinking that it might be Gibby calling to tell her he'd returned to town, she snatched it up, but her hello was answered by the one voice she didn't want to hear.

"Corey, I'm getting tired of telling you that there was nothing between you and me in the first place. And even if there was, it's over now, over and done with."

"Cassie, don't hang up. I'm begging you to talk to me. Dr. Gibson told me to give you some time, and I did that. Now I'm only asking that you talk to me."

"I don't have anything to say to you."

"Then listen to what I have to say, can you do that?"

"I'm not interested in anything you have to say, Corey."

There was a long silence on the line before Cassie sighed and spoke again.

"You're causing me to be a mean person, and I'm *not* a mean person. It's just that I've changed, and I don't want to go out with you now. It's wrong, and—"

"It's not wrong," the boy cut in, "I love you, Cassie, how can that be wrong?"

"You don't love me, Corey, you don't even know me. If I told you some of the things I've done to keep body and soul together, you'd run away from me so fast."

"I think it's you who don't know me, if you could think that."

"I don't just think it, I know it. You don't know what kind of person I am. I'm not for you, Corey."

"Is it the doctor? Is that why you're tired of me, because he has more to offer you?"

"Go to hell, Corey Hammill!" She slammed down the receiver and ran outside before she realized that she didn't have anyplace to run. Anyway, it was her house, and all she had to do was stop answering the telephone. Maybe she could get one of the machines that let you know who was calling before you picked up.

When it was time for Jess to return, she stood at the front window watching for him, wondering if there was just a tiny grain of truth in Corey's accusation. She hadn't answered the question to her satisfaction when the telephone rang again, causing her to jump and run to the kitchen. When she got there, she only stared at the shiny new wall phone, as if it were a snake she was afraid to handle.

Finally, on the sixth ring, she picked it up and pressed it to her ear. If she heard his voice, she'd just hang up, without saying a word, without encouraging him.

"Cassie? Cassie, are you there? Say something."

It was Marilou's voice, and Cassie sighed with relief before she answered "I'm here, Marilou."

"Are you okay?"

"I'm fine, what's up?" Marilou didn't usually call her during business hours unless there was some minor problem she thought she had to share with her "boss," as she jokingly called Cassie. When Marilou didn't answer right away, Cassie leaned against the counter for support, as an icy feeling of *déjà vu*

84

washed over her.

"Please, Marilou," she begged, "tell me what's wrong."

"Well . . . Jess stopped in to see me this afternoon."

"He didn't tell me he was going to the store," Cassie thought aloud, puzzled as to why an eight-year-old boy would choose to spend a bright, sunny Saturday afternoon in a dark, dreary dry goods store.

"He wasn't here too long," the woman continued, "but I had a couple of customers while he was here and I couldn't spend too much time with him. I don't know how to say this, Cassie."

"I think you'd better just go on and spit it out."

"There are some things missing. I think Jess took them." The clerk's huge sigh of relief could be heard clearly through the telephone wires, and in a strange way Cassie felt sorry for her.

"I'll be right down," Cassie said, when Marilou seemed to have said all she was going to say.

She took her father's old clunker, which, for once, started right up and didn't stall out during the entire five-minute drive. She pulled up in front of the store and was glad that this time there was no police car waiting for her. She smiled wryly, thinking how Officer Tom Barney would enjoy this, if he only knew.

Marilou was waiting just inside the door, and Cassie almost ran into her when she entered the store.

"I think I know what happened," the woman said, grabbing at Cassie's arm. "As a matter of fact, I'm sure of it. It was those Rowland kids, you know, the big family down by the feed store. They're always in trouble with somebody, and there are several girls, at least three or four. They got ahold of Jess and made him do it. I know that's what happened. A sweet little boy like Jess wouldn't—"

She stopped talking when she noticed that Cassie had raised her hands in front of her to get her attention.

"What did he take, Marilou, what's missing?"

"That's the strange part, that's why I know he didn't do it on his own."

"What's missing?" Cassie repeated, and the woman walked to the counter to consult a list.

"Three girls' party dresses, sizes seven, nine and ten. And maybe some candy, but I'm not too sure about that. I know how many bags I had, but kids are always stealing that."

Cassie stared at the woman incredulously, wanting to laugh at her stupidity. "You're accusing Jess of stealing girls' dresses?" she asked.

Marilou blushed, then squared her shoulders and met the younger woman's gaze head-on. "He was the only one here, just him and me and two customers. There was no one else that could have done it. Do you think I'd accuse Jess if I wasn't absolutely sure?"

"No," Cassie replied, the smile fading from her lips, "I'm sure you wouldn't. You'd better tell me everything."

Marilou nodded and closed her eyes for a moment, as if trying to get a clear picture of the entire incident. "He came in and said hi, and sat down on the stool behind the counter. I asked him how his doctor's visit went, and he said he was okay now, that he'd be going back to school come Monday. I asked if he wanted to take his jacket off, but he said no, he wouldn't be staying too long. Said he was just taking a little walk, out in the sunshine. Two customers came in after a while, and I went back to the hardware department with them. While I was back there, Jess went over to the comic books and picked one up. If it was any other kid, I would have thought he was acting suspicious, looking down at the book, then glancing back to me, like he wanted to see if I was watching him. I got wrapped up in hunting up a special piece of pipe for my customers, then I heard Jess yell out to me that he was going. I told him to wait, but he didn't hear me. By the time I got to the front of the store he was gone. I looked out the door, but he was nowhere in sight, up or down the street."

"When did you find out that the dresses were missing?" Cassie asked, impressed by Marilou's straight-forward recitation of the afternoon's events.

"After my customers left, I was walking around straightening the racks, when I saw that a dress was missing from the size tens. I only noticed it because I had purposely put it out in front. It was so pretty, violet with tiny white pearl buttons. I looked for it, then counted the size tens and discovered that they were one short. So I counted the other sizes and there was a size nine gone, and a size seven."

"Couldn't someone have taken them yesterday?" Cassie asked.

"Oh no, I put them out last night after I closed the store. We just got the delivery yesterday, and I thought they were so fresh and pretty that they might brighten up the store a little. I'm so sorry, Cassie. If there was any other way, I wouldn't have bothered you with this."

"It's all right, Marilou. If Jess did something wrong, I have to know, I'm his mother. Tell me something. Why do you think he would steal those dresses, except for pressure from the Rowland kids. Were they expensive? Could he sell them and make money on them?"

"Oh my, no, they were only $19.95 each. Anyway, nobody in Winter Falls would buy them from him. They'd just call us and tell us somebody was trying to set up shop and trying to compete with us, without a license."

"Why would they call us instead of the police?" Cassie wondered aloud.

"So that we could protect ourselves from unfair competition. Folks in Winter Falls are like that, Cassie."

"I believe you. Well, I'm going to go on home and wait for Jess. It's past the time I told him to be back from his walk. If he tries to tell me a story about this, I may have to call you later."

Marilou said that would be all right, but Cassie could tell from the look on her face that there were a lot of things she would rather do than call Jess a thief to his face.

Jess wasn't home when Cassie arrived there, although it was almost an hour past his deadline. She checked out the house, then sat in the living room to wait for him. She knew she should be starting dinner, but she was too shaky to think about eating, and she guessed that Jess wouldn't be hungry either, after he heard what she had to say to him.

A half hour later, she went outside and walked around the house, beat a path through the tall grass in the back, all the way to the old wooden watering trough that had never in her memory held water. She even checked under the porch, but there was no sign of Jess anywhere.

Cassie went back to the car, turned the key and hit the accelerator. This time the car wouldn't start. She got out, slammed the door hard, and started walking toward the center of town. Two blocks down the street, she saw Jess. He was shuffling along with his head down and he didn't see her until he almost ran into her.

"Mom! I was just on my way home for dinner."

"You're late, you should have been home two hours ago."

"I'm sorry. I don't have a watch anymore."

Cassie took his hand and retraced her steps back to the house. She wasn't mad at him. She was worried. After she heard what he had to say, she'd call Gibby and tell him what had happened. But maybe Gibby wasn't back yet. Then what would she do?

She hung up Jess's jacket and made him sit down on the couch. Kneeling in front of him, holding his hands in hers, she asked him to look at her. He did, raising his eyes slowly to meet hers. His eyes were so blue, so like his father's, that Cassie almost forgot her reason for wanting to talk to him. Then it all came back to her in a flood of misery, and she decided to make the whole thing as quick and painless as possible.

"Jess, Marilou says you stole three little girls' dresses from the store. I want you to tell me the truth, did you take them?"

He nodded yes, and Cassie experienced a wave of conflicting emotions: pride that he was being so honest with her, and sorrow that he had committed a crime.

"Why did you do it, Jess?"

"I did it for Wanda."

"Wanda? The girl you met at Lake Wahelo?"

"Uh-huh."

"The girl that drowned in Lake Wahelo?"

"Uh-huh."

"Why did Wanda need the dresses, Jess?" Cassie asked, playing along.

"She wanted to get out of the lake, and she needed a dress because she wanted to look pretty."

"Why did she need three?"

"Only one of them was for her."

"Who were the others for?" Cassie asked, but she already knew, and in that second while she waited for his answer, she prayed fervently that he would name the Rowland girls. If he did, she would forgive him, and never mention it again. But her prayers were not to be granted, and Jess's answer to her question would never be forgotten.

"They were for Helen and Lorraine," he said, "Wanda's little sisters."

# Chapter Nine

Jess hung out at the comic-book rack, pretending an interest in the latest issue of Batman Comics. He intended to stay there until Marilou stopped hovering over him. He stood there a long time, long enough to read the whole comic book if he'd wanted to, while she worked at a counter three feet away, unpacking new merchandise. Finally, the bell over the door tinkled, and two people came into the store, a man and a woman. They acted like they were glad to see Marilou, and spent a long time talking about almost everybody in Winter Falls before she led them to the back of the store to look at some hardware.

When they were far enough away, Jess moved slowly and stealthily around the tables stacked high with sheets and towels and blankets. He knew every department in the store, so he didn't have to hunt for anything. When he got to children's clothing, where most of his own clothes came from, he stopped. After glancing around to make sure that no one was watching, he reached out and grabbed three dresses from the revolving rack marked "party dresses." He took one from each of the sections marked size ten, size nine, and size seven. He slid whatever was handy off the hangers, not particular about color or style. They all looked pretty awful to him anyway.

He rolled the garments into a ball and stuffed them

under his jacket, which he had kept on in the store in spite of the fact that he was sweating buckets. He sneaked back toward the front of the store, turned to check that Marilou was still busy, and slid a bag of hard candy sticks into his pocket.

"I'm leaving now, Marilou," he called out.

"Wait a minute, honey," the woman answered, but he pretended that he hadn't heard her.

Once he was out of the store, he ran to the corner and rounded it, to get out of sight as fast as he could, in case Marilou came to the door looking for him. He took back streets to the edge of town, until he was on a dirt path he had discovered the last time he made the same trip.

He reached Lake Wahelo in twenty minutes, and stood on the bank wondering what to do next. Finally, he took the dresses out from under his coat and shook them out, thankful that he was alone. He pressed his hands over the fluffy pastel garments and tried to smooth out some of the wrinkles he'd put in them by rolling them up like rags.

He stood there for several minutes staring out at the lake before he saw a subtle movement. Out in the middle of the lake, the ice started to shift. He actually heard it cracking before he saw it moving. As he watched, fascinated and horrified, a thin arm reached up out of the icy water, through the ragged tear in the ice. He could see the dead white skin flapping around it, and he wanted to run away as fast as he could and never come back. But his feet were rooted to the spot, and his eyes were fixed on the hand that now moved, gesturing to him to come forward.

"I can't come out there," he yelled, "I'm scared."

"You won't fall in this time, Jess, I'll take care of you." He didn't hear the words with his ears, but he heard them in his mind.

"And you don't have to yell," the voice continued, "I can hear you when you whisper."

"Are you Wanda?" he asked, following her

instructions about not yelling. He was scared stiff, but he almost giggled. He felt silly whispering to an arm sticking up out of the water. He thought for a moment that maybe it was just a stick, that he had imagined the rest of it, and he was making a fool of himself talking to a twig or something.

But that wasn't so, and he knew it. He had seen Wanda once, when he almost drowned, and she had been putting her words in his mind ever since.

"Did you bring the things I asked for, Jess?" the voice asked suddenly, startling him. "Yes," he answered holding up the dresses as proof. He couldn't remember her asking for them, but when he'd awakened this morning, he'd known what his instructions were.

"Come on out here, Jess, don't be a scaredy cat," the voice teased.

"I'm not," he yelled, forgetting that he didn't have to yell. He crawled out to the center of the lake slowly and carefully, trembling with fear. He was aware that the girl had fully emerged from the lake to watch him, but he didn't look at her until he put the dresses in her hands.

She was narrow bones and flapping white stuff, like old skin, and her head was a skull, like he'd seen in museums. She didn't have any eyes, just holes where her eyes should have been. She was terrible and fascinating to Jess.

"Go away, Jess McCall," she said without words, frightening him even more. "I'll call you and tell you when to come back, and if you're smart, you'll come when I call you."

Jess turned and crawled back to shore, scared to death that she was behind him, reaching out for him with her awful bony arms.

# Chapter Ten

By the time Dr. Gibby reached the house, Cassie's emotions were in a turmoil. She hadn't even tried to talk to Jess, to find out whether he was lying to her or if he really believed that he had talked to a dead girl at the lake. After he had answered her question about why he'd stolen the dresses, Cassie went to the kitchen to call Gibby. Fortunately, he had just returned from New York, and promised to come over as soon as he returned some phone calls. While she was still in the kitchen, Jess came in to tell her that he had an upset stomach. She dosed him with Pepto-Bismol and tucked him into bed in her old room, which she had finally cleaned out and painted. Now it bore little resemblance to the room where she had spent so many miserable days and nights of her childhood. It was Jess's room now, and he seemed to enjoy having a room of his own for the first time in his life.

Gibby's cheeks were red from the cold, and Cassie thought what a good-looking man he was. Not handsome like some of the soap-opera stars she used to watch in Phoenix on her days off, but fit and healthy-looking. He was not the type of man she would have chosen for herself; she had always gravitated toward the dark, dangerous types or the ones with the bad-boy reputations. But she could see why any sane, sensible woman would want a man like Gibby. He was so good, and he would be so good for Jess. In her current state of emotional chaos, the thought proved to be too much for her. She turned away, but not quickly enough. As soon as Gibby draped his overcoat over the back of the couch, he came to her and turned her back to face him.

"What is it, Cassie? Oh, God, don't cry, whatever it is, I'll help you through it."

"I know you will." She smiled and wiped her eyes with a wrinkled Kleenex from her pocket.

"Come over here and sit down. You'd better tell me everything that happened while I was away."

It took only a few minutes to tell him about Jess's walk, Marilou's phone call, and the missing dresses. When she got to the part about Wanda, the doctor rose from the couch and started to pace back and forth restlessly. When Cassie finished, he continued to stand, his eyes narrowed in concentration.

"Well?" Cassie prompted after several long minutes of silence.

"I'd like to send him to a child psychologist who also happens to be a friend of mine. Don't look like that, Cassie, please." He knelt in front of her and took her hands in his. In spite of her worry over Jess, she noticed that his hands were cool and dry and smooth, and that they seemed to contain a healing power all their own. Just sitting there, with her hands in his, calmed her so that she could listen rationally to what he had to say to her.

"Dan Winslow was a classmate of mine. He's a good psychologist, and a nice guy, very good with kids. Jess doesn't have to know what kind of a doctor he is, if you don't want to tell him. I'll explain the situation to Dan before we take Jess in—"

"I don't have any money, Gibby, and I don't have any health insurance. I'm going to be making payments to the hospital for the rest of my natural life. Couldn't you just talk to Jess first and see if you think he really did see something out there? Maybe some of those Rowland kids were playing games with him, filling his head with tales about Wanda and her sisters."

"Cassie, I'm not qualified to do what you're asking me to do. I've told you before that I don't want you to worry about the bills."

"Who's going to worry about them—you? Jess is my son, not yours, and you have a life of your own."

"I'd like to make you and Jess a part of my life, Cassie."

"Don't talk that way! Just don't talk that way." Cassie jumped up from the couch and brought the doctor his coat. When he didn't reach to take it, she shoved it at him, so that he had no choice.

"There's nothing you can do tonight," she said, "I don't know why I got you over here."

"I'll call Dan the first thing tomorrow morning, then I'll let you know about the appointment. Maybe I can drive you over to Hartford myself. Tell Jess I'm sorry I missed him. I don't know when Dan will be able to see him, but I'll see you and Jess tomorrow one way or the other."

Cassie nodded and opened the door, told Gibby good night, and avoided eye contact with him. She knew that if she looked into his eyes, she would see something she didn't want to see: pain, or worse, indifference. Either way, she wouldn't be able to deal with his feelings. He had no business feeling anything for Jess and when she got control of herself, she intended to tell him so.

She spent the next half hour searching the house for a bottle of alcohol she might have missed when she dumped her father's booze down the drain. She needed a drink tonight, and she considered leaving Jess alone for a couple of minutes while she drove down to the liquor store. But what if that cop, Tom Barney, was on duty and saw her driving up to buy booze? If he found out that she had left Jess home alone, he might try to take her son away from her.

"The damned car probably wouldn't start anyway," she reasoned as she lay down on top of her bed fully clothed and closed her eyes to shut out the world.

She fell asleep and fell into the dream, which seemed already in progress, on pause, waiting for her entrance. She stood on the shore of Lake Wahelo, clothed as she had been when she lay down on her bed, in blue jeans and a dark red sweater that had been her mother's. She crossed her arms over her chest and hugged herself, shivered, and wished she had worn her new down jacket. It was a crisp, clear night, and she could see every star in the sky above her. It was a beautiful night, and she almost forgot how cold she was for a few minutes while she tried to identify the different constellations.

Then a small sound caught her attention and she dropped her eyes from the stars to gaze out across the lake. She watched for several minutes and couldn't see anything out there—but as she started to turn away, a flicker of movement caught her eye. The noise came again, a weak cry for help. There was someone out there, someone stranded on the ice in the middle of the lake.

A cold wind blew down from the hills that surrounded the town. Dry twigs and dead leaves lifted from the forest floor and skittered across the ice. The eerie sound intensified Cassie's feeling of being alone in the world, just her and someone in trouble out in the middle of the lake. Someone was trapped, maybe drowning, and Cassie stood helplessly on the shore, too terrified to try and save them.

Suddenly her mind was filled with a horrible knowledge: it was Jess who was drowning. It was Jess who was calling to her for help. He had almost drowned once, and she had begged for another chance to become a good person. She had failed, and now God was exacting His terrible punishment. God was taking Jess from her.

"No!" she screamed, "No!" She tried to run out onto the ice but her feet slid out from under her. She hit the solid ice hard and skimmed over it, sliding toward the middle of the lake at breakneck speed. Her legs and arms burned from the friction and from the near-freezing temperature of the water that was seeping inside her clothing.

Then she was in the water up to her neck, and whoever had been crying out for help was gone, drowned before she could reach them. But she knew that wasn't true. Some knowledge born of the dream convinced her that it was she who had been drowning all along.

She thrashed her arms, kicked her legs, and sank deeper into the black water. It covered her chin and caressed her mouth. When she tried to take a deep breath, it sneaked past her lips and trickled down her throat. She coughed and swallowed more water. She wanted to scream, but fear of swallowing again kept her silent. A second later, water filled her nose, covered her eyes, and closed in over the top of her head. She could feel her long hair floating straight up, as she sank deeper, her feet searching for the bottom of the lake.

She went down slowly after that, and it was almost amusing. She pictured herself sinking, a human-shaped ship with a rupture in her bow, drifting calmly downward. It hurt at first; the water made her throat feel raw. She thought her chest would burst, and she knew that she was dying. She didn't fight it. She welcomed it as an end to the pain, the beginning of something better.

A great sense of calm settled over her, a peace, a sense of well-being such as she had never before experienced. It was so easy to just let go, to give herself up to the rhythmic pull of the water. She felt herself drifting away, until a sharp pain in her leg jerked her back to full consciousness. Had she landed on a sharp rock, a shard of glass? Again, she felt the pain, and doubled over to clutch at her left calf. She rubbed her leg, eased the jabbing pain, and felt her mind start to drift again. She thought that she must have been underwater for several minutes now, and it was surely time to let go.

Something touched her face, something that felt like a human hand. Jess. He was in the water with her after all. She experienced a feeling of sadness that Jess was dying, too, when he had only lived for nine short years. Maybe if she gave him a push, he could float up to the surface. If she was to have one last stroke of luck, there would be someone there to save him.

With an effort, Cassie opened her eyes for what she thought was the last time. Instead of seeing Jess, there was a female child in the water with her, a little girl of six or seven who held a long wooden stick. As Cassie watched in disbelief, the child poked at her leg and sent the now-familiar pain shooting through her left calf. She wanted to say something to the girl, to tell her that she was being hurt by the sharp stick, but she couldn't concentrate. Someone had grabbed ahold of her shoulder and was shaking her back and forth, gently at first, then more forcefully.

"Mom, wake up. Come on, Mom, I'm sick to my stomach and I need you to help me. I'm scared, Mom. Wake up!"

Cassie woke up with a jolt and sat upright in the bed so quickly that she almost knocked Jess over.

"What is it, sweetheart?" In the dark room, his face was luminescent, pale and backlit by fever.

"I'm sick, Mom, you've got to help me."

Cassie carried him to the bathroom, where he seemed to throw up more than he had eaten in the past week. When he was finished, she changed his sheets and tucked him into bed, weak and trembling. She took his soiled sheets downstairs and popped them into the ancient washing machine. Any other time, she would have called Gibby and asked him to come over, but she knew that she had to stop

98

depending on him. This wasn't a medical emergency, it was just a virus or a case of too much junk food. She didn't need a doctor for that.

Only when the sheets were in the dryer did she have time to consider her dream and its implications. Eerie as it was, she concluded that there was no mysterious message behind it. She had been worried about Jess's obsession with the dead girls in the lake, and she had conjured them up in her own mind, that's all. Still, she thought, as she finally lay down on her bed and pulled the quilt up to her chin, it might be interesting to dig through the attic and try to find an old photograph of her aunts. It would really be weird if one of them resembled the lovely dark-haired child who had poked at her leg with a stick as she drowned in Lake Wahelo.

# Chapter Eleven

Monday morning brought a freezing rain and a dark, gloomy day to Winter Falls. Cassie was glad to have an excuse to keep Jess home from school for another day or so. She let him sleep in while she made coffee to drink while she glanced through the morning paper, which was still being delivered to the house. Her dad had never read a book in his life, so far as Cassie knew, but while she was growing up, he had sat at the kitchen table every morning, drinking bitter black coffee as he pored over the *Winter Falls Gazette*. It was an old habit that he obviously had followed until the time of his stroke.

Cassie didn't read much, but she liked to skim through the paper, scan the headlines, read "Dear Abby" and "Hints From Heloise." She poured a cup of coffee, turned up the collar of her terry-cloth robe, and stepped outside for the paper. It was in a plastic bag, wedged up close to the door so that it would stay dry. That was weird because the paper boy usually tossed it in the general direction of the porch as he flew past on his ten-speed Schwinn, no matter how raw the weather.

What was stranger still was the piece of green wax paper on top of the newspaper. Cassie bent to pick it up and saw that it contained a single red rose. She instinctively brought it close to her face and inhaled

100

the lovely fragrance, while she tucked the thin newspaper under her arm and turned back to the door. That was when she saw him. He had probably been there all along, standing off to the left of the house, several feet away. He was wearing a gray jacket and no hat, and his face bore an expression of despair that tore at Cassie's heart. Water flattened his beautiful hair, and streamed down his face. He was soaked to the skin, but he didn't even seem to notice that it was raining.

"Corey Hammil, go home before you catch your death of cold. What's wrong with you, standing out there in the rain like that?" Cassie raised her voice to him, although there was no need. He was standing only a few feet away, and the entire world seemed to have fallen silent.

She didn't think he heard her, and she debated whether it would be wise to get soaked herself in trying to reach him. She decided to go inside and drink her coffee. If he was still there when she looked out again, she'd throw her coat on, find an umbrella, and go out and try to reason with him.

Cassie felt terrible turning her back on Corey and closing the door in his face. She had turned up the heat because Jess was ill, and it was warm in the house, cozy compared to the cold rain that was falling outside where Corey kept his lonely vigil.

She poured the cold coffee into the sink and replaced it with a fresh cup. She considered tossing the rose in the trash, but decided that would be senseless. Instead, she filled a water glass from the tap and stuck the long-stemmed rose in it. Removing the newspaper from the plastic bag, she spread it out on the table, took a sip of her coffee, and began to scan the front page. A header on the bottom half of the page stopped her.

"And it isn't even Halloween!" the inch-high letters read. Beneath that, in smaller print:

Both this newspaper and the Winter Falls Police Department have been deluged with calls reporting sightings of the three ghostly little girls who are believed to have drowned in Lake Wahelo fifty years ago this month. Wanda, Helen and Lorraine McCall wandered off from their home . . .

Cassie skipped over the part of the article that dealt with the details of the girls' disappearance, all of which she had heard a hundred times before, until she reached the bottom of the column. According to the reporter, the girls had been seen walking on the approach road to the lake. Motorists claimed to have seen three small girls on the side of the road, looking lost and confused. When one man got out of his car and tried to approach them, they disappeared into the woods. He yelled out that he only wanted to help them, but they were gone. In his own words, "They just seemed to disappear into thin air."

Another motorist called the police screaming hysterically that she had seen "arms reaching up out of the lake" as she drove past. It was the same old stuff, repeated year after year, nothing new since Cassie had sneaked her dad's newspaper into her room to read the accounts ten years ago.

She folded the paper and pushed it down into the trash bag under the sink so that Jess wouldn't see it and start asking questions. It was probably people talking such nonsense that had made him steal the dresses and go out to the lake in the first place. It struck her that she never did ask him exactly what had happened to the dresses. She would love to hear his answer to that question.

In a way, Cassie couldn't blame Jess for his interest in his dead aunts. When she was a child, she had been intrigued by the romantic tragedy of the story: three young women whose lives had been cut short, who had forever lost their God-given right to fall in love and be happy. She and her girlfriends at school had cried over the terrible injustice of the tragedy more than once.

Now that she was grown up and had a child of her own, Cassie wished that the story would just go away, so that Wanda, Helen and Lorraine could rest in peace.

She tried to put all of her minor problems out of her mind and concentrate on the main one, which was to get Jess to the child psychologist Gibby wanted him to see, and find out once and for all what was wrong with the child. She telephoned Marilou to say she wouldn't be going to the store this morning, and she thought the woman sounded almost relieved. Cassie liked Marilou, and she hoped that the stolen dresses weren't going to stand between them and make it difficult for them to work together at the store.

When she went upstairs to check on Jess, he was standing at the window in her bedroom staring out into the rain-soaked morning.

"Hi, sweetheart, how are you feeling today?" she asked. She placed her hand on his forehead and smiled when she found it cool and dry.

"I'm okay," he said listlessly, moving away from the window.

"What were you looking at out there?" Cassie wondered.

"Nothing. Can I have my breakfast now?"

"Sure thing, Captain Crunch and hot chocolate coming right up." Jess left the room and Cassie followed him, but not before she took a quick glance to the window to prove to herself that the yard was empty, and Corey was nowhere in sight.

While Jess was dawdling over his cereal, the telephone rang. It was Gibby, and the sound of his voice soothed Cassie and drove from her mind the memory of Corey standing in the freezing rain, begging her with his eyes.

"Something's come up," Gibby told her, "and I won't be able to drive you and Jess over to Hartford today. I'd like to go with you, so if you don't mind waiting until tomorrow, Dan has some free time in the early afternoon."

"I don't mind," Cassie interjected quickly. "I don't feel like driving all the way over there in this rain. Anyway, the car only starts when it feels like it. I'd hate to be stuck in Hartford without a way to get home."

"That's something we'll have to discuss. It's absolutely necessary for you to have dependable transportation, especially while Jess is having problems."

"We can discuss all we want, but I can't afford to buy another car. Anyway, Jess and I will be leaving soon, and there's no way I'd drive all the way back to Phoenix."

"Okay," Gibby answered in what she imagined was a rather resigned tone of voice. "We'll talk tomorrow, Cassie. I just got a call to go over to Chick Wiley's condo. His girlfriend just called the police and said he didn't wake up this morning. Considering Chick's lifestyle, I'm betting on a heart attack. If that's the case, I'll have to examine the body, interview the girlfriend, and make out a coroner's report, so I might be out there for a while."

Gibby gave her a message for Jess, said he'd call them later, and hung up. Cassie once again found her son at the front window, staring out into the rain. She walked up behind him quietly but before she reached him, he turned to face her.

"Dr. Gibby said to tell you hi. He's busy this morning, but he'll call again later this afternoon."

She knew Jess heard her, but he didn't answer, and she could see that his focus was divided between her and something outside the house that was vying for his attention.

"What's so fascinating out there?" she asked,

104

walking around the boy and approaching the window. "Is Corey Hammil still standing out there in the rain making a fool of himself?"

"I don't know."

"Since you weren't feeling too well last night, Dr. Gibby wants to take you to see another doctor tomorrow," Cassie said, anxious to know how Jess would feel about seeing Gibby's friend, Dan.

"What kind of a doctor?" he asked, and Cassie knew that it wasn't going to be easy to get out of this one. Why hadn't she kept her mouth shut and waited for Gibby to break the news? To her surprise, Jess didn't seem to be upset about seeing a psychologist, even after she explained what that meant. The child seemed tired and resigned to whatever his mother and the one doctor he really trusted wanted to put him through.

When Gibby stopped by after dinner, he told Jess what a nice man Dan Winslow was, and how he would try to help Jess deal with the aftereffects of his near-drowning experience. When Cassie gave the child permission to watch TV for an hour, Gibby asked for coffee and Cassie obliged. She untied the string from a bakery box, cut a large wedge of cherry pie, and placed it in front of the doctor with his coffee.

"Thanks," he said, after a bite of pie and a sip of coffee. "If you stay in Winter Falls, I'll end up weighing three hundred pounds someday."

"Not much chance of that," she answered, filling her own cup and sitting down across the table. She let him eat the pie and warmed up his coffee before she asked him how his day had gone.

Gibby shook his head and leaned back in his chair. "It's the damnedest thing, Chick Wiley was only thirty-seven, never been sick a day in his life. He was drinking a couple of cases of beer a week and smoking about two packs of cigarettes a day the last time I saw him. But the girlfriend said he had been on a health kick, given up the booze and cigarettes.''

"What happened?"

"I hate to have to admit that I don't have a clue. He died in his sleep, but it wasn't a quiet death, it was horrible."

When Cassie didn't say anything, Gibby looked up at her. "You don't want to know, Cassie. I'm trying to get in touch with his next of kin, so that we can order an autopsy."

She shrugged and stood, moving to stand behind his chair. He had removed the jacket of his navy suit, rolled up the sleeves of his white shirt, and stuffed his tie in his pocket. She could tell by looking at his back that the muscles were bunched up, tied in knots. When she placed her hands on his shoulders, he tensed, then relaxed as she began to knead his sore muscles.

When she felt that he was sufficiently relaxed, she brought up the subject she wanted to discuss with him. "Gibby, I have to find out about my dad, and I need you to help me."

"I'm not sure if I can help you or not, but I'll try. What do you want to know?"

"I want to know what happened to make him turn out the way he is. I know something bad happened to him, or to my grandma or grandpa. I just don't know what it was."

"I have a letter," Gibby said after a long moment. "I think you should read it. It was written by your grandfather before your dad was born, and it explains some of the things that had happened up to that time. I don't know if it will help or not, there's still a lot left unexplained, but you deserve to read it and judge for yourself. I'll bring it over tomorrow when I pick you and Jess up."

"Thank you." Cassie stopped rubbing his back and moved away from him. He turned and looked at her, a strange expression on his weary face.

"I should be getting Jess to bed now," she explained, and the doctor grabbed his jacket from the back of the chair and left the room. She heard him saying good-bye to Jess, then heard the front door close behind him.

"Too bad," she whispered. "Too bad that I'm not in his league, but at least I'm smart enough to know it."

Five minutes later, Cassie was telling herself that she wasn't so smart, after all. Why hadn't she asked Gibby any of the questions that were filling her mind, hinting at the strong possibility of a sleepless night ahead? The two main questions that nagged at her for the next few hours were: Where did Gibby get the letter that was supposedly written by her grandfather and, secondly, *why* did he have it in his possession? Another question was, who had been the recipient of the letter? And if the letter was so important, why hadn't it stayed in her family for the enlightenment of her grandfather's descendants?

Cassie fell asleep long after midnight, only to find her dreams filled with questions about the mysterious letter. When she awoke at 7:00 A.M., she was restless and jittery, and the morning seemed endless. When Gibby finally arrived to drive her and Jess to Hartford to see Dr. Winslow, she had been pacing the floor in front of the window for hours.

Gibby jumped out of the car and came into the house to get them. He swung Jess onto his shoulders and would have left without mentioning the letter if Cassie hadn't grabbed his arm to stop him.

"Do you have it with you?" she asked. "You didn't forget it, did you?"

"Are you sure you want to read it? I looked it over last night, and I came to the conclusion that it's bad timing to give it to you now. Truthfully, I wish I hadn't mentioned it."

"But you did."

"Yes," Gibby sighed, "I did, and you have every

right to know what happened." He reached into the inside pocket of his topcoat and pulled out a white envelope. John Gibson III, M.D. was printed in raised lettering in the upper left-hand corner, with his address beneath it. Cassie ran her fingers over the letters and stuck the envelope in her purse. She was too nervous to ask all the questions she had formed the night before, and she decided that she would wait and ask them later, when they were on the way home. At the hospital in Hartford, while Gibby was preparing Dan Winslow for his meeting with Jess, Cassie sat in a starkly modern black-and-silver chair in the lobby and pulled her grandfather's letter out of the envelope.

It consisted of four pages of creamy vellum stationery, its edges and creases brown with age. The writing was a large, spidery scrawl and at first she had trouble reading it. After a couple of sentences, it became easy to follow, as if she were reading a letter from someone familiar, someone close to her, whose letters she had read many times before. She was glad that she had waited for Gibby to leave the lobby, and that she had let Jess wander down to the gift shop to buy a package of peanut-butter crackers. She had the unexplainable feeling that the letter was too personal to share with anyone, although she knew that Gibby had read it before and knew its contents.

It *was* personal, and it was not at all what she had expected. It wasn't addressed to anyone, and it read more like a diary entry than a letter. Her grandfather had been a very sensitive man, nothing like the son he had brought into the world. Cassie glanced around to see if anybody was watching her, but they weren't. Sitting in the lobby of the huge hospital, she might as well have been alone in the world. She flipped to the back page, saw that the letter had been written in 1935, two years before her father was born. She turned back to the beginning of the letter, and began to read.

I graduated from Harvard Law School in 1930, and was hired to assist the County Prosecutor. I worked part-time in that capacity during the last two summers before my graduation.

I courted Vivien and won her hand in marriage during my senior year at Harvard. We were married in the spring, in her home town of Boston, and my only reservation about our union was Vivien's reluctance to spend her life in what she called "a one-horse town like Winter Falls."

But things were good at the beginning, and when we had been married little more than a year, we were blessed with our first child, named Wanda after Vivien's mother, who had recently passed away. The following year, although the signs of a failing marriage should have been apparent, Vivien bore me another daughter. We named her Helen.

I loved my wife and children, was satisfied with my job, and I enjoyed life in Winter Falls. If Vivien had just been happy, I would have had the perfect life, with one exception: guilt over what Johnny and I had done to Jeremy haunted me every day of my life. I have never called what happened to Jeremy an accident. I am guilty, and I will carry that guilt to the grave.

I'm not making excuses for what I did, but in 1935, when Jeremy clubbed his parents to death, I was young and woefully inexperienced, and involved in a marriage that was deteriorating day by day. Add to that fact that I had convinced myself that I was as guilty as Satan himself for what had happened to my friend. I know Johnny Gibson carried the same burden, although we barely spoke for years after that night in the summer of 1928.

I worked in a small-town Prosecutor's Office,

and we were kept well-informed by the police, so that we were always on top of what was happening in our little corner of the world. When the call went out that there had been two brutal murders in Winter Falls, I was out the door in seconds. At the Winter's house I was asked to identify the bodies of Jeremy's parents, but I could not do so. They were battered so badly around the head and face that they were beyond recognition.

I found Jeremy in his bedroom down the hall, cowering in a corner. In his halting, only partly intelligible speech he confessed to me that he was the murderer. He wanted a driver's license and a car, a bright red one like the one I had driven in my bachelor days. He got angry because his parents wouldn't give in to his wishes. So, he killed them. In what was left of his mind, it was that simple.

At the time, I thought it was extremely fortunate that I had been alone in the room with Jeremy when he told me what he had done. I was able to soothe him quickly and convince him not to talk to anyone else, not a word, not a syllable. A suspect was never found, and police speculated that a drifter had done the deed during a robbery, since there was no money in the Winters' bedroom, where I swore they had always kept large sums of cash.

With the money that his parents left him in their wills, Jeremy was able to hire a housekeeper and a nurse, a muscular young man who, fortunately, never quite trusted him.

At the time I was asked to identify the bodies of Mr. and Mrs. Winter, I would have sworn that was the worst day of my life. I would have sworn that there could never be a worse day, but I was wrong.

Shortly after the birth of my third daughter,

Lorraine, Vivien left me. One evening I returned from work to find my wife's closets empty, and a strange woman looking after my children. The two smaller girls were crying. Only six-year-old Wanda was calm and controlled. It was she who handed me the note written in Vivien's flowing hand on the personalized stationery I had given her for her birthday. It was terse and to the point, and need not be repeated here. I will only say that it broke my heart and changed my life completely.

Still, there were only worse things to come, things so horrific that their contemplation boggles the mind. After all these years, I find that I cannot force myself to write about them. Perhaps another time.

Colin McCall
At Winter Falls, Connecticut
May 12th, 1935

# Chapter Twelve

Cassie found that she had no questions to ask about her grandfather's letter because the answers made no difference. After reading the message written by Colin McCall fifty years ago, she was filled with a deep sympathy for him, for what he had gone through. He had obviously loved his wife, Vivien, so much that losing her had almost driven him crazy. Add to that the trauma of Jeremy Winter's deterioration, for which her grandfather felt responsible, then the death of Jeremy's parents at their son's own hand, and it was no wonder that Colin McCall had passed a legacy of despair down to his own son.

"I want to bring him home," she said to Gibby as he guided the blue Mercedes out of the hospital parking lot and drove east on the street that would take them out of town, back toward Winter Falls.

"I thought you might like to hear how Jess feels about his interview with Dr. Winslow."

"In a minute, okay, Jess?" She turned to glance at Jess and he nodded solemnly.

"Hang in there just a minute, fella," Gibby said, catching Jess's eye in the rear-view mirror. "Okay, Cassie, let's have it."

"I want to bring my father home from the hospital. I was going to take Jess to see him today, but I think it would be better for them to meet at home. I'm hoping you'll agree with me."

"He's not ready to go home, Cassie, not physically or mentally. Taking him home wouldn't do either one of you any good."

"I know you're trying to protect me, Gibby, but this is what I want."

"I won't release him."

"Then I'll get another doctor."

"You can't do that, I've been his physician since my father died ten years ago. I was his doctor before he had the stroke, and I've since been appointed by the court to make decisions regarding his care in case he isn't capable of indicating his own desires."

"You told me he was competent," Cassie challenged.

"He is, his mind is working just fine, but it isn't easy for him to communicate with us and let us know what he's thinking."

"I'll get a lawyer and petition the court if I have to."

Gibby sighed and pulled the Mercedes to the side of the road, eliciting a blast from the air horn of a semi that had been traveling too close on his tail. He put the car in park and turned in his seat, so that he could look Cassie directly in the eye.

"I'm not going to fight you on this Cassie, but I wish you'd give it a little more thought. You seem to have the romantic notion that everything will be different now, but the stroke hasn't changed your father. He's still the same man who abused you as a child, the same man who forced you to leave home at sixteen."

"I know all that, but I'm beginning to understand that he might have had a reason for the way he acted. Anyway, Jess has the right to meet his grandpa."

"I know you, Cassie. You have some wild idea that you owe your father, and you think this is how you can atone for your imagined sins."

"You don't understand," Cassie whispered, "nobody understands."

"I'm trying," Gibby answered, reaching over to squeeze her hand. "We'll finish talking about this at home, if that's okay with you." He inclined his head toward the rear seat of the car, and Cassie realized that Jess was awfully quiet, probably listening to every word she and Gibby said.

She agreed that it would be better to finish their discussion later, and Gibby put the car in gear and eased his way back into the heavy late-afternoon traffic.

The rest of the way home, they talked to Jess and discovered that he could either take or leave Dan Winslow. To the child's way of thinking, the doctor "asked too many questions. It made me tired answering them."

When Gibby dropped them at the house, he indicated to Cassie that he planned to telephone the psychologist early in the evening to get a rundown on his therapy session with Jess. After that, he would get in touch with her to fill her in on Winslow's recommendations.

Gibby had wanted to stop for dinner on the way home, but Jess wasn't hungry, and Cassie didn't feel like sitting in a diner with the boy wiggling around and asking if they were almost finished eating. At home, she scrambled an egg for each of them and popped two English muffins in the toaster. Even as he picked at his food and managed to get a few bites down, Cassie worried over Jess's restlessness. She knew that he was bored, that he needed to go back to school to keep his mind occupied. Still, she wasn't going to let him out of her sight until she heard Dr. Dan Winslow's evaluation of his condition.

They were playing a game of old maid when the telephone finally rang around seven-thirty.

"Hold on a minute," she said to Dr. Gibby. "Jess, you can go on up and start your bath and lay out your p.j.'s while I talk to the doctor. I'll be up in a couple of minutes."

The boy reluctantly left the room, and Cassie waited until she heard his footsteps overhead before she put the receiver back to her ear.

"What did he say?" she asked.

"Nothing that I didn't expect. Jess has been through a very traumatic experience. He nearly drowned in the same lake where his aunts drowned fifty years ago. Dan says it's possible that deep down in his subconscious Jess feels guilty because he survived and they didn't. Also, there are all the tales about sightings of the girls' ghosts that could have influenced him. Children absorb a lot more from their surroundings than we adults give them credit for."

"He isn't just lying then?"

"No, he isn't making up stories, Cassie. Whatever he tells you is what he believes to be reality."

"I don't know whether that's better or worse."

"Dan isn't too worried about him. He'd like to schedule another session and see Jess again in a couple of weeks, but he doesn't think we have a real problem with the boy."

"Will it go away?"

"It may take a few therapy sessions for Dan to convince Jess that the girls aren't alive, but if he says there's nothing to worry about, I believe him. Of course, if you'd like to call another doctor, get a second opinion—"

"No, I like Dr. Winslow fine."

"Then I'll make another appointment for him to see Jess week after next."

"Good. Listen, Gibby, Jess is being awfully quiet upstairs. I think I'd better go and see what he's up to."

"Okay, Cassie, you go ahead and check on the boy, and we'll talk tomorrow."

"I still want to talk about my father coming

115

home," Cassie said, to let Gibby know that he wasn't getting away with anything.

"I thought you would."

She heard him laughing as she hung up the phone and cocked her head for a minute before running up the stairs, calling out her son's name. She heard water running in the bathroom, into the bathtub, and it shouldn't have been running that long. It didn't take more than a few minutes to fill up the old claw-foot tub, and she never filled it more than half full for Jess anyway.

"Jess, what are you doing up here? Did you forget that you've got the water running?"

Cassie glanced into Jess's bedroom, which used to be her bedroom, which still gave her the creeps sometimes. He wasn't there. The bathroom door was closed, and that stopped her. He didn't like her bursting in on him when he was using the toilet, or taking his clothes off. She pounded on the door and jiggled the doorknob. "You in there, Jess? Answer me, damn it, Jess, I'm not playing games with you."

She turned the knob and shoved the door open, then stood dead still, her mouth open but unable to form a scream, her hands clawing at her throat. Jess was floating facedown in the tub, which was overflowing onto the floor. His longish yellow hair streamed on top of the water, his arms bobbed on the surface.

Cassie's throat opened, she screamed and crossed the room in a split second. She grabbed her son by the shoulders and flipped him over, then she screamed again. Jess was smiling up at her, his cornflower blue eyes as innocent as a newborn baby's. He opened his mouth and spit at her playfully. Water dribbled out of his mouth and dripped down his chin, which had taken on a bluish cast from the cold water he had used to fill the tub.

Cassie held onto him with her left hand while she slapped him across the face with her right. "Damn

116

you, Jess," she yelled, "you scared the shit out of me, you goddamn little—"

She let go of him and he fell into the water, then she reached over him and turned off the tap. Water stopped running into the tub but it still sloshed out of the tub onto the bathroom floor. Even in her present state of shock she thought of how the linoleum floor would be ruined, and how much it would cost her to repair it.

Jess floated on his back in the tub and held onto his knees, which were drawn up to cover his private parts. He seemed to be unsinkable, and Cassie was tempted to push him down and see how quickly he would bob back up to float like an air-filled ball on top of the water. He was staring at her, his eyes bluer than she had ever seen them, the whites of his eyes red with hurt and anger.

She knelt on the wet floor and felt the water soak through the fabric of her slacks. In less than a minute her legs felt as if they were freezing, but Jess seemed to be perfectly comfortable lounging in the cold water, waiting for her apology.

Cassie knew that she had to make amends with him and get him out of the cold tub as quickly as possible.

"I'm sorry, honey." She reached to take one of his hands but he pulled it away and tucked it under his body. He sank a little lower in the water, but his legs still floated, as though they were filled with air. "I didn't mean to hit you, Jess. You know I've never slapped you before, except on your bottom when you were little. We've always been able to talk about things before, but now it seems like we have trouble doing that. I just lost my temper for a minute. Can you forgive me, if I swear I'll never do it again?"

"I want to go to school tomorrow." His voice was a hoarse croak, and Cassie's first impulse was to scold him for getting a sore throat by sitting in the freezing bath water. She caught herself in time, and said simply: "Sure if that's what you want. Hug?"

The child threw both arms around her neck and squeezed her so fiercely that she thought something might crack in her neck before he stopped. But she couldn't push him away. His body was ice cold, he had dark circles under his eyes, and he was holding onto her for dear life. She realized that she was shaking all over, and she didn't know what it was that scared her so badly. Maybe it was just that he was all she had. Except for her father, of course. Maybe soon she could get her father back home with her and Jess, and the three of them could be a family.

"Don't ever scare me that way again, Jess," she told him as she leaned over his bed a few minutes later and tucked an extra blanket around his thin shoulders.

He said, "I'm sorry, Mom," and kissed her cheek with colorless lips.

Cassie woke up the next morning hoping that Jess had forgotten her promise to let him go back to school. She looked in on him, found him sleeping soundly, and tiptoed downstairs to make her coffee. She thought she would just let him sleep and not wake him up until it was too late for him to get ready for school on time.

She figured up her bills while she drank her coffee, instead of reading the paper as was her usual custom since arriving in Winter Falls. She didn't want to go outside, to open the front door and find Corey Hammil standing in the yard looking like a sick puppy. When she finished totaling her monthly expenses, Cassie walked through the house, carrying her coffee cup with her. She really wanted to see if the new ads for The Emporium were running in the paper, and thought she might take a chance on opening the front door if Corey was nowhere in sight.

She pulled aside the far left edge of the faded gold drapes and peeked out, hoping that if Corey was out there, he would be watching the middle of the window where the sheer curtains met, not the edge of the window between the drapes and the window casing. When she saw Corey and Jess standing together in the yard, she dropped the drape and pulled back. How did Jess get dressed so quickly and get outside without her hearing him come down the stairs or open and close the front door? And what were he and Corey talking about?

She lifted the corner of the drape again, and saw that Corey had moved closer to Jess, that he was hovering over the boy, leaning toward him in what she thought was a menacing way. Then suddenly Jess shoved Corey and Corey shoved Jess back—or maybe it was the other way around. It all happened so fast that before she had a chance to react, Jess was on the ground and Corey was stalking down the street toward town.

She dropped the drapes and ran from the house but Jess was already on his feet when she got to the yard.

"What happened?" she asked, wanting to hear his version of what she thought she had seen from the window.

"Corey shoved me," the child answered in a flat tone of voice that was neither forgiving nor accusatory.

"Why would he do that?"

"'Cause I told him to go away from here and let us alone, I guess."

"Why didn't you let me handle getting rid of Corey?"

"I was only trying to help, Mom."

"I know you were, honey, but Corey's a grown man and you're still—well, you're not quite a man yet. He could hurt you pushing you around like that."

"He didn't hurt me."

"Well he could have, so next time you see him skulking around, you just call me, okay?"

Jess nodded that he would, but Cassie wasn't

119

convinced, and she told herself that she would have to keep a keen lookout for Corey from now on. If he kept bothering her, she would call the police and have him picked up for trespassing or something. And if he ever hurt Jess, she would find a way to hurt him back, she swore she would.

# Chapter Thirteen

Jess was dressed for school in Levi's and a colorful red sweater chosen from the stock at The Emporium but he was shivering either from the cold or from his confrontation with Corey. After she finished scolding him for being outside without a jacket on, Cassie fixed him a bowl of cereal and didn't rush him to finish, as she usually did. If he dawdled over his breakfast, maybe she could point out to him that it was late, and talk him into staying out of school one more day. She knew she was being irrational about keeping him at home with her, but she didn't care. Jess was her baby, and if anything happened to him—well, she wouldn't even let herself complete the thought.

To her distress, he finished eating in record time, shrugged his arms into his down jacket, kissed her good-bye, and was out the door before she had time to protest. She checked the outdoor thermometer and found that the day was a little warmer than usual, which meant that the temperature was hovering just above freezing. Still, she thought she could use the cold as an excuse to drive down to the school and pick up Jess at three o'clock so that he wouldn't have to walk home.

That decision brightened Cassie's mood a little, and she hummed as she dressed for work in navy slacks and a red sweater that almost matched the one Jess had worn to school.

Cassie felt a little anxiety about facing Marilou. She hadn't yet mentioned that she intended to bring her father home from the hospital, and she wondered if she should bring it up today or wait until she had straightened things out with Gibby and made the arrangements. When her dad came home, she would either have to quit work to stay with him, or hire a nurse to look after him for a few hours every day. She decided that would probably be the best course, since Marilou wasn't capable of running the store herself and would definitely resent a stranger taking over as her boss. Cassie made a mental note to ask Gibby if he could recommend someone to take care of her father.

At The Emporium, she found Marilou in a grumpy mood, complaining about all the long hours she'd been putting in since her "boss" was spending so much time at home. Without thinking of the consequences, Cassie offered the woman a raise of ten dollars a week. The generous gesture made Marilou happy, but Cassie worried all morning that she would have to deduct the money from the meager sum she allowed herself to take home every Friday night.

By two o'clock in the afternoon, Cassie had a splitting headache. She decided to pick Jess up early so that they could have a combination late lunch/ early dinner and get a good night's sleep. Her father's old car had started right up in the morning when it was cold, but the motor stubbornly refused to turn over in the relatively warmer afternoon temperature. Rather than go back inside and ask Marilou if she could borrow the Buick, Cassie walked the short distance to the elementary school. It was a gloomy old brick building set back from the street in a grove of tall trees, the perfect setting for a slasher film, as far as Cassie was concerned.

She had only been inside the school twice before:

122

once when she enrolled Jess on his first day of school, and once a couple of weeks ago when she went to pick up some work for him to do at home while he was recovering from his accident. She poked her head in the office, asked for directions to Jess's homeroom, then followed them to a small classroom at the far end of a long, dimly lit corridor.

As she approached the door, it opened and emitted a swarm of jabbering children who appeared to be about the same age and size as Jess. A few of them looked at Cassie, then turned to whisper something to their companions, but most of them ignored her and hurried off to wherever it was they were going. She watched the twenty or so children closely, but Jess was not among them.

*He must still be in the room,* she thought, and was about to venture inside when a tall, square woman stepped through the door to stand beside her.

"I'm Cassie McCall, Jess's mother," Cassie said, raising her eyes to look up at the taller woman.

"Yes, I remember. Is Jess all right? I hope he hasn't had a relapse. Actually, we expected to see him back in school several days ago."

Cassie's shock must have shown on her face, because the woman leaned down and touched her arm gently. "Oh, my dear, I hope nothing else has happened to Jess."

"He was supposed to be here today," Cassie stammered. "He asked if he could go to school this morning, and I let him go. Are you telling me that he hasn't been here at all today?"

"Not today, or yesterday, or—"

"I only care about today," Cassie cut in abruptly. "This was supposed to be his first day back."

The teacher nodded solemnly and started to walk down the corridor, pulling Cassie along with her. "I think we should talk to Mrs. McCambridge about this without any further hesitation."

"The principal? Yes, okay," Cassie agreed, but

when they were adjacent to the door through which she had entered the school, she freed herself from the teacher's grasp and moved away from her. Outside, she heard the woman calling out to her, but she ignored the call and ran across the parking lot and down the street to her car, which was still parked outside The Emporium. She refused to sit around the principal's office discussing why Jess wasn't in school when she could be out looking for him. She got into the old car, slammed the door, and prayed that it would start. After several tries, it did, and she roared down the street in a cloud of black smoke.

As she drove through town, trying to remember the route Officer Barney had taken the day they'd looked for Jess together, she chastised herself for not listening to her maternal instincts. Something had been telling her to keep Jess at home today, and she had let him get away with going to school because she hadn't wanted to have a confrontation with him. *I'm some mother!* she thought, then stepped on the gas, a knot of fear growing big and hard in her belly.

She drove around for an hour, systematically going up and down every street in town, before she decided to check at home and see if by some miracle he had returned on his own. After rounding the corner with as much speed as the old vehicle could muster, she jumped out, left the motor running and the car door open while she ran up the walk to the house. The front door stood ajar, and fear twisted the knot in her stomach into a tight ball.

"Jess?" She screamed out. "Are you there, Jess?"

He didn't answer, but she suddenly knew he was home. That elusive mother's instinct was kicking in again.

She took the stairs two at a time and skidded to a stop just inside his bedroom. He was there, in bed, wearing his Ninja Turtle pajamas, sleeping soundly. He was breathing hard, his chest rising and falling, his little face screwed up into a fierce grimace.

124

Somewhere in a dream he was fighting a dragon, or running from a beast-thing that devoured little boys.

She sat down on the edge of the bed and shook his shoulder gently.

"Jess?" she whispered.

"No," he said, "I don't want to. You can't make me." He struggled against the hand Cassie placed on his chest, and whimpered in fear.

"Jess!" She shook him harder, using both hands to lift his head off the pillow. When he still didn't respond, she slipped her arm beneath his shoulders and pulled him towards her. The pillow was wet, soaked, as if he had climbed into bed straight from the shower without bothering to towel himself off.

"Wake up, Jess!" She felt panic rising in her chest, squeezing her lungs, cutting off her airway. "Oh, my God, what will I do?" she moaned. Then as loud as she could, she screamed the child's name over and over, and shook him violently back and forth, as if she could force him to wake up by the power of her will.

He opened his eyes, so blue that they shocked her into dropping him back to the wet pillow.

"What's wrong, Mom? Why are you waking me up? Is it time to go to school?"

She calmed herself, hugged herself instead of him, willed herself to stop screaming inside.

"Why didn't you go to school today, Jess?"

"Didn't I?"

"No, you didn't. I went down to the school to pick you up and I talked to your teacher. She said you weren't there today."

"I don't know why I wasn't there, I can't remember."

Cassie wanted to yell at him and shake him again, shake him until he told her the truth, but she overcame the irrational urge.

"Right now, I want you to go dry yourself off while I change your pillowcase. Then we'll go downstairs and you can talk to me while I fix us some dinner."

"I'm not wet, Mom."

"Your head is wet, you must have been sweating while you were asleep. You probably dreamed something bad."

As he felt his head, a puzzled expression appeared on his face. Then suddenly, as Cassie watched, she saw a light dawn behind his eyes. He lowered his hand and avoided her gaze as he slid out of bed and headed for the bathroom.

*He knows*, she thought. *He knows where he's been today, but there's no way in hell he's going to tell me.*

She got a fresh pillow from the hall closet and laid the wet one out in the hallway to dry off. She put a clean pillowcase on the new pillow, placed it on Jess's bed, and reached over to pick up his dirty clothes from the chair next to the bed. She drew her hand back as though she had been bitten by a snake. She shifted her weight, knelt beside the chair and lifted the Levi's, the red sweater, the white socks and size ten Fruit of the Loom jockey shorts. They were all soaked, heavy with water. She thought that maybe he had come home dirty and jumped in the bathtub fully dressed. If that was what had happened, the wet clothes would still show signs of whatever it was he was trying to wash out, there would be grit in the bathtub. There would be—

She stopped herself, because she knew it was a lie. She knew where he had been. She had known since the moment that awful look had crossed his teacher's face. She could have driven there straight from the school, *should* have driven there. She had denied the truth because she didn't want to know, and even now she was afraid to face Jess with her knowledge.

She gathered up the wet clothes and carried them downstairs to wash and dry them. They were dirty, and she would wash them, the way a good mother should, but she didn't believe that she could ever get them clean again.

Bacon was sizzling in the frying pan and Cassie was preparing lettuce and tomatoes for sandwiches when she thought she heard a car pull up out front. She hadn't heard from Gibby all day, and she wondered if he was angry because she had forced the issue of bringing her father home. She turned the gas off under the skillet, laid the knife down on the counter, and walked to the front of the house where she could glance out the window and see if it was Gibby's Mercedes parked at the curb. It wasn't, and when she saw who was walking up the path to ring her doorbell, she lost her appetite.

Officer Tom Barney smiled when she opened the door, and it was a chilling sight to see his mouth split in a wide grin while his eyes remained as cold and hard as tiny blocks of ice.

"Evening, Miss McCall," he said, and coming out of his mouth, the words sounded like an insult.

"Officer," Cassie returned, wishing that she could call him any one of the several names she preferred for him.

"Hear your boy was missing again this afternoon."

"Is that a crime in Winter Falls?"

"Most parents in these parts would probably think so. But I keep forgetting that you're from the big city. I guess you look at life from a different angle than us country folks around here, huh? Anyway, I closed your car door for you. Guess you were in a hurry to see if the boy had beat you home. Here." Cassie looked down and saw that he was holding the keys she had left in the ignition when she ran inside to look for Jess. She took them from Barney's hands without touching his fingers, and tucked the keys in the pocket of her slacks.

"I don't suppose you want to talk about it?" he asked.

Cassie just stared at him until he lowered his eyes and reached for the notebook that protruded from his rear pants pocket.

"I just have a couple of questions for you, Miss McCall. It's kind of cold out here, if you could just—" He gestured toward the living room, and Cassie knew when she was licked. If she didn't let him in and listen to what he had to say she'd never get back to fixing dinner, and she'd never get to talk to Jess about where he'd been all day.

"Come on in," she said reluctantly, standing back and holding the door open wide so that Barney wouldn't have to come close to her when he entered the house.

Since she didn't ask him to sit down, the officer stood just inside the door and opened the notebook that Cassie had already grown to hate.

"Miss McCall, I have to ask you about your whereabouts on the night Chick Wiley died."

She was surprised, but anger quickly surpassed surprise to become her primary emotion. "You want to know where I was that night? Why? The man died of natural causes, didn't he?"

"Where did you get that information?"

Cassie almost blurted out Gibby's name before she caught herself. "The newspaper, I guess."

"Uh-huh. Well, just humor me and tell me where you were that night."

"I was right here, where I am every night. I have an eight-year-old son, and I don't leave him alone after dark so that I can go wandering around town looking for victims."

"Victims?"

"Well, isn't that what you're trying to say, that you think I did something to that poor man to cause his death?"

"Did you know, that 'poor man,' as you call him, made a joke of talking to your Aunt Wanda over the airwaves once a week or so?"

"I heard that, yes, but I never listened to his show."

"Not much of a radio person, huh?"

"I turn it on in the morning for the news, that's all."

128

"Young person like you, I'd think you'd want to keep up with the music. Rap, isn't that what you listen to?"

"No, as a matter of fact, I don't."

The officer smiled his thin, sick grin, snapped the notebook shut, and stuck it back in his pocket.

"Okay, Miss McCall, that's all for now. Might need to talk to you again though."

He turned back to the door and Cassie opened it, hoping that he would leave quickly so that she could spray the room and get rid of the nasty smell that was probably a product of her imagination. He stepped out onto the porch and she had the door half closed when he spoke again.

"By the way, Miss McCall, if I was you, I'd watch that little fella, keep a little better track of him." Barney stared at a spot behind her, and Cassie knew that Jess had come downstairs and was standing in the living room listening to their conversation.

"That lake's a bad place for a kid," Barney continued, "especially in the wintertime. You know, with the ice and all. Be a hell of a thing if he drowned out there while you're here taking care of your daddy—and whatever else you're doing—wouldn't it?"

The cop turned his back on her and she slammed the door hard, so hard that the plate she had saved to buy her mother for Mother's Day fifteen years ago dropped to the floor and rolled across the threadbare rug to rest beneath the statue of the baby Jesus. Cassie retrieved the plate and clutched it to her breast as she knelt before her makeshift shrine and closed her eyes in prayer. She prayed for help for Jess, and for guidance for herself. What she wished for Tom Barney, she didn't dare mention in the Lord's presence.

# Chapter Fourteen

Jess knelt on the ice, not remembering exactly how he had gotten there. Sometimes he felt as if his mind didn't belong to him anymore. Wanda talked to him in his head all day long, and she made pictures for his dreams at night.

The three little girls lured him to the dirty brown water when he was awake, and they brought the lake to his bed while he slept. It seemed like he could never get away from them.

Sometimes he wanted to tell his mom about what was happening to him, but then he looked at her and she seemed to be sad and so all alone that he just couldn't do it. If he could get away with Dr. Gibby for a few minutes, he might be able to talk about Wanda. Maybe it would be easier to tell him.

There was a splash off to Jess's right, and Wanda's arm shot up through a hole in the ice. He closed his eyes so that he wouldn't have to look at it. He didn't want to see Wanda the way she was under the water. Without looking, he knew that she was a skeleton covered by flapping sheets of too-white skin. He knew that there were no eyes in the sockets of her skull, and that her long dark hair floated like seaweed on top of the dirty water.

He shuddered and took a deep breath to hold back the nausea when Wanda put her hand in his so that he could lead her out of the water. He stood and moved rapidly across the ice toward the shore, more swift and sure-footed with each trip across the ice.

At first, he had been fascinated by the thought of knowing the three girls who lived in the deepest part of the lake. One syllable out of Wanda's mouth, and he would be at her side, day or night. But it wasn't fun anymore, and Jess really wished that they'd just leave him alone. He didn't know why they needed him to get out of their watery grave, but Wanda said they did. She said if she tried to come out without his help, she'd look the same on the shore as she did in the lake, and people would run from her. If he helped her, she could turn into a normal little girl again for a few hours. Wanda said that once he led her out, she had the power to bring her sisters out and make them look human, too.

Jess didn't understand it, but he knew that he had to do what Wanda said. She would come out of the lake and get him if he didn't. She'd look like a skeleton, and she'd come to his house in the middle of the night, and she'd make him quit breathing or something. Even worse, maybe she'd hurt his mom.

When they approached the bank, he dragged the girl out of the water, and didn't let go of her hand until she told him to. He didn't like the lake, and it was good to have the hard-packed ground under his feet again.

"Thank you for helping us, Jess," Wanda said in his head. Out of the corner of his eye, he could see her leaning toward him, and he knew that she wanted to kiss him. He didn't want her to, but he was afraid to jerk away from her. Wanda was scary, and Jess instinctively knew that he shouldn't cross her.

He stood still and waited for her cold lips to touch his cheek. He expected them to feel disgusting, like dead fish or something. To his surprise, they didn't. The dead girl's lips were warm on his cheek and soft, sort of like his mom's lips.

131

"You can go now, Jess," Wanda said without moving her lips.

"Okay," Jess answered aloud. He started to walk away, then turned back to watch Helen and Lorraine climb out of the water and gather around their older sister. He wanted to ask them what they did after he helped them get out of the lake but when they parted and looked at him, he found himself at a loss for words. They were beautiful. Their skin looked firm and smooth, their eyes clear, their hair brushed and shining. They were clothed in the dresses from the Emporium, and Jess knew that tomorrow he would go back and get them more dresses because they deserved them. They were just little girls, and they had been cheated out of their lives once. They were, after all, his aunts, and he was too nice a kid to be the one who cheated them this time around.

# Chapter Fifteen

Gibby stopped by the house while Cassie and Jess were eating their BLT's, and accepted Cassie's offer to stay and eat with them. She fixed him two sandwiches on toasted sourdough bread and filled his cup with hot chocolate.

"I don't know how you keep your figure, eating all this fattening food," he remarked, and Cassie blushed until he turned his attention back to his sandwich.

When they finished their dinner and Jess went into the living room to read a book, Cassie told Gibby about Tom Barney's visit.

"He came just short of accusing me of something," she said. "I think he was insinuating that I'd kill a man because he made fun of my dead aunt to make points on the radio. I can't say that I respected him for that, but I wouldn't kill him for it either. You know," she continued after a short hesitation, "I don't think I ever disliked a man the way I dislike your Officer Barney."

"Tom's not a bad guy," Gibby offered in Barney's defense. "Actually, he's a good cop. He just takes his job a little too seriously sometimes. He is a weird bird though, isn't he?"

They both thought about Tom Barney for a few seconds, then burst into spontaneous laughter. A minute later, they were serious again, and Cassie thought it was a good moment to bring up the subject of her father.

It wasn't easy for her to convince Gibby to see things her way, but she had her mind made up, and it was only a matter of time before he held up his hands in surrender.

"Okay, you win. I'll give him a complete physical tomorrow and if there's nothing new, I'll sign the release papers. When do you plan to bring him home?"

"As soon as possible."

"How about next week, Tuesday or Wednesday?"

"Monday."

"Monday afternoon then."

"Monday morning."

"Ten o'clock?"

"Eight."

"You are one tough lady, Cassie McCall. Nine o'clock Monday morning. You'll have to bring him home in an ambulance. I'll line somebody up to help you get him settled in, then we'll take it from there. Are you going to quit working at The Emporium?"

"No, I'll go in for a couple of hours every day to take care of the books and place orders. Marilou can handle everything else."

"You may have to give her a raise."

"I already did, ten dollars a week." Gibby looked surprised and Cassie quickly added: "It can come out of my paycheck."

"Are you crazy? It most certainly won't come out of your paycheck. I'm just surprised she didn't insist on twenty."

Cassie laughed with relief, then got back to business.

"I know I've already put a lot on your shoulders, Gibby, but could you make up a list of the supplies I'll need for my father and tell me where to buy them?"

"Get me a pencil and a piece of paper and I'll do that right now. Call my nurse tomorrow morning and she'll give you the number of the local nurse's registry. You'll need someone to come in every day while you go to The Emporium."

"You're wonderful," she said and impulsively leaned to kiss Gibby on the cheek. He angled his face and kissed her lightly on the lips, then turned his attention to the list of medical supplies. Cassie put her fingertips to her lips and stood stock still, staring at the handsome red-haired man for several seconds before she turned and hurried from the room to put her son to bed.

After Gibby left, she realized that in her excitement over planning to bring her father home, she hadn't finished telling Gibby about Jess's skipping school, and about his wandering off to the lake again. She decided to talk to Gibby in the morning when he came by to pick her up. There was so much red tape to cut through before she could be sure of having her dad released next Monday, and Gibby had offered to drive her into Hartford to put things in motion at the hospital. She and Jess would have to get up very early because she'd have to ride in with the doctor when he went for his early rounds.

She called Marilou and the woman reluctantly agreed to see that Jess got to school on time, if Gibby dropped him off at her house on the way to Hartford. Cassie could tell that Marilou felt uncomfortable with the child since he had stolen the girls' dresses from the store. She felt bad about that, but she didn't know how to approach Marilou to try and make things better.

She looked in on Jess when she went upstairs, and was relieved to find him sleeping, although he did appear to be having restless dreams again. He was talking in his sleep, and Cassie, leaning close, could have sworn she heard him say, "Wanda." She patted his shoulder and spoke to him for a few minutes, and

135

his nightmare abated. When she left his room, he was lying on his back, snoring softly.

It seemed as if Cassie had just gotten to sleep when the telephone rang, shattering the silence of the house with a violence that propelled her out of bed and across the room before she realized that it was the instrument on her nightstand that was making the awful noise.

"Hello," she answered meekly, sure that she would hear the cold, impersonal voice of a hospital spokesman telling her that her father had taken a turn for the worse.

"Cassie? I'm sorry to wake you. I thought maybe you'd be up by now."

"Gibby? What time is it?"

"A little after six. We were going to leave for Hartford at seven, remember?"

"I'm sorry, I must have forgotten to set my alarm."

"Well, it doesn't matter now. I have an emergency call that's going to keep me in Winter Falls this morning."

"Oh."

"Don't sound like that, I haven't changed my mind about helping you get your father home." Even half asleep, Cassie noticed that he hesitated just a moment too long before he went on. "There's been another death," was all he said before he fell silent.

"Who?" she asked, then realized that it might not be any of her business.

"Bob Graham. Maybe you saw his byline in the *Gazette*?"

"Yes, he wrote the article about Wanda, Helen and Lorraine being sighted at the lake last week."

"Bob was the one who kept the legend alive."

"I didn't know that."

"Well, anyway, he died in his sleep, so I have to go out there and fill out a death certificate."

"He died in his sleep? Just like Chick Wiley?"

"I haven't seen him yet, so I don't know if the

136

deaths were similar or not," Gibby answered carefully.

"But you think they are."

"I didn't say that, Cassie."

"You said the first one was mysterious, even before you saw the body."

"I didn't say that, did I? Anyway, it doesn't matter, I'm sure it's just a coincidence that we've had two men die in their sleep within such a short period of time."

"Two young men."

"I don't know exactly how old Bob was, but I'd say he was in his early fifties. At that age, it could have been a heart attack. I don't want you to get yourself all excited thinking there's been foul play involved in these deaths. I've ordered an autopsy on Chick and I'm sure we'll find a natural cause of death."

"It's just that I worry so much about Jess. How can I let him wander around town alone if—"

"Don't even say it, Cassie."

She didn't, not to Gibby, but after she hung up she went over all the terrible possibilities in her mind: a communicable disease, a rare virus, a cloud of illness that would kill off the entire town one person at a time. If there was one more death, she wouldn't hesitate to take Jess and board the next flight to Phoenix.

She woke Jess up at seven but after taking one look at him, she knew he wouldn't be going to school. She laid her hand on his brow, expecting to find him burning up with fever. Instead, his forehead was cold and clammy, as if his fever had already broken.

"Oh, honey, do you feel really bad?" she asked. Jess seemed to be struggling to sit up, and her thoughts flew back to the two men who had died of God knew what disease.

"I think I've got a cold," the boy answered. Then he smiled weakly. "I'll be okay, Mom."

"Well, I'm going to make you a bed on the couch

137

where it's warmer. You can stay home today, and tomorrow morning we'll both go into Hartford with Dr. Gibby."

"Do I have to see that doctor again?"

"No, sweetheart, I have to sign some papers so that we can bring your grandpa home."

"Grandpa's coming home?"

That news seemed to give Jess strength that he hadn't had just moments before. "He'll be a family with us, won't he, Mom?"

"Sure he will," Cassie answered with a lot more confidence than she felt, "but we'll talk about this later. Right now I want to get you downstairs where it's warm."

Jess didn't want any breakfast, and a few minutes later he started vomiting. There didn't seem to be anything in his stomach, just something brown and watery that scared his mother half to death. She called Gibby's office and left a message that she'd like him to look at Jess, but it was late in the afternoon when she heard his car pull up in front of the house.

When she opened the door to let him in, she was shocked. She had never seen him look so tired and so—she had almost said "defeated," but it couldn't be that.

"Is he still vomiting?" the doctor asked, heading straight for the couch and the small, still figure that reclined there.

"He's been throwing up every twenty or thirty minutes all day," Cassie answered.

"Is he eating or drinking anything?"

"Just a few drops of water, nothing else."

"Hi, Jess, how're you doing, partner?" Gibby's whole demeanor changed when he approached the sick child, and Cassie experienced a feeling that she couldn't identify, almost a feeling of pride in him, like she felt about Jess when he did something that warmed her heart and made her glad to be his mother.

138

Gibby examined the child, then led Cassie to the kitchen. "Fix him a cup of weak, warm tea and see if he can get a little of that down. I'm going to call in a prescription for something to stop the nausea so that he can get some sleep. If he's still like this tomorrow, we'll let them look at him in the E.R."

"Why don't you just look at him?"

"I did look at him, Cassie," Gibby answered, smiling indulgently, "but if the nausea doesn't go away overnight, we may have to get some tests run in the E.R."

"Oh." She felt stupid for questioning him, and not for the first time wished that she was a sophisticated, intelligent woman who would be a match for him.

"I think I'll fix *you* a cup of tea, too," she said, turning away from him so that he couldn't see her face.

"Good idea, but make mine strong. I'll call this prescription in and see if they have anybody there to deliver it. If they don't, I'll pick it up for you."

Two minutes later, he was off the phone, telling her that the prescription would be delivered within ten minutes. He drank his tea and waited around until Jess had sipped his weak tea and taken a dose of the medicine. Then he insisted on carrying the child upstairs and helping change his pajamas since the ones he was wearing felt damp to the touch.

The doctor didn't say anything else about Jess's condition, but Cassie sensed that he was more than a little worried about the boy.

Back in the living room, Gibby picked up his overcoat from the chair where he had put it when he arrived, and Cassie remembered that Bob Graham had died.

"Was it just like the other death?" she asked.

"What? Oh, as a matter of fact, it was. That doesn't mean I want you worrying that Jess has some mysterious illness. Neither of those men were sick for a day before they died, and their deaths have nothing to do with Jess, do you understand that?"

"I'm not stupid."

"No, you're certainly not, but you are bullheaded where your son is concerned."

Cassie let him leave without telling him good night and after she heard his car pull away, she let the tears—that had been threatening all day—run down her cheeks.

She turned out the lights and sat in the living room until she had regained her composure, then walked through the downstairs, checking to see that the doors and windows were locked, the gas and water turned off in the kitchen. She climbed the stairs slowly, thinking about her reaction to Gibby's teasing—because she was sure now that was all it had been. She thought that maybe after Jess got to know her father, it would be better if they hired someone to stay with him and went back to Phoenix. They had a life there, she had her job, and Jess had his friends in school. Maybe she would meet someone, a man who would want to take care of them and be a father to Jess.

She intended to enter Jess's room, to see if the medication was working and he was sleeping soundly. She started to step through the doorway and ran into a wall that shouldn't have been there. She put her hand up in front of her and pushed on what felt like a solid barrier erected between Jess's room and the hallway where she was standing. She pounded on the obstruction but it didn't give a quarter of an inch.

Then her eyes adjusted to the darkness of the upstairs hall, and she saw what it was that she was fighting. It was a wall of water, solid across the open door-frame, liquid and moving inside her son's room.

"Jess!" she screamed. "Get up, get out of there, you'll drown."

She ran up and down the hallway, looking for a

weapon, for anything that might break through the obstacle that was keeping her away from Jess. Finally, in desperation, she picked up the heavy wooden clothes hamper and flung it against the water-wall. It bounced off, and several damp towels scattered in the hallway. She kicked them aside and attacked the wall with her hands, to no avail.

Cassie fell to her knees and rested her head on the strange barrier. She thought of running to the phone to call the police or the First Aid Squad, but she knew there wasn't time for that. She closed her eyes to clear her vision; when she opened them again, she still could see the water flowing back and forth in Jess's room. It covered his furniture and surrounded the bed where he had gone to sleep sick only an hour before. Now he might be dead, drowned in his own bedroom, drowned in a crystal-clear illusion in his frightened mother's mind. The water filled the small room from floor to ceiling, from wall to wall. No, Cassie decided, it isn't an illusion, it's real, and the water isn't clear. It's dirty, like la—

"No! Oh, God, Jess, what's happening to you? Wake up, Jess, get out of there!"

She pounded on the wall and fell forward into the room. Her momentum carried her to the side of the bed, where Jess lay perfectly still. His small features were relaxed in sleep, and he looked like an angel in pale blue pajamas, which were as dry as dust. Cassie fell to her knees and gathered him into her arms, waking him in the process.

"Mom?" he asked. "I was dreaming about the lake. I was dreaming I was underwater, and it was so nice. I wished I could just stay there forever and ever."

"Don't say that, Jess, don't ever say that again."

"What's wrong, Mom? It was only a dream."

The child started to cry, and Cassie hugged him tighter. She began to rock him back and forth in her arms, as she had done when he was small.

"I'm sorry, sweetheart, I didn't mean to make you

cry. Mommy loves you, Jess, and she never wants to lose you, that's all.''

"You won't lose me, Mom, I'm going to stay with you forever, even when you're an old, old lady."

Cassie pushed him away, so that he could see her smile, then pulled him back against her chest. When her face was hidden from his gaze, she closed her eyes in pain and fought the fear that was tearing at her heart.

# Chapter Sixteen

Cassie and Jess rarely saw Dr. Gibby on weekends, mainly because she tried not to impose upon his free time. It was bad enough that he stopped by to see them almost every evening. He surely deserved to have his weekends free when he wasn't on call.

This particular weekend she was glad that he only called once to check on Jess's condition. She needed the time to get used to the thought of having her father home—the thought of her living in the same house with him for the first time in ten years. She was scared, there was no denying that, and if Gibby saw how frightened she was, he might change his mind about letting her dad come home.

Every time she closed her eyes, Cassie could hear the awful reverberations of her last weekend at home: her father shouting, her mother crying, a cacophony of sounds that seemed to fill the entire world with rage. He had struck her that day, slapped her hard across the face, knocking her to the floor at his feet. Then she had felt his heavy boot on the small of her back, and she knew that if he exerted pressure, she would probably either die or be paralyzed for life. That was the second she decided to leave, and she had never been sorry, not once. Her only regret was that she couldn't have taken her mother with her.

Thinking about her mother and remembering the rare moments she had smiled and enjoyed life, Cassie went up to the storage room and opened her mother's trunk. She removed the red velvet robe from its golden box and took it into her parents' old room, which was now her room, and laid it across the end of the bed. Gibby had told her that her father would never be able to climb the stairs again, so she knew the robe was safe from him there.

In anticipation of Connor McCall's homecoming, Gibby had rented a hospital bed and a wheelchair, which had been delivered early Saturday morning from a hospital-supply house in Hartford. Friday afternoon, after returning from the hospital, she and Jess had cleared out the dining room and stored the furniture, which had seen better days, in the garage for disposal. She had stayed up half the night cleaning the room, scrubbing the walls and the carpet. She couldn't have explained why she was doing it, since she could never remember her father being an exceptionally clean person. But she could remember him striking her mother when she left dirty dishes in the sink, so maybe that was her motivation. Strange still, because Connor couldn't lift his arm to strike her now, not if his life depended on it.

Cassie knew that morally she was doing the right thing. She had talked to Jess and told him not to expect too much because his grandpa was old and sick. Now she could only hope that the reality would surpass her expectations, and that the three of them could truly become a family.

By Monday morning, she thought she had worked it out, at least as well as could be expected. She and Jess were up at the crack of dawn, dressed as if they were going out for a fancy dinner. She knew that the ambulance wouldn't be there until around ten-thirty, so at nine o'clock she made french toast for Jess and thought she might even be able to

144

stomach a slice herself.

She placed a cup of cold water in her new microwave, set the timer for two minutes, and pressed the button. Laying her Tetley teabag on the table, she told Jess she was going outside for the newspaper. Moments later, she staggered back inside, clutching the *Winter Falls Gazette* to her chest.

"What's wrong, Mom?" Jess asked between bites of french toast dripping with butter and syrup.

"Nothing, Jess, just finish your breakfast and go watch for the ambulance."

"What's in the paper, Mom?" the boy persisted.

"When I tell you to do something, I wish you'd just do it instead of disobeying me," Cassie said in a tight, disapproving tone of voice.

"Okay, I'm going." Jess pushed his empty plate aside and walked out of the room, watching her face for a clue as to what was bothering her.

When he was at the other end of the house, she opened the paper and reread the headline. She shook her head in disbelief and ran her hand over the words, to make sure they were real: "University student missing. Corey Hammil, a nineteen-year-old Pennsylvania boy who is in his junior year at the university, has been missing from his dormitory room for at least a week, according to his roommate. Local authorities were made aware of the boy's disappearance when his parents telephoned them to inquire about their son's whereabouts."

There was more, but that was enough. Against her wishes, she saw Corey's handsome face before her eyes, and heard his pleas. Were she and Jess the last people to see him? Was he still hiding out in the tall weeds behind the house? He couldn't be in the garage, because she and Jess had just cleaned it out a couple of days ago, and he couldn't be living outside in the yard, so where could he be? She finally decided that he was probably on his way home to see his

145

parents. They could have panicked and called the police when they hadn't heard from him for a few days.

*Is it my fault?* she wondered. *Am I responsible for every fool that wants to sleep with me? The police would probably say that I led him on, and maybe I did. Oh, God, why can't I learn the truth about men without having to suffer through every kind of humiliation possible?*

She was still worrying about Corey when Jess yelled that Dr. Gibby was there, followed by another yell that the ambulance had arrived. She wiped off the counter one last time and hung the rag over the faucet, then dried her sweaty hands on a paper towel and went to greet her father.

It took over half an hour to remove Connor from the ambulance and install him in the hospital bed in the dining room. He looked bigger to Cassie out of the wheelchair, and she felt a wave of fear sweep over her as she saw him lying in the high, narrow bed. What if he recovered fully and got his strength back? What if he hit her again? What if he hit Jess? What would she do?

"Cross that bridge when you come to it," Gibby suggested in her ear, reading her thoughts. He put his hand on her shoulder and turned her to face him. "This is how he'll be the rest of his life, Cassie, but if you don't want him here, just say the word and back he goes."

"It's his house."

"That makes absolutely no difference."

"What would the hospital say?"

"Why do you care what they'd say? I don't."

She looked into Gibby's eyes and saw that he spoke the truth, and that strengthened her resolve.

"I want him to stay right here, where he belongs," she said, and she meant it.

She had purposely stayed away from Connor up until now, waiting in the living room, or standing back against the far wall of the dining room while Gibby and the attendants moved the older man and tried to make him comfortable. Now the ambulance driver and his partner were getting ready to leave, and she knew that Gibby would have to follow them.

"What happened to the nurse you hired?" she asked suddenly.

"She'll be a little late, but she'll be here before your dad needs to be bathed or moved around."

"She? I thought you were going to try and get a man." Cassie wondered why Gibby had contacted the Nurses' Registry himself instead of letting her do it, as they had originally planned.

"Mrs. Bower is as strong as an ox. She won't have any trouble lifting him around, if that's what you're worried about."

"What if he has to go to the bathroom before she gets here?"

"Cassie?" Gibby leaned down and looked into her eyes, pinning her with his gaze so that she couldn't turn away from him. "Are you getting cold feet about this? Mrs. Bower is only going to be here for a few hours every day. The rest of the time you're going to have to handle your dad by yourself. That's the way you said you wanted it. Have you changed your mind?"

"No." She drew in a long draught of air and let it out slowly, then repeated the procedure several times.

"Cassie?"

"I'm fine now. This is what I want, it really is. I'm fine with it."

"Still, I think I'd better stay with you until Rose gets here."

"Rose Bower? She sounds like she belongs in a flower garden or something."

Gibby's warm breath touched her ear as he whispered: "Well, she doesn't look like it. She's about six feet tall and built like a brick—well, I'll leave it up to your imagination."

147

"I get the picture. But seriously, you don't have to stay until she gets here. I'm fine now, I promise."

"Okay, if you say so. You can get me on my beeper if you need me." He wrote the number on a pad of paper, tore off the sheet and gave it to her.

"Thank you for everything, Gibby. I don't know what Jess and I would do without you."

"Well, don't spend any time worrying about that because you don't have to do without me."

He walked over to the bed and leaned over into Connor McCall's line of vision.

"How're you doing, Connor? Are you comfortable? I'm sure you're aware that you're back home, with your daughter, Cassie, and your grandson, Jess. They're going to take good care of you, and Rose Bower's going to come in every day to help out. You've known Rose for a good many years, so I expect you'll be satisfied with her, but if you don't like her, we'll get you someone else."

Gibby turned to glance at Cassie, and she knew why. He wanted to know if she had seen the look on her father's face when he mentioned her name. She had, but she wasn't going to give up and admit that she'd made a mistake in bringing her dad home.

"I think he's tired," she said, stepping up to stand beside Gibby. "Maybe we'd better let him rest for a while." The old man's eyes shot daggers at her, but she continued to exert her authority by taking Gibby's arm and steering him away from the bed.

"Good going," the doctor said, then he squeezed her hand, whispered some last-minute instructions, and strode through the living room behind the two men from the ambulance. "I'll drop by later and see how you're getting along."

Due to the confusion and chaos of the past forty minutes, Cassie had forgotten about Jess entirely. She looked for him now, and found him standing at the foot of the bed, staring at his grandfather. The man's eyes were closed, but Cassie knew he wasn't sleeping. He was avoiding making any contact with them until he had to.

*Well, old man,* Cassie said to herself, *there'll be a time when you'll need us, and I can hardly wait for that day to come.*

When she turned her attention back to Jess, he was slouched against the bed. He'd been feeling all right for the past few days, but now he looked tired again. She led him into the kitchen and made him some soup for lunch, not happy at all with the damp, clammy feel of his forehead or the unnatural brightness of his eyes.

After Cassie got Jess settled with his soup, she took a bowl into the dining room and stood at Connor's bedside, willing him to open his eyes. He did, finally, and she tried to spoon some of the lukewarm chicken broth into his mouth. When he saw the soup coming, he glued his lips shut and refused to open them, even when Cassie tried to pry them open with the spoon. After several tries, she gave up and returned the bowl to the kitchen. Mrs. Bower could heat it up in the microwave if the stubborn old man would eat it for her.

Back in the kitchen, she found Jess's bowl still three-quarters full sitting on the table, and the boy nowhere in sight. The back door wasn't completely closed, and she guessed that he'd slipped out to avoid another confrontation with her over the soup. A jacket, not as warm as his green down one, was missing from the hook inside the kitchen door, which only confirmed Cassie's suspicions. If he didn't return by the time Mrs. Bower arrived, at least she knew where to look this time.

She found him there, on the lake shore, two hours later. He was watching a group of children play ball toward the edge of the woods, a wistful expression on his small face. She called his name and was rewarded by a smile before he realized where he was and that he

149

had been forbidden to go to the lake without permission.

Cassie walked over to where he was standing and reached for his hand.

"We've got to go home, Jess. We've got your grandpa to take care of now, remember? You're going to have to grow up and show a little more responsibility."

"There's something out there," he said, and she caught the fear in his voice.

"Where?" She shaded her eyes with her hand and peered out in the direction where Jess was staring, toward the middle of the lake. "I don't see anything."

"There," he said, and pointed to a specific spot a couple of hundred feet away from where they stood.

"There's something there," he repeated and she had to admit that there was something, but she couldn't tell what it was that was bobbing on the surface of the water between the sheets of ice that covered almost the entire lake.

"You stay here," she instructed Jess, "and I'll try to go out there and see what it is."

"You can't do that, Mom," the child answered excitedly. "The ice isn't as thick as it used to be. You could fall in."

"I'll be careful," she promised, as she placed one foot on the ice and tested her weight before starting out slowly and carefully to walk toward the patch of blue that floated in the middle of the lake. From such a distance, she couldn't tell whether it was a blue ball or a blue jacket or something else entirely. Her stomach contracted as she remembered the red jacket that floated under the water when Jess fell into the lake. She only hoped to God that she wouldn't find a child when she reached her destination. She wasn't sure she could handle that.

"Be careful, Mom," Jess called out behind her, and Cassie nodded her head. She continued moving forward, taking her time, knowing that there was no hurry to reach the blue object. She was horribly sure of that, the larger it loomed in her field of vision.

Finally, after a long time, she stood over the floating patch of blue, and she knew what it was. It was a heavy nylon windbreaker, the kind hundreds of kids from the university wore all the time. She crouched down and stared at the thing for several minutes without making any move to touch it. She could hear Jess's voice coming to her from far away, asking her what she had found.

With a trembling hand, she reached out and touched the nylon. It moved because there was an air pocket between it and whatever was underneath it, and Cassie drew her hand away. It wasn't an empty jacket. There was something under it, something solid, something that had once been alive. There was a head under the ice. A head with thick, sandy hair, the kind that would keep falling into a man's eyes.

She half stood, slipped, and almost fell into the hole on top of the body. Catching herself in time, she ran across the ice, sliding precariously, by some miracle keeping her balance until she reached the shore.

"Come on," she told Jess, grabbing his hand and pulling him away from the sight that seemed to hold him entranced. "We'll call the police from the nearest pay phone."

A mile down the road toward town, the boy spotted an old-fashioned black box on the side of the road and Cassie pulled over. She had to repeat the story twice before the police dispatcher could understand her, before he promised to send a car right out.

The cop on duty was Tom Barney, and he stayed dry on the shore while a diver made his way out to the middle of the lake and ascertained that there was indeed a body floating under the ice. Then Barney sighed, laid his clipboard on the hood of his car for safekeeping, and tiptoed out to the spot where the diver waited.

Within five minutes, another patrol car drove up, carrying two more divers. They were no sooner in the water than a team of paramedics arrived, lights flashing and sirens blazing.

"Shut that fool thing off," Barney ordered, "no rush for this one."

The men on shore waited in silence for the divers to pull the body out and drag it in. Barney had told Cassie to wait until he had a chance to talk to her, and she had the feeling that he wanted her to be there to see the boy's body pulled from the lake and placed on the bank.

*He knows,* she said to herself. *Barney knows who it is and he wants to see my reaction. But I can't act surprised, I'm not that kind of a person.*

Cassie told Jess to stay put and climbed out of the car. She reached the bank in time to watch the paramedics turn the body over onto its back, and she didn't have to worry about her reaction. She took one look at Corey Hammil's blank, staring eyes and crumpled to the ground.

# Chapter Seventeen

When Cassie came to, she was lying on a stretcher in the first-aid vehicle, with a blood pressure cuff on her upper arm. A young paramedic sat on a stool beside her, and he smiled when she opened her eyes and looked at him.

"Hi, you okay now?"

"I think so. What happened?"

"You took one look at the body and passed out. Typical female civilian reaction."

"Corey's dead," Cassie said to herself, and the remark caught the paramedic's attention.

"You knew the guy? I think you'd better tell Tom Barney."

"I'm sure Officer Barney knows."

"Officer Barney knows everything," Tom Barney said from the doorway of the van, "and what he doesn't know, he aims to find out. How ya feeling, *Ms.* McCall?"

"Fine," Cassie answered.

"Think you can make it home, or should I have somebody drive you?"

"I can drive myself home."

"Suit yourself. I'll be by to talk to you in a half hour or so. Stay around home till I get there."

The young paramedic helped Cassie sit up, and held onto her arm while she stepped down from the vehicle. Corey's body was still lying on the sand, only now somebody had covered it with what looked like a tarpaulin. With a jolt of nausea, she realized that they were waiting to load the body into the medical van, to place it on the stretcher where she had been lying only moments before.

She hurried to her father's car, opened the door, and literally fell into the driver's seat. Jess was huddled in the passenger seat, and she gathered him into her arms.

"I'm so sorry, honey. Have you been sitting here by yourself all this time?"

"That policeman came over to talk to me. He wanted to know when was the last time we saw Corey. Corey's dead, Mom." The boy started to cry and Cassie rocked him for several minutes before he straightened and told her he was all right. After a few stall-outs, the old car's motor caught and kept running. As she shifted into drive and pulled away, she happened to glance in her rear-view mirror. Tom Barney was standing on the bank, staring in her direction. In one hand, he held his clipboard. With the other hand, he was making an obscene gesture.

Ten minutes later, Cassie arrived at the house to find Mrs. Bower pacing the floor, and when Mrs. Bower paced, the entire house shook. The no-nonsense woman stood at least six feet tall and must have weighed over two hundred pounds.

"I told Dr. Gibson I could only stay an hour or so today," she complained in a grating voice. "I still have a day or so to finish up on my old job. After that, I can stay longer."

"I'm sorry," Cassie apologized, "the doctor must have forgotten to mention it to me."

The look on Mrs. Bower's face said quite clearly that she didn't believe that for a minute, but at least she stopped whining. She was efficient though. She had left a report of everything she'd done for Connor, and of his reactions to her ministrations. According to what she'd written, the man much preferred her help to any he got from Cassie or Jess. He had sipped a cup of tea, eaten a bowl of soup, and used the bedpan before closing his eyes for a late-afternoon nap.

Cassie could only hope he would sleep for an hour or so longer, so that she could pull herself together and get the sight of Corey's dead body out of her mind before she had to face her father. She knew that Tom Barney wouldn't tell her anything, even when he found out what actually had happened to Corey, whether he had been murdered or had committed suicide. If he took his own life, would Barney blame her? There was another possibility, maybe the boy had met with an accident, slipped and fallen into the water while he was—was what? What could he possibly have been doing out on the ice in the middle of the lake? Not fishing. There was no fishing pole or tackle of any kind near the body. Not skating. Corey was wearing the high-topped sneakers he always wore, no matter how raw the weather. Cassie had teased him about that, told him that a grown man should have enough sense to wear boots in the snow, but Corey just laughed it off and said he preferred his Nikes.

Tears welled up in Cassie's eyes as she pictured Corey laughing, tossing his thick hair out of his eyes, reaching to pull her close to him. She wanted to cry for him, to share the loss that his family must be feeling now, after a telephone call from Tom Barney. But she felt that she didn't dare let Jess or her father see her pain, which was a private thing she didn't want to exhibit.

Jess wasn't hungry and neither was she, so she offered to play a game of hearts with him to help get his mind off what had happened at the lake. When Gibby called to say that he would be stopping by kind of late to check on Connor, Cassie hated to let him hang up. She held onto him for a few seconds longer, and Jess used that time to run upstairs and use the bathroom. He came back into the kitchen two or three minutes later announcing, "Grandpa's awake now," and ending the card game for the evening.

"Hi, Daddy." Cassie forced herself to sound cheerful as she approached the bed.

Connor rolled his eyes up into his head so that he wouldn't have to look at her.

"I know you've always been unhappy with me, Daddy, but I've never known why. Maybe we can figure that out now, and work things out between us. We have a lot of time now, we—"

Cassie jumped backward as the old man leapt up in the bed, reminding her of a fish thrashing on a hook.

"All right," she said when she had regained her composure, "we won't talk about it now, but that doesn't mean I'm going to forget about it. I'm going to get you something to eat. It's just leftovers, but tomorrow I'll cook you a real meal, like Momma used to make. And you can have a chocolate milkshake for dessert."

Her father dropped his eyes and stared into hers, and it wasn't hard for her to read his message: "You left home," his eyes said, "and she died of a broken heart. You aren't fit to speak her name."

As she went to the kitchen to fix dinner, Cassie wondered if those thoughts really belonged to her father, or if they were reflections of her guilt that she was attributing to him.

Despite the fact that the leftover casserole was delicious, Connor refused to take a bite of it. He did sip a little water, but only after Jess stepped forward and took the glass from his mother's hands. Cassie sent Jess upstairs and turned the downstairs lights off around nine-thirty, sure that Gibby wasn't going to show up. She sat in the dark living room and thought about Corey Hammil's short life and the unfairness of his death until she saw headlights coming down the street around ten-fifteen. Since there were seldom any cars on the street after nine in the evening, she was sure that the headlights belonged to Gibby's Mercedes.

She opened the door for him and whispered that her dad was asleep but when Gibby approached the bed she heard him say, "Hi, Connor, what's the matter, can't you sleep tonight? I'd think being back in your own house would take away some of the stress of the hospital environment. Okay, let's see what I have in my bag. I guess I can help you out a little bit tonight. Do you need anything else while I'm here? Bedpan? Drink of water? Okay, then I'll stop by and check on you tomorrow. Relax and try to get a good night's sleep now."

Gibby came back to the living room and silently motioned toward Cassie's down jacket, which hung on the coat tree just inside the front door. She threw it around her shoulders and followed him out to the porch.

"How are you two getting along?" he asked, as soon as they were out of earshot of her father.

"He hasn't eaten anything since Mrs. Bower left, and he wouldn't take any water from me, but he did take a few sips for Jess."

"He'll come around in a couple of days. In the meantime, just hang in there and try to keep the atmosphere stress-free."

"Isn't skipping meals bad for him?"

"He didn't eat much in the hospital either. Sometimes, just one meal a day. Maybe you could make him a little jello tomorrow. He likes that."

"Okay."

Gibby took her hands in his and rubbed them gently.

"You're cold, I've got to get you back inside."

"I'm not used to this weather yet."

"Cassie, I'm sorry about Corey, and I'm especially

sorry that you and Jess had to find the body."

She nodded, whispered, "I know you are," and realized that she was thoroughly exhausted. She wanted to lean against the strong doctor, and let him hold her until the pain of Corey's death abated.

"Is Jess okay?" Gibby asked.

"He cried a little but he's not too upset. I guess he didn't really like Corey very much. Corey was just a kid himself, he didn't know how to handle a little boy like Jess."

"You have nothing to feel guilty about, you know that, don't you?"

"How did you know I'm feeling guilty?" Cassie asked, looking up into his eyes.

"Because I know you, Cassie McCall, and you think you're responsible for the ills of the world."

"Maybe I am," she joked.

"I'm glad you're all right." Gibby kissed her cheek and shoved her toward the door. "Now get inside before I have to treat you for pneumonia tomorrow."

"That's an old wives' tale," she shot back at him, "that you get sick from being out in the cold. Cold's good for you, it's just uncomfortable, that's all."

"Thank you, Dr. McCall."

She went inside and closed the door, but she swore she could hear the doctor's laughter as he walked across the yard and climbed into his car. She started up the stairs, then stopped and gazed across the dark room toward her father's bed.

"Good night, Daddy," she whispered, but the figure in the bed made no response.

Cassie woke up in the morning to an insistent pounding that she finally identified as someone knocking on the front door. She thrust her arms into the sleeves of an old terry-cloth robe and ran down the stairs. Her father was awake, staring straight ahead of him, his eyes cold and blank. If he had the power of speech, she was sure that he would be screaming: "See who's at the God-damned door, girl.

You'd better learn to move faster than that, Missy, or you won't be gettin' anything to eat today."

It was a shock to find Officer Barney on the doorstep when the sun was barely up, and the sight of the man appearing before breakfast didn't set well on Cassie's stomach.

"Yes?" she said through a crack in the door, "What is it?" Only now did she remember that he had sworn to stop by and question her yesterday. She had been so preoccupied with thoughts of Corey and with caring for her father that she had totally forgotten everything else.

Barney pushed the door against Cassie's breasts and sidled through the narrow opening.

"You have a good night's sleep, Miss McCall?" he asked, and Cassie realized that she had never feared anyone the way she feared this man who disliked her so intensely. Every question he asked, no matter how casually, was a trick question.

"I went to bed very late," she answered, then was sorry she had volunteered even that much information about her personal life, which was none of his business.

"Mind if I sit down?" he asked when Cassie didn't offer him a seat. She indicated a rather uncomfortable, threadbare chair but Barney sat on the couch instead, and placed his clipboard on his crossed knees.

"How well did you know Corey Hammil?" he asked without preamble.

"We went out a couple of times."

"How did you meet him?"

"He came to fix my roof. It leaked when it rained hard."

"Did you sleep with him?"

"Yes, I did, and if that caused him to be killed, I'm sorry," Cassie blurted out.

Barney stopped writing and stared at her intently. "For a civilian, you seem to know an awful lot about people gettin' killed, don't you?"

"I don't know anything. Jess and I saw something floating in the lake and I went out to see what it was, and it was Corey, that's all I know."

"Don't get all excited now, nobody's accusing you of anything. Yet. But come to think of it, a lot of bad things started happening in this town once you and your boy came back, didn't they?"

Cassie just stared at the cop and didn't bother to dignify his ridiculous question with an answer.

"The boy upstairs?" Barney asked, inclining his head toward the ceiling.

"He's sleeping."

"Doesn't go to school much, does he?"

"He's been sick."

"Is that a physical sickness or a mental sickness?"

"He's had the flu," Cassie lied.

"Well, just tell me when and where you last saw the Hammil boy alive, and we can call it a day here."

"I don't remember exactly when it was, a week or so ago, I guess. I looked out the front window and he was standing on the lawn, talking to Jess. I went out, but Corey was gone by the time I got out there."

"What'd you go out for?"

"I don't understand the question."

"Why did you go outside? Did you want to talk to him about something?"

"I just wanted to tell him to leave Jess alone."

"Was he bothering the boy in some way?"

"He shoved Jess and knocked him down. They'd been arguing about something. I don't know what."

"Umm-hmm. Maybe I'll have to talk to the boy about that sometime."

Barney rose from the couch and before Cassie realized what he was doing, he had strode into the dining room and was standing at the end of her father's bed.

"Hi ya, Connor. They treatin' you right here? If they don't, you just let me know and I'll run them in.

Keep up your spirits, things are gonna change for the better soon, you can count on that."

*Now what in the hell does he mean by that?* Cassie wondered as she showed him the door. *Everything the man says seems to be a veiled threat of some kind.*

Cassie tried to put Tom Barney's nastiness out of her mind as she prepared breakfast for Jess and her father. True to her expectations, Connor refused her attempts to feed him oatmeal and he spit out the tea which she managed to get in his mouth.

"Suit yourself," she said finally, thinking that maybe she wouldn't be able to keep her father at home, if he steadfastly refused sustenance. But when Jess came downstairs, greeted his grandfather and asked if he'd like some hot tea, Cassie thought she saw a barely perceptible movement of the man's head. Evidently, Jess saw it, too.

"Grandpa wants tea, Mom. He wants me to feed it to him, don't you, Grandpa?" Again, there was the slight movement that could have been taken as a nod. Maybe it was just a tic, something over which the man had no control, but Cassie fixed the tea anyway and took it into the bedroom.

She placed the cup on an old nightstand she'd put beside the bed and Jess patiently spooned small portions into his grandfather's mouth. Connor seemed to have a hard time swallowing, and he tired quickly. After several spoonfuls he managed to turn his head a little to the left, away from Jess.

Cassie was excited about these small hopeful signs, and she told Gibby about them later in the morning.

"We've always known that he should be capable of much more movement than he's shown," he told her. "Maybe having Jess around will give him the incentive to push himself harder."

"I hope so. Wouldn't it be wonderful if they became friends, like a real grandpa and grandson?"

"It certainly would," Gibby agreed, "and if it

happens, the credit is all yours."

Cassie was elated, but after Gibby left and Mrs. Bower had come and gone for the day, she was once again faced with a stubborn man who refused to eat or drink or even use the bedpan while she was in charge. More than once, she caught him watching her with a malevolent stare that sent chills down her back. When she turned to face him, he made a grimace that mimicked his smile, the one she remembered from her childhood. The evil smile that was the harbinger of a tongue-lashing or a hard slap across the face, or a beating with the belt he would slowly remove from his trousers. Or worse.

But Cassie refused to think about that. She hadn't thought about it for ten long years, years that she might not have survived had she stayed in this house with the man who now lay helplessly inactive in the big hospital bed. There were good things to think about, and she forced herself to enumerate them: spring was coming, and she and Jess had a real house to live in. She would plant flowers along the front walk and make a garden out beside the house. Gibby would come for lunch, and they'd eat on the back porch, after she cleaned it up and painted it, of course. And her father was home again. Maybe he would recover and he and Jess would share family things with each other. But what would her father share with her? Would things revert to the way they had been ten years ago? Would she become afraid of him again?

*What do you mean by again, Cassie?* she asked herself. *You're afraid of him now.*

# Chapter Eighteen

The next two days passed quickly, with Connor sipping a little tea and broth for Jess, and eating his main meal of the day for Mrs. Bower. She helped him use the bedpan, bathed him, and with Cassie's assistance, got him into the wheelchair. Sometimes he fell asleep in the chair and they left him there for several hours, until Dr. Gibby made his daily visit. Together, Cassie and Gibby would lift Connor back into bed, where he would stare over their heads at a spot on the wall until he dozed off again, exhausted from his long stint in the chair.

Gibby indicated that Connor's progress was slow and that, starting the following week, he would begin daily sessions of physical therapy.

Helping Mrs. Bower and Gibby handle her father was a traumatic experience for Cassie. She couldn't remember ever holding his hand or hugging him as a child. She had to close her eyes and psych herself up before Mrs. Bower called her for assistance. Otherwise, she was afraid that she might shudder and show her distaste when the time came to stand behind Connor and place her hands under his arms to lift him into the chair.

On Friday, Mrs. Bower came to the house early and planned to stay until late afternoon so that Cassie could accompany Jess to his second appointment with Dr. Dan Winslow. Cassie worried about how the nurse would handle Connor by herself, but the woman didn't seem to be worried by the prospect.

Since Dr. Gibby was tied up with a heavy patient load, Cassie borrowed Marilou's Buick and set off for Hartford with Jess. She was determined to make the trip an adventure, with a stop at one of his favorite fast-food restaurants on their way home.

They arrived at the hospital early, but Dr. Winslow was already there waiting for them.

"Hi, Jess, come on in and sit down. If you'd like to wait outside, Cassie, I'll speak to you when I finish with Jess."

Cassie nodded, and admitted to herself that she was rather intimidated by the doctor's dead-serious, formal manner. The thought crossed her mind that Dr. Winslow was certainly nothing like Gibby, and a moment later she felt a flush brightening her face. *You know you're in trouble,* she said to herself, *when you start comparing other men to a man whom you hardly know. The only reason you do it is that he's a good person who treats you with kindness.*

Angry with herself, Cassie pushed all thoughts of Dr. Gibby out of her mind and concentrated on Jess. He wasn't looking well at all today, and she was determined to spend more time taking care of him. He was still out of school, and just yesterday she had received a telephone call from the principal, a polite inquiry as to why he wasn't there.

"He's sick," Cassie had blurted out. "He's still seeing a doctor almost every day." And I don't trust you to take care of him, was what she wanted to add. I don't trust you to keep him away from the lake, away from—the lake, that's all.

Doctor Winslow spent a long time with Jess before he called Cassie to come into his office.

"How about you waiting for us outside, Jess?" he suggested when Cassie was seated in a beige Danish-modern chair on the opposite side of his desk.

"I won't be long, sweetheart," she promised.

Once the door was closed, the doctor folded his hands on his desk and regarded Cassie as if he were trying to read what was on her mind.

"He's a good little boy," he said finally, "and he really wants to please you. I think he's holding something back because he's afraid of upsetting you."

"What has he told you?"

"He talks about his relationship with you quite freely. He knows the truth about his father, and he seems to admire you for raising him as a single mother. He doesn't seem to be aware of any traumatic incidents in his life before the near drowning. He does admit to going to the lake frequently and even to taking the dresses from your father's store. But there's something he isn't willing to discuss regarding his trips to the lake. I can sense his reluctance to let me inside the barriers he's erected."

"Barriers? You mean like he's trying to hide something?" Cassie asked.

"Maybe not 'hide' exactly. I feel that he's attempting to be protective of someone or something. He appears to be a very noble-minded little boy."

"Do you think we can find out? Do you want to see him again?"

"Most definitely. And you can do your part by talking to him often and very gently trying to get him to open up to you. I'll see him . . ." Dr. Winslow consulted a black leather diary on his desk and thumbed through a few pages. "How about a week from today, same time?"

Cassie nodded and held out her hand to take the little appointment card the doctor filled out and handed to her. She began to rise from the chair, anxious to get out to the waiting room and collect Jess, but the doctor stopped her.

"There's more, Miss McCall."

"Oh." She let her body drop back into the chair.

She had known it was too good to be true, had known for days that there would be more.

"There are a few things that bother me, and I'd like to be frank about them."

Cassie nodded again, afraid to speak.

"I'd like to suggest that you check Jess into the hospital for a complete physical. Wait, wait, there's nothing that serious involved. One thing I'm concerned about is that Jess has a short attention span for an eight-year-old boy who has a history of being an A-student. He also seems to have difficulty focusing. Both of these problems could be due to neurological damage dating back to his accident."

"There's more," Cassie stated simply, and the doctor nodded.

"His color is bad and his temperature fluctuates wildly. Contrary to that, his eyes look feverish. I think it would be smart to have him checked over before something more serious develops."

"I'll talk to Dr. Gibson this afternoon," Cassie promised, thinking about Jess waiting in the room outside, probably wondering what was taking her so long.

"I know you're anxious to get back to Jess. I'm sure Dr. Gibson will notify me of your decision."

The doctor rose and accompanied her to the door.

"Where is he?" Cassie asked after a quick scan of the waiting room failed to reveal Jess.

"He probably went to the restroom. Or maybe he found the candy machines."

"I told him to wait." Cassie ran up and down the corridor calling out Jess's name until the doctor stopped her.

"This won't help, Cassie. I'll see if he's in the men's room. If not, we'll check out the cafeteria and the candy machines. You stay right here until I return."

The wait seemed an eternity but within five minutes by her watch, the doctor was back with Jess in tow. His head and face were damp and Cassie could tell from the scraps of white paper in his blond hair that the doctor had tried to dry off the boy's hair with paper towels.

"What were you doing in there, Jess?" Cassie asked, then she felt stupid for asking such a ridiculous question, and decided to rephrase it: "Why are you all wet?"

"It seems that Jess decided to wash his hair while he waited for you and me to finish," the doctor answered when Jess didn't have anything to say.

"It's cold outside," Cassie said, knowing that she wasn't reacting in a normal way.

"I have a cap you can borrow to get him home," Dr. Winslow offered. He led them back to his office and fetched a blue, knit ski-hat from the top of a shelf.

"I'll bring it back to you next week," Cassie said, accepting the hat and covering Jess's hair with it.

"Don't worry about it, I never use it anyway." The doctor smiled thinly and shook her hand, but she could see that he was troubled. She didn't ask him about what he had found Jess doing in the men's room because she already knew. Every time the child got near water, he buried his face in it and pretended that he was drowning. He sucked the water into his nose and let it flow down his throat. He swallowed as much of it as he could as he relived the horrifying moments he had spent in Lake Wahelo.

She decided not to say anything in front of Jess, but she knew that she would have to talk to the doctor privately as soon as possible. She didn't like the look on his face as he watched Jess walk down the hallway toward the outside door. The perfect Dr. Dan Winslow suddenly looked very puzzled, and very ineffectual.

Despite the disturbing events at the hospital, Cassie stopped at a burger restaurant and convinced Jess that he was hungry. For once, he did eat most of his food, and he jabbered on about his grandfather for most of the drive back to Winter Falls.

"He likes me, Mom, I can tell. He wants me to feed him. Do you think he likes me, Mom?"

"Of course, he does, sweetheart. Who wouldn't like you?"

Cassie managed to keep up her end of the conversation, but she was distracted by the memory of Jess standing beside Dr. Winslow in the hospital corridor, his face damp, his hair matted down, his eyes bluer and clearer than ever. She didn't know whether something was really happening to Jess, or if she was being an overprotective mother, or both.

When they arrived at the house in the early afternoon, she let Jess turn on the TV, which she had moved up to his room after Connor came home. She had asked Gibby whether her father might like a little TV of his own, but Gibby said the man had somehow indicated that he didn't like to watch television anymore.

Connor was sitting in his wheelchair, looking better than he had since Cassie's return to Winter Falls, and Mrs. Bower was beaming.

"Your father is a model patient," she said enthusiastically, before Cassie even had her coat off. "He's so alert today, I can just tell he's listening to every word I say. And I swear I saw him move his lips, like he was trying to tell me something. It won't be long now, and the dear man will be talking to us again, mark my words."

"That's wonderful," Cassie said, turning to smile into her father's glaring eyes.

"Oh, don't mind how he looks, dear," Mrs. Bower advised, patting Cassie's arm. "The old dear just can't control his facial muscles yet, that's why he looks like an old bear. But he's not, are you Connor?"

Cassie thought her dad looked as if he would throttle the nurse if he had the power to do it, but she kept her thoughts to herself.

Since there was nothing else to do for Connor, Cassie let Mrs. Bower rattle on for a few more minutes before she suggested that they get her dad back into bed. When that task was successfully concluded, she showed the nurse to the door. Then she made a cup of tea and sat down in the living room, around the corner from Connor's bed, so that she couldn't see him and he couldn't see her. She missed having the TV downstairs. She would have liked to turn it on, just for the noise.

The day was gloomy, and the living room was dark. She couldn't hear the TV going upstairs, and it wasn't more than a few minutes before she closed her eyes and gave in to the exhaustion that claimed her. It was harder than she'd thought, taking care of her dad, but in a different way than she'd imagined. It wasn't hard on her physically, only a little more laundry and the struggle to help lift him in and out of bed a couple of times a day. But it was hard on her emotionally, having him in the house, catching him watching her, wondering what was going on in his mind. The house seemed to be at peace only when he slept, and she was never sure when he was faking that.

The sound of Gibby's voice woke her, and she sat up with a start. Her neck and back protested the cramped position she had forced them into so that she could sleep.

"It's a good thing you don't lock your door," Gibby said, "I've been standing out there for a full five minutes."

Cassie shook her head to clear away the cobwebs. "I wonder why Jess didn't answer."

"He's probably watching TV and thinks the pounding is part of the soundtrack," Gibby joked.

"We have to give your television back to you," Cassie said, suddenly remembering that the set belonged to Gibby.

"I gave that to Jess," the doctor answered.

"No, you didn't. You can't give him things like that."

"I didn't mean to offend you, I just wanted Jess to have it. I never watched it anyway."

"I can't let him keep a gift like that, Gibby. It's nothing personal against you, you're just too good to us, that's all."

Gibby obviously decided to shelve the subject because he nodded towards the dining room, whispered, "How is he today?" and without waiting for an answer walked in to check on Connor. He spent ten minutes or so talking to the man, then went to the kitchen, where Cassie was looking through the cupboards, searching for the makings of an easy dinner.

"I'm buying tonight," he said. "How do you feel about Kentucky Fried Chicken?"

"Are you sure?" she asked and when he said he was, she expressed her desire to eat Kentucky Fried Chicken until she burst.

"I'll take Jess with me while you set the table and make some of your good hot cocoa—deal?"

"Deal."

Gibby took the steps two at a time and Cassie smiled to herself as she laid out place mats, napkins and the forks which she and Jess would ignore in favor of using their fingers for the greasy chicken that they both loved. She heard the doctor calling Jess's name, then heard his footsteps on the stairs again.

"He isn't upstairs," Gibby said, rushing into the kitchen slightly out of breath. "Are you sure you didn't give him permission to go for a walk or something?"

"Of course, I'm sure."

"Well, you were asleep. Maybe he wasn't able to wake you up. Would he have left a note?"

"No, probably not. Gibby, he knows he's not allowed to go out without permission, not in a

170

strange town, not in the wintertime, not when it's almost dark outside."

"I'll find him."

"I'm going with you."

"Somebody has to stay here with your dad, Cassie. Trust me, okay?"

"Okay."

"I'll bring him home."

"Do you know where to look?"

"Hey, I was a boy myself, remember? I know all the places a little boy would go."

"There's only one place."

They looked into each other's eyes for several seconds before Gibby nodded and left the room. Cassie followed him through the house and took up her vigil at the front window, her happy dinner-plans forgotten.

# Chapter Nineteen

Gibby was gone less than half an hour but for Cassie the clock stood still from the moment he walked out the door until she saw his car careen around the corner at breakneck speed. He didn't stop at the curb, and for a moment she thought he was going to drive right into the living room and kill both of them. The big Mercedes jumped the curb without slowing down, and barreled across the lawn until it came to a stop just inches from the front door.

By the time Cassie got to the door and pulled it open, Gibby was shouldering his way inside. She took one look at the dripping bundle in his arms and cried out. There was an answering rumble from the dining room, and she knew that she had awakened her father from his nap. She tried to be quiet as Gibby laid Jess on the couch and extracted him from the heavy blanket she had previously seen in the back-seat of the Mercedes.

"What happened to him?" she whispered urgently. "Is he going to be all right?"

"He's sleeping, passed out from sheer exhaustion. Can you get some dry clothes for him and a couple of towels? Move it, Cassie!"

She raced up the stairs, tripped and fell onto the second-floor landing with a thud. She was running again before she was back on her feet, gathering the thickest towels she could find from the bathroom, clean underwear and blue flannel pajamas from Jess's room.

Back in the living room, she watched as Gibby dried the boy and dressed him in the warm clothing. She looked at them together, as Gibby's red hair mingled with Jess's blond hair, and wondered if Gibby had a stake in Jess's life now. In both their lives.

"He was in the lake, wasn't he?" she asked when she saw that the child's eyes were open, that his blue-tinged lips were moving.

Gibby nodded and propped Jess up in a sitting position. "Do you feel a little better now?" he asked the boy.

"I want some answers," Cassie interrupted, raising her voice, "and I want them now."

Gibby looked up at her, and she was shocked to see the pain in his brown eyes, pain that was a direct reflection of the pain she felt.

"I don't have any answers, Cassie," he said, "but I'm as anxious to get some as you are. Would you mind fixing something hot for Jess to drink? I'll check on your dad while you do that."

"Will Jess be all right?" she asked, and for the first time in all the years she had known Gibby he seemed to be at a loss for words.

Later, after Connor was fed and tucked in for the night, Cassie and Gibby sat in the kitchen with Jess.

"Sweetheart," Cassie pleaded, "you have to tell us why you keep going to the lake. If we understand, maybe Dr. Gibby and I can help you."

Her son stared into her eyes, and once again she was almost overwhelmed with his beauty, a beauty in which she felt she had no part. She was as surprised as the doctor when Jess began to talk rapidly, his words and sentences running into each other.

"Wanda wants her daddy, and I don't know where to find him. She says her daddy went off and left her and her sisters all alone. She wants me to find her daddy for her."

"That's crazy," Cassie cut in, "that's just plain crazy, Jess. Wanda's daddy—"

At Gibby's eye signal, Cassie quit speaking and put her hand over her mouth to hold back the words that wanted to tumble out.

"Did Wanda tell you where to look for her daddy?" Gibby asked.

"Stop this," Cassie demanded, jumping to her feet. "You're talking like you think there really are girls out there."

"As far as Jess is concerned—" Gibby began, but Cassie cut him off again.

"Are you a psychiatrist now?" she asked.

"I'm a friend, Cassie. Or, at least, I'm trying to be one."

"I want this over with. Now. Tonight. I don't want to hear any more talk about dead girls and their daddy. I'll dry your blanket for you, and you can pick it up sometime tomorrow. Jess and I are going to bed now."

She picked Jess up in her arms and marched through the house with Gibby at her heels. "Hysterics aren't going to help Jess," he said in a conversational tone of voice that emphasized how her own voice had risen.

"I'm not hysterical," she said with control.

She sat Jess on the couch and picked up the blanket from the floor, together with the boy's clothes. They were all coated with thick lake-bottom mud.

"Oh my God, your car. What this must have done to the seats. Will you be able to get them clean? Your beautiful car."

Gibby grabbed her by the upper arms and shook her back and forth. "Forget the damned car. I don't care about the car. A car is a piece of metal. I care about you and Jess, can't you understand that?"

The shaking helped. Cassie felt the gears mesh in

her brain, felt things tumble back into place.

"I'm all right now," she said, stepping away from Gibby, avoiding his touch when he reached for her again. "Go home now, please. Go home, and we'll talk some other time."

Gibby pleaded with his eyes, but his glance at Jess's exhausted face must have convinced him that she was right. In spite of her wish to have him gone, the doctor leaned to kiss the little boy's cheek before he left the mother and her son alone.

The next morning, Cassie sheepishly called Gibby to apologize and to tell him about Jess's visit with Dr. Winslow. When she told him about his friend's recommendation that the boy have a complete physical at the hospital, Gibby readily agreed.

"I'll schedule it and get back to you," he told her. "And, Cassie, I'm the one who should be apologizing to *you*. I have no business interfering in your life."

She didn't know what to say, so she simply said, "Thank you," and hung up quickly, before he asked more of her. She knew that she needed Gibby until whatever was wrong with Jess got better. She also knew that she wasn't ready to make a commitment to him at this time, not even a commitment of friendship.

Cassie was supposed to go in and do the books for The Emporium today, but one look at Jess's pale, wan face changed her mind. He looked sick, as if some ugly parasite were eating away at his insides. She brought him downstairs where she could keep an eye on him, even though that meant no television to keep him occupied. She gave him books to read, and tried to keep up a conversation with him while she tended to her father.

She straightened Connor's sheets and tried to get him to sip some tea and eat a soft-boiled egg she had prepared for his breakfast, but the man wouldn't cooperate. He moved his lips just enough to slobber the egg down his chin onto his pajama top. Once again, Cassie got the impression that her father had the ability to move but was holding back for some unexplained reason.

Maybe he needs the attention, she thought to herself. Maybe he's afraid that if he gets better, Jess and I will go away and leave him. Maybe he needs our reassurance that we'll be here for him, no matter what. Her thoughts flew to the red velvet robe, still lying on the bed upstairs, and she decided that she would bring it down later in the day and try to put some color back into her father's dreary life.

She was carrying the uneaten egg and the cup of tea back to the kitchen when Jess's shrill little-boy's voice called her name.

"Hold on, sweetheart, I'll be right there," she told him. She continued on to the kitchen, scraped the egg into the garbage can, and rinsed the plate in cold water.

"Hurry up, Mommy."

"I'm coming, Jess."

By the time she got to the living room, the child was twisting and turning on the couch, as if he were in agony.

"Jess, what's wrong? Where does it hurt?" She bent over him and started to run her hands up and down his arms, then his legs, looking for a place to concentrate her energy.

"I have to go to the lake," he mumbled. Then louder, screaming: "I have to go to the lake."

"You can't go to the lake, Jess."

"I have to. You don't understand, I have to." Sweat stood out on his smooth brow, and there was a fine sheen on his upper lip, although it was a cold morning, with the temperature in the mid-teens.

Cassie tried to hold the boy down, but he thrashed at her with his arms, and kicked her when she got within reach of his feet.

"You stop it now, or I'm going to punish you," she shouted to be heard over the sound of his moaning and wailing, but the threat had no effect on him.

With every minute that it continued, the boy's "fit," as Cassie thought of it, got worse. There had been an epileptic boy in one of her high-school classes, and the way Jess was behaving reminded her of that boy. The child seemed to have no control over his arms or legs. Even his head was weaving back and forth on the thin stem of his neck.

"Stop!" Cassie screamed. "Stop, or you'll hurt yourself. You'll break something."

The boy's agony continued until finally Cassie had an idea. "Come on," she yelled, "come on, help me." She managed to get him up in her arms by pinning one of his arms behind her body and letting the other one wave freely back and forth in front of her. He was still kicking at her, but she ignored the blows and half carried, half dragged him up the stairs.

In the bathroom, she literally dropped him into the old claw-foot tub. He tried to clamber out, but she held him down with one hand while she used her other hand to turn on the faucet.

The water came out in a slow trickle, even though she had opened the faucet all the way. "Come on, come on," she begged, and the rusty water rushed down into the tub.

As soon as he heard the roar of the water, the boy quieted down. He looked up, not at his mother, but at the cascading water. Then he began to inch closer to the steady stream that ran down the stained walls of the old tub. When he was close enough, he stuck his head under the flow. When his head was soaking wet, he turned it to one side and let the water fill his eyes, his nose, his mouth. Then he turned over completely, so that he was lying on his back in the tub, his nice blue flannel pajamas turning dark with water stains.

Cassie watched in horror as her son placed his mouth directly under the water flow and closed his eyes in ecstasy. The water filled his mouth and his throat. He swallowed. According to the laws of nature, he should have been drowning, gasping for air, sputtering and spitting out the offending liquid.

But the water in his throat and lungs didn't bother Jess. Cassie could see that he loved it, that he needed it. She still didn't know where the idea had come from to put him into the bathtub. She had watched him throw that tantrum or fit or whatever it was, and her mother's instinct had taken over and told her what to do. He said he needed to get to the lake, so it followed that maybe he needed water—or thought he needed water.

She knew that if Gibby found out about this, he'd swear that she believed the tales about her aunts still being in the lake. After what she had just done, she must believe that since his near-drowning experience Jess needed water in his lungs to survive. She didn't believe that, she couldn't believe that, but Gibby would swear that she did. And if she did believe that, it was only one step further to believe that her baby spoke to a little dead girl named Wanda who was searching for her daddy.

# Chapter Twenty

Cassie finally coaxed Jess out of the bathtub and into her arms. She held him and rocked him until he pulled away, frightened and embarrassed by her intensity. He changed his clothes while Cassie cleaned up the bathroom, then she took his hand to walk downstairs.

It was surprising to find Mrs. Bower skulking around at the bottom of the staircase, obviously trying to hear what was going on between Cassie and Jess.

"He had a high fever," Cassie explained, "so I put him in the bathtub to bring it down." If it's any of your business, she added to herself.

"I let myself in and found your father alone down here," the woman said, accusingly.

"He was fine when I took Jess upstairs."

"He shouldn't be left alone, Mrs. McCall."

"He's alone all night long, every night," Cassie insisted.

The nurse squared her broad shoulders and turned her back on Cassie, which suited her fine. It gave her a chance to regain her composure while she straightened Jess's bedclothes on the couch and promised to bring him comic books from The Emporium before Mrs. Bower left for the day.

It worked out fine because the nurse was glad to get

179

rid of her, to be left alone to fuss over Connor while Cassie made an appearance at the business that still gave her a weekly paycheck despite the fact that she hadn't been there for quite a while. Marilou was glad to see her boss and started right in on how she had fallen behind on her work the past two weeks.

"Our inventory is low," she complained, "and we have a special order to place for the police department. Officer Barney was in asking about the rainproof covers for their hats and some good leather gloves he wants to order. I told him to write down what he wants, and you'll take care of it next time you come in."

"Where did you tell him I was?" Cassie asked, as she chose several comic books for Jess from the dwindling supply on the rack.

"Why, I told him you were at home, of course," Marilou answered, "what else would I tell him?"

"Did he ask you a lot of questions about me?"

"No, he didn't, Cassie. At least, not exactly. You know how Tom Barney is, always talking about something."

"What was he talking to you about?"

"Oh, he's a little worried about Jess, wandering off to the lake all the time and all."

"I see. I'm not going to be able to stay today, Marilou. Jess isn't feeling well, and Mrs. Bower has her hands full with my father."

"How is Connor anyway?" the woman asked, dropping the subject of Tom Barney's visit. "I thought maybe I'd stop by and see him one of these days. If it's all right with you."

"You're welcome anytime, Marilou. I'm sure my father would be glad to see you."

"Well, when are you coming in to place that special order and go over the inventory?" Marilou called out as Cassie headed for the door.

"Next week, I promise."

"I'll bet," Marilou mumbled, just loud enough for

Cassie to hear her.

After a quick stop at the supermarket for supplies, Cassie headed home. As she rounded the last corner, she was surprised to see Gibby's Mercedes parked in front of the house, and Mrs. Bower's gray Honda nowhere in sight. She opened the door and walked in on a scene that stopped her in her tracks.

Gibby was sitting on the couch, with Jess pressed up close to him, and he was reading to Jess from a book that sounded like a Star Wars adventure. Connor was sitting in his wheelchair, which had been pushed over to the couch. He, too, seemed to be enthralled with the story Gibby was reading in the deep, powerful voice of a born storyteller. It was a minute before they noticed her presence, and Cassie wished she'd had a camera to capture the scene on film. Then she would have a picture to take out late at night when she was lonely, and imagine that she had a family like the one in the photograph, a husband who would be coming home to warm her bed, and a father who loved her.

"Mommy," Jess said, breaking the spell and calling both Gibby's and Connor's attention to the fact that she was standing in the doorway watching them.

The feeling of contentment that she had momentarily felt didn't last long. Gibby handed the book to Jess and steered her to the kitchen, where he immediately started asking what had happened to the child that morning.

"Mrs. Bower has no right telling you my business," she said angrily.

"She wasn't telling me so as to be mean, Cassie, she was concerned about Jess."

"That's all I hear, how everybody is concerned about Jess, and I don't believe a word of it. Tom Barney and Mrs. Bower and even Marilou—I think they're all a bunch of nosy busybodies who don't have a life of their own."

"You don't mean that."

"How do you know what I mean?"

"Are we going to fight every time we see each other?" Gibby asked, "—because if we are, maybe I should turn Jess's care over to another doctor."

Cassie shrugged, mumbled, "I don't care what you do," and turned away from him, so that he wouldn't see the tears in her eyes.

"I'm sorry, Cassie, I didn't mean that. It's just that I'm concerned—oops, there's that nasty word again. Does that make me one of those awful busybodies?"

"Nosy busybodies, I called them nosy busybodies."

"So you did." Gibby turned her to face him and dried the tears that still wet her cheeks, even though she was laughing.

"I have to check in at my office now and see a couple of patients leftover from this morning, then I'm on my way to Boston for a conference. I should be back sometime tomorrow afternoon, if you need me. You have my home number, if you can't reach me in the office."

Cassie nodded, followed him to the living room and helped him lift her father back into the high, hospital bed. Then she showed him out the door and went back to sit with Jess until it was time to start dinner. She read to Jess from the Star Wars book, but her mind wasn't on what she was reading. She was thinking about Gibby, about the fact that she had never seen the house he lived in, and knew next to nothing about his personal life, even though he was so much a part of hers.

At five-thirty, she decided to start dinner—minute steaks and baked potatoes with sour cream. When she passed through the dining room on her way to the kitchen, her father's face was turned in her direction, and she felt his eyes fixed on her face.

"Hello, Daddy," she said, and for once he didn't jerk his head and try to turn away from her. She noticed the color of his eyes, a warm, chocolate brown like her own. She wanted to touch his hair and pat it down where it was rumpled from the pillow, but she didn't. It was too soon for that kind of personal attention, but she felt that it wouldn't be long before she and her father were making contact and behaving like members of an ordinary family.

She smiled at her dad, and hurried on to the kitchen. She hadn't been bothering to cook for him in the evening because he never ate the food she prepared, but tonight was different. Tonight he had looked at her, really looked at her. She threw an extra steak in the skillet for him, and put three potatoes in the microwave, humming as she went about her tasks.

Even though she was in an optimistic mood, she was surprised that Connor actually ate a few bites of his dinner when Jess offered it to him. She didn't have enough nerve to try and feed him herself. Some part of her was still skeptical about her father's acceptance of her, and she didn't want to chance rejection. But Jess, with the complete innocence of childhood, approached his grandfather as though they had never been apart.

"Look, Mom, he likes the steak. He likes the potato, too, but he doesn't like sour cream."

"You know, I remember now, he never did like it," Cassie answered, "but how can you tell?"

"He spits it out, but he likes the potato if I give it to him plain."

"He isn't eating very much."

"I just give him tiny bites. That's what Mrs. Bower told me to do."

"Oh. Well, she should know how to do it."

"Why don't you like her? She's a nice lady, Mom, and she's a nurse."

Cassie laughed and ruffled Jess's hair on her way past him to straighten the living room. "You're right, I should like her because she's taking such good care of your grandpa. Maybe I'm jealous."

"Sure, Mom," Jess teased, but Cassie wondered if it might be true. Maybe that was why she had taken such an immediate dislike to the woman. Maybe she *was* jealous.

After she finished cleaning up, Cassie told Jess to stay downstairs with his grandfather while she took a shower and got ready for bed. The house was cool, and when she stepped out of the water she was hit with a chill that permeated her entire body. She wrapped a bath towel around her waist and stepped into the hallway. As cold air wafted around her upper torso, she crossed her arms over her breasts to protect them. Her room was a few degrees warmer, but the thought of her desert-weight terry-cloth robe wasn't inviting. She dropped the towel on the floor and stopped to stare at the red velvet robe that lay draped across the foot of the bed.

Is he ready for this? she wondered. She closed her eyes and ran the scene in her mind: she walked into the living room where her father was sitting in his wheelchair (how he had gotten out of bed and into the chair, her imagination didn't reveal). His eyes lit up at the sight of her, wearing the robe that had belonged to her mother, the robe she was sure her mother had never been allowed to wear. "Do you like it, Daddy?" the dream-Cassie asked, and her father overcame his paralysis to nod his head. He smiled, and she noticed that there were tears in his eyes— tears of regret and joy. He beckoned to her and she went to him, knelt before his chair and rested her head in his lap. It was only a minute before his frozen hands moved and his gnarled fingers rested in the mass of thick dark hair that was her legacy from his side of the family. He wove his fingers in and out of her hair. "So beautiful," he murmured, "my daughter is so beautiful."

"Mommy . . ." The sound of Jess's voice broke into her dream, shattering the pictures in her mind and bringing her harshly back to reality. She opened

184

her eyes to find the room moving in front of her, and it took her a few seconds to realize that she was swaying back and forth. She planted her feet firmly, and she abruptly put a stop to the rocking movement of her body.

"Mommy . . ." The call came again, and this time Cassie answered back. "I'm coming, Jess," she yelled, then reached for the red velvet robe.

When she walked into the living room, Jess looked up from the story he had been writing and dropped the yellow number-two pencil. It hit the couch, fell to the floor, and rolled out of sight.

"You're so beautiful, Mommy," he said, echoing her dream.

"Thank you, sweetheart." She leaned to kiss his forehead and whispered in his ear: "Let's go in and see Grandpa for a few minutes."

"I think he's probably asleep."

"Let's just go see."

"Okay," the boy answered, but he didn't seem to be too enthusiastic over his mother's idea. When he stood up, he nuzzled his head into Cassie's stomach and rubbed his cheek on the rich velvet, then he took her hand. She wasn't sure whether the physical contact was to reassure her, or if the boy needed reassurance for himself.

The dining room was lit by a night light that threw long, uneven shadows into every corner. It took several seconds for Cassie's eyes to adjust to the dimness. She moved close to the bed and stood over her father's still form, expecting to find him sleeping. Maybe hoping that he would be asleep, she wasn't sure. Suddenly his face seemed to jump into her line of vision, and she saw his eyes, open and alert. She saw not the soft brown eyes that she had noticed the day before. Now her father's eyes were dark and watchful as they moved from her eyes to the blood red robe and back again.

He tried to speak, and the sound was terrible, like

185

the growl of a wild animal. The word that came out sounded like, Yu . . . yuuuuu. You.

*You look just like your mother, Cassie.* When she closed her eyes and shut out his face, she could imagine him saying that.

"He doesn't like the robe, Mom." Jess was tugging on her arm, trying to drag her away from the bed.

"Yes, he does, Jess, he doesn't know how to tell me, but he likes it fine."

"You like the robe, don't you, Daddy? You think it's beautiful, just like you think I'm beautiful. Look at my hair, Daddy." She threw her long hair over her right shoulder and leaned close to the old man who was her father. "Can you smell it? It smells like flowers, doesn't it, Daddy? Did Momma have flowers on her grave that smelled like that?"

"Cut it out, Mom, okay? Grandpa's tired, so let's you and me go up to bed now." Jess was getting frantic, pulling on her hand, acting as if he was afraid to touch the robe again.

"I haven't even been to visit her grave, Daddy. All these weeks here in Winter Falls, and I haven't even been to visit her grave. When I was in Phoenix, that's all I thought about, visiting my momma's grave, bringing her flowers. Did you ever take her flowers, Daddy?"

Connor's body jerked and moved several inches in Cassie's direction. His eyes were terrible, bloodshot, with veins bulging from concentration.

Cassie reached for his hand and pulled it toward her. She could feel the resistance as he fought her with his mind and willed his body to follow his instructions.

"Touch me, Daddy. Touch the robe I sent to Momma. I wanted her to wear it, but you never let her, did you? It's so soft, Daddy. I bought it at Goldwater's and I spent way too much money on it. But Momma loved it, didn't she? She couldn't write and tell me, because you wouldn't let her. But I know

186

she loved it. She could have worn it, and you could have touched her, Daddy. Now you can touch me. Touch my arm, touch my shoulder, touch my stomach."

She was jerking the old man around in the bed, forcing him to put his hand on the soft material. He was resisting harder, fighting with all his will to pull his hand away from her.

She glanced down at Jess, who had grown silent, and still as a statue. She could see that he was torn between running from the awful scene, and staying to see the final outcome.

"Go, Jess," she whispered, "there isn't any more to see. I thought I wanted him to love me, but I didn't. What I really wanted deep inside was to make him pay for what he did to Momma. But I can't do that either, because he isn't capable of feeling anything. Your grandpa is a man without a heart, Jess. He didn't love your Grandma, and he sure as hell doesn't love me. So my plan backfired, didn't it, Daddy? You win again, but in the end you're the one who's the big loser because I have Jess for my son, and I have Gibby for my friend, and you don't have anybody at all."

"Come on, Jess, let's go upstairs." She put her hand on her son's thin shoulder and turned him from the sight of his grandfather's misery. She was following him out of the room when she heard a noise that made her turn back to the bed. Her father was leaning half out of the bed, using sheer willpower to move his body. He was trying to say something, and finally, after long minutes of struggle, it came out.

"Ca . . . cas . . . sie." The word was slurred, and it was dragged out into several syllables, but it was her name, spoken by her father. She walked back to the bed, and a bud of joy bloomed in her chest when she saw him smiling.

"Oh, Daddy . . ."

She leaned over the bed and put her face close to

his, positioned her lips to touch his pale cheek. She was only an inch away from kissing him. "I'm sorry, Daddy."

She felt the blob of spittle hit her lips before her mind registered what he had done. She touched it with her fingers, smeared it, felt it drip down her chin and drop onto the red velvet robe. Then she realized what had happened. With an effort, she focused her eyes on his face. He was smiling.

Cassie stood very still, afraid to make a sudden move. If she moved, she thought that she might lose control. He was an invalid. It would be a sin to strike him, but that's what she wanted to do. She was a human being, and this man had been demeaning her for her entire life.

She tasted the bitterness of his spittle in her mouth, and knew that she hated him more than one human being should ever be allowed to hate another. She raised her arm and wiped the offensive slobber from her face, never taking her eyes from his. Then she pulled down the zipper on the robe and stepped out of it. She stood before her father as naked as she had been the day she came into the world.

"This is what you always wanted, isn't it, Daddy? This is why you hated me, because I wouldn't show myself to you. You beat me because that gave you an excuse to rip my clothes off and stare at me and touch me with your eyes. Do you know what's funny, Daddy? I never would have remembered if you hadn't spit on me. I never would have remembered what a bastard you really are."

# Chapter Twenty-one

Jess stood on the lake bank, his eyes fixed on a spot in the center of the large body of water. His legs were so tired that they barely held him up. He was watching for Wanda and, after a long time, she finally made her appearance.

He saw her arm emerge from the water first: no more than a long, narrow bone that should have fallen out of her shoulder socket years ago. Then her body broke through the ice, and Jess shuddered uncontrollably. Flaps of dead white skin fluttered in the breeze, and flapped against her skeletal frame.

The thing that called itself Wanda rotated in the water, until the empty eye sockets in its skull fixed on Jess. He knew that somehow she was staring at him without eyes, seeing him, envying him his life force.

"Jess!" Her voice reverberated through the boy's head, and he threw both hands over his ears, as if that could shut her out. He slid down the bank and stepped into the cold water. It was getting slightly warmer now that it was February, the ice cover no longer met the bank, and into the narrow space between the ice and the bank Jess placed his sneakered feet.

Immediately, he felt his body begin to adjust to the colder temperature. His blood flowed thicker in his veins, his skin coarsened and became slimy to the touch.

He knelt and began to crawl across the ice toward the spot where Wanda waited with growing impatience. He was very tired, his legs and arms felt heavy, his eyelids wanted to close and not open again until he was fully rested. But he didn't know if it was possible for him to feel rested again, unless he died, and that thought was really scary. Still, he could have lain down and fallen asleep on the ice, but he knew that Wanda wouldn't stand for that.

He crept across the ice until he was right next to the hole through which the dead girl made her entrance into the world of the living. Her skeletal arm shot out, and Jess closed his eyes. He cringed with terror as her bony fingers closed on his arm, and a wave of nausea washed over him. The girl's strength was phenomenal; he knew that she could easily break his arm if she wanted to. His stomach churned and he heaved, but nothing came up because he hadn't eaten anything all day.

He crawled back to shore with Wanda in tow. With her so close to him, he felt what was left of his strength ebbing away. He was as weak as a baby and he felt as if he could just lie down and sleep for hours, or days—or forever. He knew that Wanda was draining the strength from his body, that she was getting her strength from him, but he didn't know what to do about it.

Jess wished that the ice would melt away, so that he could lie down and float in the cool lake water. When spring came and the earth warmed up, the water would still be cold. It would remember the ice that held it captive all winter long, just as Wanda remembered the times with her daddy, the times before everything went wrong and she was dead, buried under the ice.

He felt sorry for Wanda, and for her pitiful, silent sisters. But he couldn't keep giving his energy to the girls so that they could get out of the lake. He knew what was happening to him, and he had to find a way to make it stop. He couldn't count on his mother or Dr. Gibby. It was up to him, Jess McCall. His dead aunt Wanda was killing him, and he had to find a way to make her stop before it was too late.

# Chapter Twenty-two

Cassie woke up coughing, and knew that she had finally succumbed to the cold that had been nagging at her for days. She glanced at the clock on her nightstand and saw that she had slept in. Mrs. Bower would show up in less than an hour, starched and prim and looking down her narrow nose at a twenty-six-year-old woman still in her bathrobe so late in the morning.

Cassie sat up and flung her legs out of the bed, slipped her icy feet into scuffs, and wondered what she should prepare for breakfast. Jess wanted nothing but cold cereal, but her father—

The memory of what he had done to her the night before hit her like a ton of bricks. She dropped her head into her hands and pressed her fingers to her temples, trying to shut the memory out, but it wouldn't leave. She would remember it always: the look of pure hatred on her father's face, the shock in Jess's eyes. What Connor had done was bad enough, but she had multiplied the horror by stripping naked in front of her father and her son. She truly wondered if she had damaged her son for life by her thoughtless actions.

Cassie wanted to cry, but she refused to give her father that much satisfaction. He had humiliated her and devastated her son; that was enough.

She slipped on a pair of jeans and an old John Lennon sweatshirt, making plans as she combed out her thick dark hair and brushed her teeth before going downstairs. She was determined to get through this one day somehow, to keep up appearances for Mrs. Bower's sake. Later, she would tell Gibby exactly what had happened, and ask him for advice. One thing she knew for sure: she would not be able to continue to care for her father, or to live in the same house with him.

She would ask Dr. Gibby to find a live-in nurse or a full-time housekeeper and a nurse who came every day like Mrs. Bower. Then she and Jess would board a jet for Phoenix and go back to their old life. She would miss Gibby, there was no denying that, but she'd get over it. There was no future for her in Winter Falls, and she was smart enough to know it.

Downstairs, she walked through the middle room without looking in Connor's direction. If he was awake, he made no sound, and she now knew that he was capable of both sound and movement. She boiled water and spooned instant oatmeal into it, stirred the mixture, and removed it from the heat. She didn't know what she'd do about feeding her father, unless Jess woke up and offered, although after last night she wouldn't blame him if he didn't. In that case, she'd leave the chore for Mrs. Bower. The old bastard can wait for his breakfast, she said aloud, and half hoped that he heard her.

Jess didn't come downstairs, and the oatmeal sat on the stove, thickening and hardening into unappetizing lumps. Cassie drank two cups of coffee, and avoided going back to the front of the house as long as she could. Finally, she walked into her father's room, stopped beside his bed, and forced herself to speak to him.

"If you're hungry, Mrs. Bower should be here in

five or ten minutes. Jess hasn't come down yet, and I know that you don't want me—"

The man in the bed made a grunting noise and turned his head to the far wall. So that was that, no contrition, no apology, no sudden change of heart. Cassie smiled grimly and walked into the living room, where Mrs. Bower was coming through the front door. Since being given a key in case of an emergency, the nurse never bothered to knock or make her presence known before she barged in and took over. Cassie resented the woman's actions, but didn't have the nerve to tell her that she wanted her to knock or ring the doorbell before she opened the door and walked in.

"How's my favorite patient today?" the nurse asked in a stage whisper.

"Connor is fine, Mrs. Bower, but he hasn't had his breakfast yet. I wonder if you'd take care of that for me?"

"He hasn't had his breakfast? Why it's almost lunchtime." She straightened her uniform and bustled into Connor's room, where she was soon talking to him in soothing tones, promising to see that he got better care in the future.

Cassie was glad to leave them to each other. She ran up the stairs and into Jess's room, planning to hustle him out of the house for a couple of hours. She intended to do everything she could to take the child's mind off his grandfather's cruelty and his own health problems.

"Jess?" she called, "Get up you sleepyhead. Come on, let's see if we can get the rattletrap started and go for a spin. What would you like to eat. What—"

He was gone, missing. His bedclothes were rumpled: sheets twisted, blankets on the floor, pajamas in a blue pool. Jess was nowhere in sight. The bathroom door yawned open. Cassie fearfully approached the tub, but it stood dry and empty.

She flew down the stairs, taking them two at a time, threw open the door, and almost trampled her son.

"Where ya going, Mom?" he asked innocently.

"I was going to look for you, Jess. Where in the hell have you been?"

"I went for a walk."

"Where? Where did you walk?"

"Nowhere, just around."

"Well, at least you wore your coat. Are you wet?"

She knew what the answer was when none was forthcoming from the child.

"Go up to your room and change into some dry jeans," Cassie instructed, and he went, past the curious eyes of Mrs. Bower.

"Where has he been this time?" the woman asked, but Cassie ignored her and passed Connor's bed without seeing him.

She was grateful that Mrs. Bower was long gone and her father sleeping when Gibby arrived for his daily visit.

"Things are falling apart, Gibby. Jess and I have to go home, we can't live here anymore. Jess will be all right in Phoenix, in the middle of the Arizona desert. This water thing will go away when we get home."

"I hope you're right, Cassie, because I'm going to miss you and Jess. All day I look forward to these few minutes I can spend with you."

"Thanks for saying that, even if it isn't the exact truth," Cassie answered. "Anyway, there's more I have to tell you and when you hear what happened last night, maybe you won't want to come by and see me again. I won't blame you if you don't."

She told him about the red velvet robe, about her father's reaction, about her father spitting on her. Gibby said, "Oh, Cassie," and reached for her but she slid her chair further away from his.

"Let me finish, please," she begged, and she could

see from his eyes that he knew something bad was coming.

"I took my clothes off in front of my father," she recited in a monotone, and Gibby's eyes flashed dangerously.

"I want to know exactly what went on here last night, Cassie. I don't want you to leave anything out."

"I want to tell you, Gibby, but it's hard. When he spit on me, I started to remember things. I remembered him . . . watching me. Touching me. Bad things."

"Connor? Oh, dear God, I never dreamed—"

"Nobody knew but me. And him, of course. My mother never knew about it, it would have killed her."

Something clicked in her mind and Cassie raised her brown eyes to meet Gibby's blue ones, which once again reflected the pain she felt in her soul.

"Do you think he told her after I left? Do you think he's that sick, that he'd tell her the one thing he knew would kill her?"

"The best thing you can do is forget about it, Cassie. It's too late to save your mother now, whatever he did. I'll find a home for him, I'll start looking tomorrow morning. As far as I'm concerned, this house belongs to you and Jess. I wish you'd stay here in Winter Falls—with me."

She shook her head and walked away from him, handed him his coat in the living room and suffered the brotherly peck he gave her before he left. Then when she was alone she cried, for her mother and for herself. For all the things they had lost, for all the things they had never known. Like love.

Mrs. Bowen telephoned early the next morning to inform Cassie that she had contracted a bad cold and would not be coming to care for Connor today. Since her own throat was sore and her cough worse, Cassie couldn't say that she didn't understand, although the woman's timing couldn't have been worse.

She had just hung up the phone when Jess wandered into her room to tell her that he was under the weather, too. His eyelids were pasted shut, so that his eyes were narrow blue slits filled with misery. He told Cassie that he was tired and just didn't feel good. He followed his mother downstairs and lay down on the couch so that he could be close to her, but he refused her offer of breakfast, and fell asleep again while Cassie was still talking to him.

She prepared Cream of Wheat, spooned it into a bowl, and carried it to her father's room.

"It's you and me this morning, Connor," she said, unable to use the word "father" when she spoke to him. "I don't want to feed you. Believe me, I don't want to have anything to do with you. But I can't let you starve to death, and if you want to eat, you'll have to let me feed you. It's up to you."

The man turned his face away from her, but Cassie couldn't detect a grimace, or the hatred that usually filled his eyes. She wondered if he, too, had caught a cold or a mild case of flu from either her or Mrs. Bower. She placed the bowl of cereal on a table beside his bed and covered it with a saucer to keep it warm.

"Let me know if you change your mind," she said, hoping that he wouldn't. Then she left him alone to go check on Jess's condition. While she was talking to the child and taking his temperature, she heard a series of gagging noises coming from her father's room. She hurried to his bed, to find that he had vomited all over his sheets and, judging from the awful smell that assaulted her nostrils, he had had diarrhea, too.

"You picked a great day to get sick," she accused. "I can't let you lie there until tomorrow, not the way you smell, so I guess I have no choice but to clean you up. And you have no choice but to let me, like it or not."

Connor refused to meet her eyes, but he was docile when she removed his pajamas and sponged off his emaciated body. He even tried to help her when she rolled him to the unsoiled part of the bed, sat him up, and lifted him into his wheelchair. There was one rough moment when she staggered and thought she might drop him on the floor, but she finally managed to get him into the chair. She shoved two clean pillows in front of him to prop him up, then pushed him into the living room so that he could look out the window.

"There isn't much to see out there," she said, "but I don't know why I'm apologizing. It was you who made us live in this godforsaken place all our lives, so I guess you must like it."

She stripped the bed next, then sprayed the mattress and the entire room generously with Lysol Spray, to kill the germs and cover the odor. A glance into the living room assured her that her father was staring out the window, concentrating on something he either saw or thought he saw in the front yard. Jess was sound asleep, his hands clenched into small fists, his eyelids moving to the rhythm of a dream.

"I'll be back in a few minutes," she said to the room, in case either of them could hear her. "I have to go down to the basement and soak these sheets before I can wash them. As soon as I come back, I'll put clean sheets on your bed, and try to get you back into it, Connor."

There was no entrance to the cellar from the inside of the house. Taking a flashlight with her, Cassie went out the back door, across the porch and down the steps, and lifted the cellar door that lay flat on the ground.

She hadn't put a jacket on over her thin sweater, and she was surprised that it wasn't colder. She

198

hadn't heard the weather report, but it seemed to be surprisingly warm for February in Connecticut.

Peering into the dark basement, she could see only the edges of the steps that led down. Using the flashlight, she moved her feet slowly, got both feet planted solidly on the first step, then moved one foot at a time to the second.

Finally, she stood on the packed-dirt floor and illuminated with her flashlight the blue metal tub that her mother had used to soak stubborn loads before washing them in the old wringer washer that stood next to it. During the ten years Cassie had been gone, Connor had evidently sprung for a new automatic washer and dryer set, which he had squeezed into one end of the kitchen. An act of kindness toward her mother? Cassie doubted it. He had probably purchased the new appliances only when his wife became too ill to make daily trips to the basement to wash his clothes.

Cassie threw the soiled laundry in the tub, started filling it with cold water using the hose that hung on the wall above it, and remembered that she had forgotten to bring the borax down with her. She ran up to the kitchen, grabbed the box from the shelf above the washer, and stopped to listen for sounds from the living room. She thought she heard something, but it was jumbled or garbled, and she couldn't make out who was talking, Jess or Connor.

Oh well, maybe they're talking to each other, she thought, aware that she had left the water running in the basement and that the tub would soon be full to overflowing. "I'll be right back," she called out, then quickly retraced her steps to turn off the water and add the borax to her father's soiled laundry.

When she got back to the kitchen a few minutes later, the house seemed to be filled with a palpable silence. Cassie felt as if a huge vacuum had sucked the life out of the house and filled it with emptiness. She dropped the box of borax on the counter and ran into the living room, heading straight for the couch where she had left Jess.

He was still asleep, talking to himself, saying "No" over and over. He was shaking his head back and forth, and a light sweat had broken out on his forehead.

"You're having a bad dream, sweetheart," Cassie said, using her hand to wipe away the light film of perspiration from his upper lip. The child opened his eyes and looked at her, warily at first, then with recognition.

"Is Grandpa all right?" he asked, and Cassie remembered Connor, sitting in his chair in front of the window.

She had her back to the window, but she inclined her head in that direction, and said "Sure he is," and kissed Jess on the forehead. For some reason, everything she did seemed to be in slow motion. Later, she would remember her every movement, in exact detail. She kissed Jess on the forehead, smiled at him, used her hand to push herself up from the couch. She stood and turned, slowly. She glanced over to the window—how many feet away from where she was standing? Five? Six? What she saw should have panicked her immediately, but it took a long time to register. Her father was gone. His chair was gone. There was no sign of him in the living room or in the middle room, which had been the dining room until he came home from the hospital.

"Did you move Grandpa?" she asked Jess.

"What?"

"Grandpa's chair is gone. Did you take him somewhere else?"

"I was asleep, Mom."

"But—" *But he's gone,* she thought, *and I was in the cellar, and you're the only one here.*

"What's wrong, Mom?" Jess climbed off the couch

200

and started walking around the living room as if he were a sleepwalker.

"Where's Grandpa?" he asked after several minutes.

The simple question snapped Cassie out of her trancelike state and spurred her to action. "Check upstairs," she commanded, and Jess looked at her quizzically. "He can't get upstairs by himself," he said, and Cassie lost her patience. "Just do it," she yelled, "just do what you're told for once."

Seconds later, the boy yelled down that his grandpa wasn't up there. By that time, Cassie had gone through the downstairs and confirmed that he wasn't down there either.

"Outside," she said to herself. But who would have taken him out without telling her? Was it possible that Connor could walk, that he had been able to hide such an accomplishment from all of them?

"Stay here," she said to Jess, who had come back downstairs and was watching her as if he suspected her of getting rid of his grandfather while he was asleep.

"He's okay," she reassured the boy. "I'll just go look outside and . . ." Her words trailed off when she realized that she wasn't making any sense at all.

She went out the front door and looked up and down the street, but there was no sign of her father, and no car parked close to the house except his own, the one that she and Jess had been using. She ran over to the car and looked inside, was tempted to go back to the house for the keys to the trunk. But she pounded on it instead, and it sounded hollow, so she was pretty sure that it was empty.

She walked through both side yards, which were narrow and overgrown with high weeds and grass. More weeds than grass, she decided. No place for a grown man to hide, especially a grown man in a wheelchair. The back yard was the same, weeds two feet high, abandoned household gadgets and appliances that threatened to hurt or maim if you stepped on one of them. She and Gibby had talked about getting a teenager from the neighborhood to clean it up and cut down the weeds when the weather got a little warmer.

There was a shed at the back of the yard, and Cassie headed for that. She was only a few feet from the back porch when she saw it: her father's wheelchair, lying on its side in the tall growth, one wheel spinning. It was empty.

# Chapter Twenty-three

She kicked a wooden box out of her way and reached the wheelchair in seconds, sure that her father would be lying in the grass in front of it. He wasn't though, and that opened up horrible new realms of possibility. Standing there, trying to collect her wits and reason out the mystery, Cassie noticed something else that was really strange. There were no ruts in the ground like those the wheelchair would have left if it had been pushed to its present position. And the grass and weeds that surrounded the chair weren't flattened.

Her heart beating doubletime, she pushed the tall growth out of her way and headed for the back of the yard.

"Connor?" she called, "Connor, can you hear me? Try to make some kind of a sound, to let me know where you are."

She stood very still then, listening intently, but there was nothing to be heard. She thought again of a giant vacuum, drawing all the sound from the world, filling it with silence.

"Connor!" she called again, "Please!" And that was when she saw him. He was lying on his stomach, his head and shoulders raised to an odd angle, his pajama top pulled up across his chest. Her first thought was that he must be cold. Her second thought was that it didn't matter. As she moved closer, she could see that his head was resting in the old wooden trough. That was why his shoulders were elevated in an unnatural way. The old wooden trough that wouldn't hold water was filled to the top with dirty brown liquid, and her father's nose and mouth were filled with it.

She didn't want to touch him, but she knew she had to do it. What if he wasn't dead yet? Maybe she could save him. She grabbed the neck of his pajama top and pulled his head up, but she couldn't move the body enough to lift him out of the water. It wanted to hold onto him, it exerted suction that pulled him back when Cassie tried to lift him out of the trough. Finally, she let go and his head fell, striking the wooden edge before it hit the murky water. Cassie's feet and legs were wet, her clothes dripping. The brown water froze on her arms and between her fingers.

She tried again, this time using one hand to lift his head, the other to yank on his arm. His head fell and struck the side of the trough again, but it fell on the outside, then bounced onto the ground.

"What happened to Grandpa, Mom?" Jess's voice gave her such a start that she almost screamed out loud.

"He's hurt, Jess," she finally managed to say. "You go inside and call Dr. Gibby. Tell him that we need him right away."

"What if Dr. Gibby can't come?"

"Jess, please, he has to come, tell him that."

The child left, backing away, never taking his eyes from his grandfather's face, which was gray and sagging, its tongue lolling, its wide-open eyes staring up at the gray winter sky. The man had fallen on his side, and Cassie rolled him over onto his stomach. She tried to remember how the paramedics

204

had worked over Jess, what they had done to try and save his life, but her mind was a blank. Still, she straddled her father and pumped on his back with her hands, trying to imitate something she'd seen on a TV live-rescue show.

Finally, when no water came bursting out of his lungs the way she thought it should, Cassie rolled her father over onto his back. She bent over him and put her mouth on his. She was immediately repulsed, and had to turn her face away so that she wouldn't gag. But she forced herself to use mouth-to-mouth resuscitation to try and revive this man who had planted his seed and caused her to be born. It was a useless maneuver and she knew it somewhere deep inside, in the place where despair breeds in the dark before it grows and breaks through to bloom on the surface of our minds.

"Daddy, don't die," she pleaded, leaning over and whispering close to Connor's ear, "you can't die when we don't have things settled between us." There was no response from him, no flicker of life in his staring eyes. She put her fingers on his neck, then on his wrist, and could detect no sign of a pulse.

"Daddy, please," she begged, "I'm sorry for everything I said. Don't die, please don't die."

When Gibby arrived five minutes later, he found her lying on top of her father's corpse, hugging it, crying hysterically.

The police arrived in several additional minutes, but Gibby had her inside by then. She sat on the couch, hunched over, drained of tears. Gibby had draped a blanket over her shoulders, since she wouldn't go upstairs to change into dry clothing. Jess sat beside her, not quite touching her, and she thought he might be trying to decide whether she was to blame. His chest heaved, and his small body shuddered with grief.

"Tell me exactly what happened, Miss McCall,"

205

Tom Barney said, standing in front of her, his crotch at exactly eye level.

Cassie related the events of the morning, which had seemed so insignificant at the time: Jess wasn't feeling well, Connor had thrown up, she had put him in his chair while she stripped the bed, etc.

"Have you ever followed that procedure before?" Barney asked, pen poised over his notebook.

"Procedure? What do you mean?"

"What I mean, Miss McCall," Barney said patiently, "is did you ever before leave Connor alone while you went down to the basement to do laundry?"

"His sheets were soiled, I told you that. No, I never left him alone before, because I never used the tub down there before."

"But you knew it was there?"

"It was there when I was sixteen. I thought it might still be there, so I went down to see."

"Uh-huh." The cop took two steps to the right and viewed Cassie from a different angle. "Do you really think I believe that someone broke into your house while you were downstairs, carried your father out to the back yard and drowned him, all in the time it took you to throw a couple of sheets in a washtub?"

"That's what happened," Cassie answered calmly, not caring whether the cop believed her or not.

"There were no tire marks in the grass," Barney persisted. "Do you expect me to believe that someone carried the man and the wheelchair out there and sat them down in the weeds before they killed him? Or maybe you want me to believe that Connor fell out of his chair and just happened to fall face-first in the water and drown?"

"Tom," Gibby interjected from his position behind the couch where Cassie was sitting, "what if there were two people? One of them could have carried Connor while the other one carried the chair."

The cop raised his hand and thrust it out in Gibby's direction. "Gibby, you and I have known each other for a long time. This is probably the first time I've ever had to ask you to mind your own business, but I'm doing it now."

Gibby rose to his full height and advanced to within a foot of Tom Barney's position. He towered over the smaller man, and Cassie thought she saw a flicker of fear on the cop's face.

"I'm afraid I can't let you ask Miss McCall any more questions today," he said formally. "She's very distraught over the death of her father."

"If that's the way you want it," Barney said, snapping his notebook closed. "Just don't either one of you decide to leave town without telling me."

"Are you insinuating that I'm a suspect in this investigation?" Gibby asked incredulously.

"If you lie down with snakes—" Barney said, turning his back on them, and Gibby would have socked him if Cassie hadn't intervened. She grabbed the doctor's arm with both of her hands and pulled it down to his side. Fortunately for Gibby, the cop didn't notice what had transpired behind his back.

Barney's barely veiled accusations brought Cassie out of her shock long enough to deal with the practical arrangements that had to be made for Connor's funeral. She sat down in the kitchen and made notes for herself, while Gibby helped with the removal of the body from the back yard, and with loading it into an ambulance for transportation to a local funeral parlor.

It bothered her that Jess didn't come around, and she asked Gibby to look at the child before he left.

"His body temperature is very low," the doctor advised after a rather lengthy examination. "Of course, it's colder than usual in here from all the opening and closing of the door this morning."

"I don't like the tone of his skin either," Gibby told Cassie when they had moved a few feet distant from the couch. "The skin has no elasticity and it feels—"

"Feels what?" she asked, suddenly alarmed.

"Damp," the doctor answered reluctantly, "damp to the touch, but that's nothing to be upset about. I want you to fix him some breakfast and I'll try to talk him into eating it."

Cassie poured some Count Chocula into a bowl, added milk, and sloshed about a third of it out onto the counter trying to pick it up. When she got back to the couch, Jess was sitting up, leaning against Gibby, looking pale and weak.

"Jess is going to eat some cereal for his old friend, Gibby," the doctor said, motioning for Cassie to bring the cereal closer. "This stuff looks pretty good, I might try some of it myself. What do you call it, anyway?"

The boy mumbled something that might have been "Count Chocula," and Gibby repeated it. "You like this stuff, huh, slugger?"

Jess nodded, a tiny movement of his head, and obediently opened his mouth when Cassie came forward with the spoon. He took a small amount of cereal and milk into his mouth and tried to chew it. He moved his jaw up and down awkwardly, as if eating were a new skill that he was trying to learn. Chocolate milk ran out of his mouth and down his chin before his mother caught it with a paper napkin.

"Swallow it, Jess," she said, and he tried. She could see him trying, see the concentration on his face, the serious effort he was exerting. He gagged and the cereal/milk mixture erupted from his mouth, splattering Cassie's face and hands.

"Sorry," the child mumbled, and both Cassie and Gibby assured him that it was all right.

"We'll try something else later, champ," Gibby told him. "Right now I'm going to drive past the pharmacy and pick up something to settle your stomach." Gibby hesitated, then leaned closer to the child and spoke again. "If you need to talk to someone about this, Jess, just have your mom call me. I know this is a tough one for a guy to handle alone, losing your grandpa when you were just getting to know him."

"I hated him," Jess said.

Gibby glanced at Cassie before he spoke again, but she kept her silence. "He was your grandfather, Jess, you didn't hate him."

"He wasn't really. He wasn't really my grandpa."

"Yes, he was, Jess. I'm sure your mom agrees with me that you should try to think well of your grandfather now that he's dead, and try to forget any of the harsh feelings you had for him. You're not doing yourself any good with this attitude."

"I'll talk to him when he's feeling better," Cassie intervened, but she didn't talk to him either that day or the next. The medication Gibby prescribed helped settle his stomach and he managed to keep a little chicken-noodle soup down, but he stayed on the couch until it was time to go to bed. He was still asleep, or pretending to be, when Cassie looked in on him the next morning before going downstairs to make final preparations for her father's burial. The second day saw little or no improvement in the boy's condition, but Gibby didn't seem to be as worried about it as Cassie was.

That afternoon, a small graveside service was planned for Connor, and Cassie had no intention of making the boy get up and dress for that.

Marilou closed The Emporium and draped the door with black bunting. She had helped Cassie compose an obituary, and it was sad for Cassie to think that the other woman knew more about her

209

father than she did. Cassie found a black dress in the back of her mother's closet, a straight, high-necked, long-sleeved funeral dress. She had no coat other than the down jacket she'd bought when she first came back to town, and Marilou insisted on lending her an out-of-style relic that partly covered the dress and kept her warm.

The service was held on what turned out to be the coldest day of the year, with thick black thunderheads lying low in the sky and a fierce wind whipping through the trees that lined the road into the cemetery. Cassie was grateful for the coat, and she smiled at Marilou as the woman clung to her. Cassie was touched to see that there were tears in the other woman's eyes and, not for the first time, she wondered if Marilou had been in love with Connor sometime in the past.

Gibby stood directly in front of the closed coffin, his arm draped protectively around Cassie's shoulders during the brief ceremony. A small knot of mourners (curiosity seekers?) listened to the minister from the Winter Falls Presbyterian Church extoll Connor's virtues and wish him a safe passage to the next life. It didn't last more than ten minutes; ten minutes to say good-bye to a lifetime of grief and misery.

Cassie threw a rose on the coffin as it was lowered into the earth and she whispered her good-byes. She wondered if it was really over, if it could possibly be over that simply.

She hurried home to Jess, who was under Mrs. Bower's professional care. The nurse had been devastated by the loss of her "favorite patient," and blamed herself for missing work the day he was killed. "If only I had been here," she mumbled over and over, until Cassie thought she would go mad if she heard the phrase one more time.

That night, the night after her father's burial, Jess

210

had a nightmare that woke Cassie from a troubled sleep. He screamed and thrashed in the bed, even after his mother arrived at his side to try and calm him.

"I'm drowning," he screamed. "I'm dying. I don't want to die, Mom."

"You're not drowning, sweetheart," Cassie soothed. "You're right here in your own bed, in Grandpa's house. You're safe, Jess, you're safe."

But her son wasn't safe, and Cassie knew it. Neither was she. Her father had carried a legacy of horror that had haunted him for his entire adult life. She knew, beyond the shadow of a doubt, that the legacy would be passed to her and, finally, to Jess.

# Chapter Twenty-four

For the next few days, Cassie moved in a trance. She called the hospital-supply company to pick up the bed Connor had used, and cleaned out the former dining room to the bare walls. Since the old furniture that had previously been in there wasn't fit to put back, she left the room empty until she could afford to refurnish it. Anyway, she hadn't decided what she and Jess would do; her plans were up in the air until the reading of her father's will at his lawyer's office in Hartford.

It surprised her that the man even had a will. Surely, he didn't have much to leave anyone, although Gibby still insisted that he was better off than Cassie imagined. And who could he possibly name in his will as heirs? He had obviously hated her and Jess, and he had no real friends in Winter Falls since Gibby's dad died. On the day after Connor's death, Cassie had spent hours on the phone in an attempt to locate long-lost relatives, with no success.

Still, the lawyer had called and said that it would be necessary for her to be present in his office on such-and-such a date, and Gibby had agreed to accompany her.

Mrs. Bower had literally moved into the house to take care of Jess, and Cassie was seriously thinking of buying a studio couch so that the nurse could sleep over. "I'm not going to be responsible for another tragedy in this family," Mrs. Bower told anyone who would listen. Taking care of Jess for the past week, she had become attached to the boy, and Cassie knew that when Mrs. Bower was there, she didn't have to worry about her son.

The child had wandered away twice in the past week, but due to the nurse's diligence, he hadn't been gone long either time. Gibby was threatening to put the child in the hospital for diagnosis of his "condition," as the doctor called it, but in the meantime Mrs. Bower took a great load off Cassie's shoulders.

It was a week to the day after Connor's death that Cassie kissed Jess good-bye and settled in Gibby's Mercedes for the trip to Hartford. She was nervous and a little apprehensive about the reading of the will. What if she was asked to pay back the money she'd taken from the business? Gibby and Marilou both assured her that she was entitled to "wages," but she had always doubted that her father would agree. And what if there was some kind of a clause that only gave her and Jess so much time to get out of the house? She hadn't been taking full paychecks for the past several weeks, and she barely had enough money in the bank to cover airline tickets to Phoenix, let alone enough extra cash to get her and Jess a place to live and tide them over until she got a job.

An hour after she entered the lawyer's book-lined conference room, Cassie exited in a daze. She was aware that Gibby shook the elderly lawyer's hand and said something about letting him know her decision soon. Then they were back in the Mercedes, looking for a place to have lunch.

At a restaurant on the outskirts of Hartford, Cassie sipped a glass of white wine and wished she had a cigarette. Gibby raised his glass and made a toast "to Cassie McCall, a very well-to-do young lady."

"I still can't believe it," she said, shaking her head.

"You know how he felt about me. Why would he leave me anything at all?"

"Who knows what went on in his mind? You and Jess are family, maybe that was enough."

"What should I do, should I sell The Emporium or try to keep it open?"

"You don't have to make any decisions today."

Cassie shook her head again to clear it. "I can't believe that Jess and I won't have to worry about where our next meal is coming from ever again."

"Well, believe it, because it's true."

"Gibby, what about the key?" she asked, remembering her surprise when the lawyer handed it to her.

"It looks like the key to a portfolio, or a diary of some kind."

"I found a diary in my mother's trunk, and it was locked. Do you think it could be the key to that?"

Gibby shrugged and gestured to the waiter. "Let's order, so that we can get out of here. When we get back to your house, we can try the key in the diary."

"My house . . . it really is my house, isn't it?"

When they arrived home in midafternoon, Cassie and Gibby completely forgot about the diary. Jess was gone, and Mrs. Bower was beside herself. It took her several minutes to remember that she had taken an important message for Gibby. When he called his office he found that he had an elderly patient who needed his immediate attention. Mumbling about why he hadn't been contacted on his beeper, Gibby kissed Cassie on the cheek, told her to call the police immediately, and headed for the clinic. Cassie was left alone to deal with what was becoming a constant problem: bringing Jess back from the lake, where he swore that he was summoned daily by Wanda.

She started to leave the house, saying a prayer that her father's old car would start, when the doorbell rang and Mrs. Bower hurried past her to answer it.

"Oh, thank God," she said, and Cassie reached around the woman to sweep Jess into her arms.

"Honey, I thought you promised me that you wouldn't go back out there," Cassie told the boy, and he shrugged his thin shoulders. He was damp and miserable, and Cassie's heart went out to him, in spite of her annoyance. When she released him and looked up, she was staring straight into the keen brown eyes of Officer Tom Barney.

"Found him standing by the lake," he said over Cassie's head to Mrs. Bower, as if the boy belonged to her. "Standing and staring, soaking wet. Coughed all the way back in the squad car."

Mrs. Bower took the boy by the hand and herded him up the stairs for a change of clothes. As soon as they were out of earshot, Barney laid into Cassie.

"I'd think you'd be watching that boy a little more carefully, after what happened to Connor."

"He was with Mrs. Bower. I thought she'd be watching him."

"Mrs. Bower still work for you?" Barney asked.

"Yes, she does," Cassie said, refusing to offer an explanation as to why she needed a nurse for Jess.

"You watch him, do you hear me? There are some mighty strange things going on in this town, and they all started after you and the boy moved here. Just 'cause you've managed to come into some money, don't start thinking you can get away with murder, 'cause you can't."

"Get out," Cassie demanded. "Unless you want to arrest me for something right now, get the hell out of my house."

Barney left, slowly, with a shit-eating grin plastered on his face. If his intention had been to get a rise out of Cassie, she had fallen right into his trap.

"See you again, Miss McCall," he called out, just before Cassie slammed the door and shut off the grating sound of his voice.

The next time Tom Barney returned to Cassie's

house, very early the next morning, he had Gibby with him. When she opened the door and saw the two men standing there, she turned and glanced at the staircase, her heart racing with fear.

"Is it Jess?" she asked, and felt herself go limp with relief when Gibby said it wasn't.

"But something terrible has happened, Cassie, and I wanted to be the one who told you."

"Wait just a minute, Gibby, let's see if Miss McCall already knows what's happened before you go telling her."

"I don't know what you're talking about," she answered, turning to Gibby for help. What could it be? she wondered, could something have happened to Marilou? "Not Marilou."

"No, it's your father's grave."

"Something happened to Connor's grave?"

"You could say that," Barney interjected. "Looks like somebody tried to blow it up to me."

"We don't know what happened," Gibby said, giving Barney a warning look. "Where we buried Connor—there's not much left but an empty hole. The casket is in pieces. There's dirt and debris all over the graveyard."

"The body?" Cassie asked, afraid to hear but needing to know.

"The body's still in one piece," Barney said, trying to get her attention back from the doctor. "Messed up a little, but that don't mean shit to a dead man."

Gibby grabbed the cop by the front of his jacket and almost lifted him off the ground.

"One more inappropriate word out of you, and I'll gladly go to jail for assault, Tom."

"Okay, okay, I didn't mean any harm."

"I think now that you've delivered the message, you can go on about your business," Gibby told him.

"Not so fast, you're not getting rid of me until I find out where the boy is."

"*The boy* is upstairs in bed," Cassie answered,

almost wishing that Gibby had choked the man.

"Afraid I'll have to see that for myself," Barney said, edging past Cassie into the house. "Oh, don't bother, I'll find my way."

"Are you sure he's up there?" Gibby whispered when the cop was out of hearing range.

"Of course, I am. I just checked on him ten minutes ago. What is this—my God, he doesn't suspect Jess of tearing up my father's grave?"

"Tom suspects everyone of everything."

"But Jess is only a little boy."

Gibby glanced toward the stairs and Cassie turned to see Tom Barney descending into the living room.

"Were you both here in this house the entire night?" Barney asked, and when Cassie nodded, he added: "Can you prove it?"

Gibby showed him to the door quickly, before she had a chance to react to his latest insensitive question. When they were alone, Cassie started to pace up and down the room, shooting off questions of her own.

"Was this something that was done, you know, on purpose?"

"Intentionally? I have no idea, Cassie."

"Could it have been an accident? A gas line or something?"

"Under the cemetery? I seriously doubt it."

"The ground is frozen solid. How strong would an explosion have to be to rip apart a heavy coffin like that?"

Gibby shook his head and extended his hands, palms upward, to indicate that he didn't have a clue.

"Were any other graves damaged?"

"Just your father's."

As soon as Gibby left, Cassie called up to Mrs. Bower that she had to run an errand, and left the house. She wanted nothing so badly as to go up and sit with Jess, and hold him until he stopped shivering and fell asleep, but she couldn't allow herself that luxury. Connor's old car started and she drove to the cemetery, which was out of town several miles to the east. At the gate, she noticed that the area around her father's grave was cordoned off, and that a uniformed policeman stood guard.

The cop watched her suspiciously from the second she turned into the drive, and he stepped forward to block her when she got out of the car and started toward the tarpaulin spread on the remains of the snow that had fallen several days ago.

"I'm his daughter," she said, inclining her head toward the outline of a body under the tarp.

The cop nodded but stood his ground, obviously having been instructed to keep everyone away from the body.

"Why is he lying out here like this?" she asked, suddenly angry. "Why can't you get another casket out here? This is indecent."

"I don't even know for sure who you are, lady, but the sergeant said they're sending another box out, and the cemetery people are going to take care of it."

Cassie supposed that he was telling the truth; he was young and seemed to be slightly intimidated by her presence. However, when she took a step to the left to see what he would do, the cop took a step in the same direction.

"I just want to look around," she said, but he shook his head and told her that he had been given orders: "No one crosses the police line."

Cassie left then and went back after dark, with a powerful flashlight from The Emporium. Marilou was at the house with Jess, who hadn't spoken or eaten since his return from the lake in the morning. Cassie was worried sick about him but she couldn't pass up her chance to see exactly what had been done to her father's grave. As she drove out of town, she only hoped that the new casket hadn't already been delivered and the damage to the grave repaired, or

218

that Barney had decided to post a twenty-four-hour guard.

The cemetery looked different at night, spookier. The tall leafless trees that lined the road threw eerie shadows onto the graves. There was a brisk wind, which bent the trees into bizarre shapes and carried a low, moaning sound across the sunken plots of the dead. She had no trouble finding Connor's grave. It was still an empty, gaping hole in the hard-packed earth. She imagined her father lying in a box inside that hole, covered by dirt, and for a moment she felt as if she were the one who was dead. She clawed at the neck of her jacket and ripped the zipper halfway down, then took several deep, cleansing breaths to clear her lungs.

When her breath started coming in measured gulps again, she noticed the moist black scattered on top of the snow. Then she noticed the splinters of wood, and the small pieces of what looked like the metal that had covered the wooden shell and reinforced Connor's casket. The undertaker had shown her samples of that material when he explained the benefits of paying a little more for an "almost indestructible" casket.

Shaken, Cassie looked around and noticed that a tree six feet or so to the left of the grave had been damaged, light strips of newly exposed bark evident even in the dark. She picked her way gingerly across the slightly sunken graves of her father's neighbors in eternity and put her hand on the tree at the point of impact. Her hand came away sticky and she stuck it under the flashlight beam to examine it.

She retched and frantically rubbed her hand on the far side of the tree trunk until she felt her own blood flowing from her palm, carrying away whatever gross human gore she had touched.

She looked around once more, and suddenly felt that she wasn't alone in the cemetery. She had the distinct feeling that someone was watching, a malevolent spirit waiting for the right moment to pounce. She ran to her car, slammed the door, turned the key, and hit the accelerator, as if the hounds of hell were pursuing her. The motor didn't turn over. She locked both doors, checked to see that the windows were rolled up tight, and waited several long, drawn-out seconds before she tried again. On the second try, the motor wheezed and turned over slowly before it died. On the third try, it caught and kept running, even though it sounded as if it wasn't going to last long enough to get her home.

She did make it to the house though, and she made another mad dash to the front door, where Marilou stood ready to let her in. One look at Cassie's face, and Marilou knew where she had been.

"Why did you go out there, Cassie?" she asked, as she led her friend to the couch and sat her down.

"I had to, Marilou," Cassie answered, "I had to see for myself what happened, what Jess or I might be accused of."

"It was bad, wasn't it?"

"It was worse than bad," Cassie answered, remembering the gore she had touched on the tree trunk, and the feeling of being watched and pursued to her car. "It was much worse than bad." Before she could consider the idea and examine it, it bounded into her mind, a fugitive from the dark jungle of irrational thought: Wanda was out there, waiting for me, watching me. It wasn't an ordinary ghost, or the spirit of someone who was recently buried there. It was Wanda.

# Chapter Twenty-five

Jess woke up thinking that he was in the lake with Wanda and her sisters, and a great sense of relief washed over him. He swallowed, and the smelly lake water ran down his throat, easing the dryness and the pain. It had been a bad night, but he would be all right now.

He had been too weak to make it to the bathroom last night, and his mother didn't know what to do for him. If she had only known to put him in the bathtub, to let him fill his lungs with water. But how could she know? She didn't know what Wanda was doing to him. He had tried to tell his mom, but he didn't blame her for not believing him.

He turned his head and felt it hit something solid. Opening his eyes, he saw that he was lying on the front lawn, in a puddle of brown, muddy water. He wasn't at the lake, after all. As he realized where he was and what was happening, the sense of relief was replaced with a feeling of panic. Maybe I'll die now, he thought, and the thought was overwhelming.

He almost blacked out, but he pulled himself back with sheer willpower, and raised his head to look around him. She was there, just as he'd known she'd be, standing in the middle of the street staring in his direction. Her two smaller sisters clung to her legs and watched him with huge, frightened eyes. They were such pretty little girls when they were out of the water, so quiet and gentle. Sometimes Jess got the feeling that they didn't want to go along with Wanda's ideas, but that they didn't have a choice. Maybe all they wanted was to be really dead, and buried like ordinary dead people. It was probably weird to feel sorry for them, but he did.

A sudden sharp pain sliced through Jess's temples, and he knew that Wanda was saying something to him. If he didn't want the pain to come again, he had to listen.

"I don't need you anymore, Jess McCall," the shrill voice echoed through his head and although he couldn't actually hear the words with his ears, he understood them.

"Then go away and let me alone," he managed to say aloud before his strength gave out.

"You belong to us now, Jess, so we can't just abandon you, can we?"

He moaned, and wished that his mother would come out of the house looking for him. Maybe if she took him back inside, she'd get the idea to put him in the bathtub again.

"You need water to live now, Jess, just the way we did before you helped us out of the lake. It hurts, doesn't it, being without water? But don't worry— when they bury you in the graveyard, we'll come and get you and take you to the lake with us. You'll like it under the ice, Jess, you'll like being there for all eternity with us."

Jess didn't answer her because he was suddenly aware that it had rained, and that the puddle he was lying in was not a trick of Wanda's, but a gift from God. He wriggled backward until his head was in the depression that held the puddle, then he turned and buried his face in the saving liquid. He gurgled and sputtered and inhaled the precious water through his nose and mouth, then rested his face in the puddle and felt his strength start slowly to come back.

222

"It won't do any good, Jess," Wanda shouted in his head. "It won't keep you alive for long. We need our revenge, and you're the only one left. If you come to us at the lake, we'll make it easier for you to die."

"No, I don't want to die," Jess whined, overcome with the knowledge that Wanda could kill him anytime she wanted.

"Nobody wants to die, Jess," Wanda screamed, her voice reverberating through the child's head. "I remember how we died now, it's all come back to me, and nobody wants to die that way. Nobody. I can't wait until your mother sees you die, Jess. Maybe she'll die, too." Wanda laughed hysterically, and it was the worst sound the boy had ever heard, but there was no way to shut it out of his head.

Jess closed his eyes and when he opened them again, Wanda and her sisters were gone, but his head was still echoing with her threats and her laughter. And there was something worse now. There were pictures running through his mind like movies, pictures of Wanda bending over his grandfather and Corey, and then two men Jess didn't even recognize. She bent over them, watching them struggle, watching them stop breathing. As the men's lungs filled with water, Wanda watched them drown, looking as if she enjoyed every second of their agony. When watching became too much for Jess, he closed his eyes and gave in to the peaceful black void that had been waiting for him.

# Chapter Twenty-six

Cassie convinced Marilou to sleep over and go home in the morning. She couldn't let her friend venture out into the dark night, not knowing who or what might be waiting for her out there. If there had been something, Wanda or something else, at the cemetery, suppose it had followed her home? She had always believed in the supernatural, in ghosts and ghouls and things that go bump in the night. Why was it so impossible to imagine that something she had always known existed had now turned on her?

Marilou slept in Cassie's bed (not downstairs on the couch, not so far away), and Cassie crawled in with Jess. She slipped her arm under his thin shoulders and pulled him close to her. His little body was so cold, so clammy. Cassie hugged him as tightly as she dared and feared to fall asleep, lest something come and take her child away from her while her guard was down.

Sometime in the middle of the night she remembered the key, and although she hated to leave Jess's side, she was anxious to know if the key fit the lock on the diary she had seen in her mother's trunk. Minutes later, she was kneeling on the floor in front of the trunk, the diary in her hands. It was exactly as she remembered, pale blue cloth with metallic blue flowers woven through the fabric.

Despite her exhaustion, Cassie felt her excitement growing as she took the little key from the pocket of her robe. It looked as if it would fit, both the key and the lock being a rather tarnished pale gold, both being small and delicate. She held the diary in her left hand and inserted the key into the lock with her right. It went in so far, then stopped and would go no further, even after she jiggled the key back and forth to try and make it fit.

Cassie was so disappointed that she wanted to toss the key into the garbage but she knew she would regret that action with the morning light. She replaced the key in her robe pocket and trudged back to the bedroom, where she collapsed into Jess's bed and fell asleep before her head hit the pillow.

Marilou awakened Cassie before dawn to tell her that Jess's breathing was becoming more labored with each hour of the night. From across the hallway, the terrible sounds had kept her awake for hours. Cassie called Gibby and reached him at home. It amazed her that the doctor sounded wide awake, even though it was only five-thirty in the morning.

"I'm so scared, Gibby," she told him, "what if he just stops breathing? I don't know how to give CPR. I might have been able to save Connor's life if I did."

"Connor was already dead when you found him in the yard, Cassie, but we'll discuss that later. Right now, let's concentrate on Jess. I'll send an ambulance to get him in about an hour. That will give you time to get organized before they get there. I'm going to admit him to the hospital in Hartford, the same floor he was on after his accident. You can ride over with him, and I'll meet you there."

"What do you think it is, Gibby, what's wrong with him?"

"To be honest, I don't know what it is, but if it's humanly possible to find out, we will, I promise."

Cassie dressed hurriedly and when she went back to check on Jess, he was awake. She sat down on the edge of his bed and told him about the trip to the hospital.

"I don't want to go, Mommy."

"It's not something I want either, sweetheart, but we have to find out what's wrong with you so that Dr. Gibby can fix it."

"He can't fix it."

"Sure he can."

"Nobody can fix it, Wanda said so."

"Do you know what's wrong with you, Jess?" Cassie asked, expecting him to say no. But the boy nodded and Cassie leaned closer to him so that she wouldn't miss his answer. "She used up all my energy to get out of the lake. Now she can stay out all the time and she doesn't need me anymore. She says she could give my energy back, but she won't. So I'm gonna die from not having my energy back."

"Oh, Jess, you're not going to die, don't say that ever again, promise."

"Okay," the child answered feebly. His head fell back against the pillows and his eyes closed, so Cassie left the room, to let him rest until the ambulance came.

Marilou was waiting for her in the kitchen with a list of questions about The Emporium, which Cassie tried to answer. To her surprise, the older woman seemed to be very interested in whether or not the store was going to be put up for sale.

"Are you interested in buying The Emporium, Marilou?" Cassie asked, pouring coffee into two stoneware mugs.

"I didn't say that, Cassie, but I do have a little savings, and I could probably get a second mortgage on my house."

"I'm sure we could work something out that would be easy on both of us." Cassie set her mug down on the table and cocked her head. "What was that noise?" she wondered.

"I didn't hear anything," Marilou answered after

listening for a few seconds.

"You're probably right," Cassie said, but she walked through the house and looked out the front window, just to be sure.

"Oh, my God!"

"What is it, Cassie?" Marilou ran into the room and approached the window to stand beside Cassie. "Did you see them?"

"I don't see anything."

"They were there, standing in the street, about halfway down the block."

"Who was there?" Marilou asked, craning her neck to try and see what her friend had seen.

"Three little girls. Three little girls in pastel dresses, standing right there in the street."

"There's nobody there now. Cassie, do you think you might—"

"Whatever you're thinking about saying, don't," Cassie cut in. She pushed Marilou aside and ran past her, out the front door and onto the grass.

She bent over the child and felt his forehead; it was as cold as the frozen ground upon which he lay.

"How did he get out here with us right there in the kitchen?" Marilou asked from behind her, but Cassie couldn't answer through her tears.

Between them, the two women were able to get the child back inside and into dry clothes before the ambulance arrived.

"How do you suppose he got so wet?" Marilou asked several times, and Cassie had no answer. At least, no logical answer.

Several hours later, she told Gibby over a tuna-salad sandwich in the hospital cafeteria that she had seen Wanda and her sisters. The way he looked at her, she knew exactly what he was thinking.

"I'm not crazy, Gibby, I saw them with my own eyes, standing in the street in front of the house."

"How do you know it was them and not some neighbor's kids out for a walk?"

"In February, with no coats or hats? Anyway, they were just standing there, staring at Jess." She didn't want to tell him that she had seen one of them before, in a dream.

"Why do you think they finally let you see them now, if they've been around all along?"

"They've only been around here since Jess's accident," Cassie explained patiently, "and I think things are coming to a head now, so maybe they actually want me to see them."

"Things are coming to a head? How do you know that?"

"Because they can stay out of the lake now, without Jess's help."

"Then where in the hell was he trying to go this morning when you found him on the lawn?"

"I think Wanda still has a hold on him. He says he hears her voice in his brain."

"Cassie, I don't know—"

"That's right, Gibby, you don't know. Nobody knows, really. Stranger things than this have happened."

"Okay, I'll grant you that. But what is it you think these girls want from Jess, or from you, for that matter?"

"They want revenge, that's the only thing they could want. I think they came back to get their revenge on whoever it was that killed them and put them under the ice.

"At first I thought it was my grandfather," Cassie went on, "and that that was why they went after Connor. But now he's dead, and they're still not at rest, so I don't know what to think."

Gibby stared at her for a couple of minutes and then shook his head to clear it. "I can't believe that we're sitting here in this white, well-lit room discussing dead girls seeking revenge on the living."

"Laugh at me if you will," Cassie answered, "but if believing is what it takes to save Jess from those girls, then I'm a believer."

Having finished their sandwiches, they collected the trash from their trays and dumped it before leaving the cafeteria and heading back to Jess's room. When they got there, Marilou was sitting in a chair beside the child's bed, watching him closely.

"Did you find out anything yet?" she asked, and Gibby shook his head.

"I'll be back in a couple of hours, Marilou," Cassie said, "I have to find out what it is that key fits, and an hour should be all I need to go through the house. Since Connor left me that key when he died, it must be important, and I think that maybe if I find whatever it is he wanted me to find, I might be able to help Jess."

She noticed Gibby and Marilou exchanging glances, but she ignored them. After she kissed her sleeping son on the forehead, she set off down the corridor. A moment later, she heard Gibby's soft footsteps behind her.

He was silent on the drive back to Winter Falls, only using his voice to form an answer when Cassie asked a question. After several miles, she couldn't stand not knowing what was wrong, and she said so.

"Cassie," Gibby answered, "there's something I haven't told you."

"Something about Jess?"

"No, nothing about Jess." He patted her hand, which rested on the seat between them. "This is about the deaths that occurred recently. Not Corey's, the other two."

"The disk jockey and the reporter," Cassie remembered.

"Right, Chick Wiley and Bob Graham."

"What about them?"

"We got the autopsy results."

"Today?"

"Last week. I didn't want to tell you."

"I'm not following this at all, Gibby."

229

"Chick Wiley and Bob Graham died of drowning. There was water in their lungs."

"But they died in their beds. That's impossible, isn't it? I mean that just proves that Wanda—"

"Hold on a minute. There is a way to kill a person and make it appear that they drowned. So far as I know, it's never been used, but the know-how was in our chemical warfare arsenal during the Persian Gulf War."

"What chemical?"

"I'd rather you didn't know. Trust me, Cassie, if you had ever taken a high-school chemistry course, you'd be in jail right now. Tom Barney has been over your entire life with a fine-toothed comb."

"Why are you telling me this now, Gibby? You obviously didn't trust me with this information last week."

"It wasn't that. I was going on the theory that a little knowledge is a dangerous thing. If Tom Barney had asked you if you knew that a person could drown without setting foot in an inch of water, I wanted you to be completely innocent of that knowledge."

"So, to repeat my question, why are you telling me now?"

"Because you seem to believe that what Jess has been telling you about Wanda is true, and if there's even the most remote possibility that it is—"

"Then Wanda could have made these people drown in their beds."

"It staggers my mind to think that it could be true."

"But it could."

"There's one more thing. I sent the water we pumped from their lungs to a lab in Hartford to be analyzed. I should be able to get the results this afternoon."

Cassie jumped up and kissed the surprised doctor on his cheek, causing him to lose his concentration and let the Mercedes veer into the lane of oncoming traffic. When he had maneuvered it back to its own lane, Gibby patted her hand again. This time, he didn't take his hand away, but let it rest on hers for the remainder of the drive to Winter Falls.

He dropped her at the house, intending to go to his office while Cassie spent the time searching for a diary or something else with a small golden lock, something that would be her last legacy from her father. She let herself into the house, threw her coat down on the couch, and started looking through the downstairs. Since the dining room was empty to the bare walls, that left only the kitchen and the living room on the first floor. In the kitchen, she dumped the meager contents of drawers onto the counter, then moved to the living room. Fifteen minutes later, she was tired and frustrated, having found nothing in either room.

Upstairs, she went through the drawers in both bedrooms and took every item out of her mother's trunk, even trying the key in the lock on the diary again, just to make sure that it didn't fit. There was nothing in the narrow linen closet but sheets, towels and washcloths, nothing in the medicine chest but aspirin and Band-Aids.

Next, she took a flashlight and made her way down to the basement, even though it was late afternoon and beginning to get dark. It was so black down there that she could hardly see her hand in front of her face, and so cold that her teeth chattered. Thinking of her mother washing clothes down in that damp, gloomy cellar made Cassie hate her father all over again. She let the flashlight's beam travel up and down each wall; she saw nothing but old paint cans and abandoned small appliances that hadn't made their way out to the yard. It didn't take long to see that the cellar held nothing valuable enough to be kept under lock and key.

Disappointed, Cassie went back to the kitchen and started looking through drawers and cabinets again, trying to be more thorough the second time. She had only been at it a few minutes when she thought she heard a horn honking in front of the house. Although the horn didn't sound again, a quick glance at the kitchen clock told her that her time was up, and that it was undoubtedly Gibby waiting patiently for her to come out.

She took time to wash her hands, shrug into her coat, and take an apple from a dish on the kitchen table. Halfway to the door, she ran back and grabbed one for Gibby.

"Find anything?" he asked when she climbed into the front seat of the blue Mercedes and handed him the apple.

"Nothing. But there's something there, something I'm not seeing."

"Tomorrow's Saturday, maybe I can take a couple of hours and help you look tomorrow night or Sunday."

"Does Jess have that long?"

Gibby obviously hadn't been expecting the straightforward question. He hesitated and looked away, staring out the front window of the car at the horizon. "I wish I could say he does, Cassie," he answered finally, "but our tests are still coming up negative."

"He's dying, isn't he? Tell me the truth, Gibby, a true friend would do that for me."

"Yes," he said, and his voice reflected the defeat that he had tried to hide from her. "Yes, he's dying. I'm sorry, Cassie."

When Cassie didn't answer, Gibby put the car in gear and pulled out from the curb. Neither of them spoke, and they were outside the municipal limits of Winter Falls, on the highway that would take them to Hartford, when Cassie touched the doctor's arm and shouted "Turn around!"

Instead, he pulled the Mercedes to the shoulder, expertly avoiding a collision with the traffic that had

232

been following close behind them.

"What did you forget?" he asked patiently.

"I forgot to look in the shed, the shed behind the house."

"I don't think anyone has used that shed for years, Cassie, it's literally falling apart. You might not even be able to reach it through the weeds and grass that have grown up around it."

"I have to try."

Without another word to try to convince her otherwise, Gibby made a U-turn and started back. Within ten minutes they were back at the house, and Cassie was running through the side yard, trampling the tall weeds as she ran.

Gibby followed her and tried to get in front of her to lead the way, but she held him off.

"Cassie, slow down and let me help you," he called out, but before he could catch up with her, she had beaten down the weeds and was lifting the rotted door away from the shed.

"Let me get that, at least," Gibby offered, "the hinges are completely rusted away." He set the door to the side and examined the outer walls of the shed. "Be careful in there," he cautioned when he realized that she was already on her way in.

Cassie stepped inside and took a few seconds to let her eyes adjust to the dark. When they did, she almost wished they hadn't. The little windowless room was filthy, with cobwebs hanging from the ceiling and several inches of dirt and rat droppings on the floor.

There was an ancient lawnmower in one corner, keeping company with a broken-handled rake and a rusted axe. There was a table, probably a work table at one time, and on top of the table was a box. A locked box. Cassie swallowed her distaste for stepping on the littered floor and made her way quickly to the table. Getting closer to it, she could see that the box was a large toolbox, and that the lock was large, too large, and silver in color. Her heart sank, and she turned to Gibby, who was right behind her.

"Wrong lock again," she sighed, and Gibby nodded—then he walked to the far corner of the shed and picked up the axe. "Stand back," he ordered, returning to the table with the axe lifted over his shoulder like a weapon. Cassie did as she was told, and Gibby swung the axe, hitting the silver lock and smashing it. He removed what was left of it, and the lid swung upward. Inside the tool box there was another box, a long narrow one that looked sort of like a fancy tie-box. Cassie leaned over it, and her heart did a flipflop in her chest. That box, too, was locked, and the lock was small, delicate, and pale gold in color.

# Chapter Twenty-seven

As soon as Cassie saw it, she knew it was what she'd been looking for all along. It wasn't a diary or a journal in the usual sense. It was several sheets of paper, folded carefully and tucked into the narrow box that seemed to be custom-made for its contents. Each of the sheets was covered with Colin McCall's large, spidery scrawl which she would have recognized anyplace.

She went back to the house and sat down on the porch to read, passing each page to Gibby as she finished it.

I am completely alone in the world and although the fates will most certainly deign that I live a long life, I feel as if I am already dead. My friends have deserted me, my wife has left me, and my three precious daughters have been taken away from me. They are dead, bludgeoned, violated and murdered as they played in the woods beside Winter Falls Lake. They were murdered by the monster who used to be my friend, Jeremy Winter.

Cassie gasped, but she just shook her head when Gibby asked what was wrong. She continued to read, lost in the lines penned by her grandfather fifty years in the past.

Less than a week ago I left them—my darling Wanda, who took such good care of me, my sweet Helen, and my tiny Lorrie. I buried them beneath the ice, abandoned them to the elements and the vagaries of time. I gave up their innocent bodies to the fishes that seek the icy depths to scavenge for food.

I have resigned my position as County Prosecutor. I could not live with the pity and the kindness, the averted eyes, the joking conversations that end abruptly when I enter a room. I have decided to open a small dry-goods store to keep body and soul together. I deserve no better.

When Jeremy came for me, to confess to me, I followed him into the woods beside the lake. I did not call the police, although I knew the procedure to be followed better than almost anyone.

I looked at my darling children, the lights of my life, and listened to my friend's halting explanation of his horrific acts. He had only wanted to play with them, to touch them. They knew Jeremy well, and they wouldn't have resisted his attempts to play with them until he became too insistent. I could see them in my mind's eye: their fear growing, their tears, their entreaties. And I could see Jeremy, not understanding . . . only wanting to play with them.

Wanda tried to protect Helen and Lorraine. Jeremy killed her first, holding his hand over her mouth until she stopped struggling. Then he raped her, probably not even realizing that she was dead.

He raped the little ones, too. They were hardly more than babies. When I think of their

236

fear, of how they must have suffered, I go mad with rage.

With Johnny Gibson's help, I buried my daughters' bruised and bloody bodies beneath the ice that was soft and melting that day. I was a coward, but I couldn't stand the thought of exposing my babies to curious eyes, and to the coroner's tools. Within twenty-four hours, the warm spell had passed and the cold weather returned. No one thought to look for the girls beneath the ice, although the search parties looked for days in every corner of the county.

After a week, the search was called off, and I held a private service to say good-bye to my beloved Wanda, Helen and Lorraine.

When I came back from the church, I drove Jeremy Winter out to the woods. On the exact spot where he had killed my children, I beat him senseless (poor choice of words) and covered his body with the new-fallen snow. I left him there, hoping that his flesh would rot, that his bones would not be found until summer, and that I would not be suspected. I had the wild thought that getting away with the crime would somehow eradicate my guilt and vindicate me for hiding my daughters' murders.

That seemed to be the end of Colin's scrawls, and Cassie turned the paper over in her hands, looking for more.

"But what happened?" she asked Gibby when he finished reading the last page. "I don't understand. If my grandfather killed Jeremy Winter, why didn't he go to jail when they found the body?"

"Wait," she held up her hand to stop Gibby's answer. "I have a lot of other questions, and I have to get them out before I forget what they are. Why didn't Colin report Jeremy to the police? An even better question: why didn't he turn Jeremy in for killing his parents? Why would he try to protect a madman like that?"

"Good questions, Cassie, but no one knows the answers to any of them. These three men were like brothers before Jeremy's accident, and their families suffered through so many tragedies. If your grandfather had turned Jeremy in to the police for killing his mother and father, he probably wouldn't have killed the girls, but, of course, Colin didn't have any idea at the time that anything so terrible would happen in the future."

"How could my grandfather continue to live with that knowledge? Even killing Jeremy couldn't have been enough, because it couldn't bring the girls back."

"I imagine Colin went a little mad after his daughters died."

"And that madness has been passed down from generation to generation. Don't deny it, Gibby."

"I don't deny it, but wouldn't it be best to let it alone now, to let it end with Connor's death?"

"It's not up to me to let it end, Gibby, my child is caught up in it. I can't just walk away from it, not until Jess is free."

"Jess is ill, Cassie. We don't have a name for his sickness yet, but we'll continue to do every test possible until we—"

"It's Wanda, Gibby. That's the name for his disease, if you have to have a name: Wanda."

"Cassie, don't."

"No! Don't look at me that way, and don't try to shut me up. I don't understand this any more than you do, but somehow my dead Aunt Wanda has been sapping Jess's energy and using it to get out of the lake where she was buried by her own father fifty years ago. Now she doesn't need Jess any more and he's going to die if we don't find a way to get rid of Wanda and reverse whatever it is she's been doing to him."

"Cassie, listen to yourself." Gibby stood up and walked down the porch steps, then came back to put his hands on the porch on either side of Cassie and lean close to her as he spoke. "You're talking about getting revenge on a dead girl, a girl who died before your father was born."

"A girl who has found a way to come back and kill my son," Cassie said, keeping her voice level, "along with several other people."

"What?" Gibby asked incredulously. "That's ridiculous, Tom Barney would never believe—"

"Fuck Tom Barney," Cassie said in the same even tone of voice, "and fuck you if you don't believe me."

# Chapter Twenty-eight

The drive back to the hospital seemed to take hours. Cassie felt as if they had been gone too long, and she was afraid that Jess would wake up and miss her. She wanted to say something to Gibby, but every time she started to open her mouth, her emotions got in the way. Maybe it would be impossible to explain exactly how she felt. He was a good friend, a wonderful man, and she respected him, but Jess was her life.

They were on the outskirts of Hartford when Gibby spoke. His deep, sensitive voice warmed Cassie's heart and helped her find the courage to go on.

"I'm sorry, Cassie, I don't know what else to say. I want you to know that I'll do anything, believe anything in order to save Jess, even if it goes against my medical training and the beliefs of a lifetime."

"Why?" Cassie asked, as tears welled up in her eyes and streamed down her cheeks. "Why would you do that for Jess?"

"Because I love him," Gibby answered simply, "because I love both of you, and I want to take care of you. I want to be a father to Jess, and I want to be your lover, your husband."

Cassie laughed through her tears, as a deep, abiding joy pushed her sadness aside. "You're crazy,

240

Dr. Gibson. Only a crazy man would want to marry an ex-barmaid when he could have his choice of pretty nurses and female doctors. And I know that's true, I've seen them look at you."

"So you think I'm crazy, do you? Well, someday you're going to look in the mirror and see what I see when I look at you: a beautiful, kind, loving woman who has filled up a deep void in my life."

Cassie slid across the seat when Gibby held out his arm and she snuggled against him as he drove the last few miles to the hospital. In the parking lot, he turned off the motor and pulled her into his arms for a deep, satisfying kiss before he helped her out of the car and across the lot to the hospital entrance.

Gibby refused to let go of her for a minute, so Cassie accompanied him to his office for a quick check of his messages before they went upstairs to see Jess. There was one message that seemed to be important, and Gibby sat down at his desk as he read it over several times before handing it to Cassie.

"What is it?" she asked after looking over the yellow sheet filled with words that she didn't understand.

"It's the lab report on the water samples from the lungs of the drowning victims."

"Well? What does it say?"

"It says the water in the lungs of Chick Wiley and Bob Graham came from Lake Wahelo."

"Oh, my God!"

"We'd better get up to check on Jess right away."

Gibby left his office door open and ran down the corridor with Cassie at his heels. He punched the elevator button several times and cursed when it didn't appear immediately at their floor. When it finally arrived, he grabbed Cassie's hand and pulled her inside, then hit the number for Jess's floor.

"You're afraid she'll come for Jess, aren't you?" Cassie asked from her position just inside the elevator doors.

241

"No, of course not. Yes, damn it, I am afraid. If those girls could kill four grown men, they could kill Jess, too."

"Thank you, thank you for believing."

"I should have believed you a long time ago."

Gibby was struggling to push the doors apart before the elevator had made a complete stop, then pulling Cassie out into the fifth-floor corridor. As soon as she saw the security guard standing outside the door of Jess's room, she knew that they were too late.

"What the hell's going on here?" Gibby yelled, and a middle-aged nurse exited Jess's room and approached them.

"The boy isn't in his room, Dr. Gibson. I'm afraid we don't know exactly where he is, but we're conducting a search of the hospital and the grounds now."

"Where's Marilou?" Cassie asked, moving closer to look around the security guard to the interior of the room. She was trying to stay calm, to let Gibby handle things, but the familiar feeling of panic was rising in her throat, pounding in her head.

"Miss Johnson went home when you didn't return after several hours," the nurse explained calmly.

"Then what happened to the private nurse I hired?" Gibby asked, his temper dangerously close to exploding. "I told you that I didn't want the boy left alone for more than a few seconds at a time."

"Miss Ryan took over when Miss Johnson left, Dr. Gibson. Around ten o'clock, she walked out to the nurse's lounge to get a cup of coffee. She couldn't have been gone more than two minutes. When she returned to the room, the boy was gone."

Gibby pushed the nurse aside and entered the room, as if he thought he might find Jess inside, in spite of what he had just heard in the corridor. Cassie followed him in, and they stood looking around the empty room, then at each other for several seconds before Gibby went into action.

"I want everyone we can spare, to go look for this child, even you," he shouted at the nurse. "I want the police alerted in every jurisdiction between here and Winter Falls. Continue to search the hospital and the grounds, even though it's not very likely you'll find him here. Come on, Cassie, I think we both know where we'll find him."

Cassie followed Gibby back to the elevator, which was being held for them by the security guard. To her surprise, Gibby punched the number two, which was where the walkway began that led to another wing of the hospital, the wing where her father had stayed after his stroke.

"Where are we going?" she asked, breathless from trying to keep up with Gibby's long strides.

"There's someone you have to meet," the doctor answered, barely slowing his pace when he noticed that she was falling behind.

"Gibby, for God's sake, slow down. Can't you have some other doctor do this for you? I don't want to meet anybody, I just want to find Jess."

"Trust me, this person may be able to help us."

Completely out of breath now, Cassie slowed down and followed at her own pace. Gibby noticed that she wasn't behind him, and he waited for her at the door to a room in the convalescent wing. When she was standing beside him, he opened the door and ushered her inside. For Cassie, it was like going back in time and stepping into her father's hospital room all over again. The room was dark, and the frail old man sat in a wheelchair close to the window. The light from the ceiling fixture played on his white hair, giving him the look of an aging angel praying in the dark.

"No," she said, "he's dead. He's dead, Gibby, he can't be here in this room alive. He can't be."

"It isn't your father, Cassie, it's an old friend of your grandfather Colin's."

243

Cassie approached the chair and peered into the old man's face. It was creased with wrinkles and puckered with age, but it contained the most beautiful, clear blue eyes that she had ever seen. When those eyes turned to focus on her face, she was transfixed. She didn't move until a clawlike hand grabbed at her blouse and the old man smiled, freezing her heart.

She cried out and tore at the hand until Gibby put his hands over hers and spoke gently. "Jeremy, you're being bad again," he said, as though he were speaking to a naughty four-year-old. "This is Cassie, your friend Colin's granddaughter, you can release your hold on her now."

The man frowned and furrowed his brow, as if there was something he was trying to remember, but he let go of Cassie so that she could move out of his range.

"Jeremy?" she asked Gibby. "Not Jeremy Winter! He couldn't be alive, my grandfather killed him."

"Colin didn't kill Jeremy that day in the woods, he just thought he did. He left Jeremy for dead, but he was found the same day and taken to the hospital where he survived his injuries. We don't know exactly what happened, and we never will. Jeremy hasn't spoken for the past fifty years."

"The authorities must have known that my grandfather tried to kill him."

"My guess would be that they know but they didn't care. After what Jeremy had done to Colin's three daughters, who could have blamed him for taking the law into his own hands?"

"I don't know why you wanted me to see him now, Gibby," Cassie said, sincerely puzzled, "when the only thing that matters to me is finding Jess and saving his life."

"We're going to take Jeremy with us," Gibby announced, taking off his own coat and draping it around the old man's bony shoulders.

"I've never said 'why' so many times in one day before, but I can't understand why you'd want to drag this man who can't even speak out to Lake Wahelo in the middle of the night."

"Very simply," Gibby answered, "I think the shock of seeing Jeremy Winter again might be what it will take for Wanda to forget about Jess and retreat to her underwater lair for another fifty years."

Cassie nodded and helped Gibby tuck the coat around Jeremy's body, then held the door while he pushed the wheelchair through.

"Are you allowed to do this?" she asked.

"Hell, no, I'll probably lose my medical license and go to jail. Come on, we don't have any time to waste chatting about consequences."

Five minutes later, Jeremy had been stuffed into the backseat of the Mercedes, his wheelchair loaded into the trunk. Cassie had no sooner slammed the passenger door than Gibby put the car into gear and sped out of the parking lot, heading for Winter Falls.

On a dark stretch of road just outside of town, Cassie thought she felt something crawling in her hair. She swatted at it frantically, and hit Jeremy Winter's hand, knocking it back into his lap.

"What the hell's going on?" Gibby asked when Cassie screamed and threw herself forward, slamming into the dashboard.

"He was touching me, he had his hand in my hair," she explained, still trembling from the contact.

Gibby touched her hair himself, smoothing it down, caressing it. She stopped trembling and relaxed, but she wouldn't let herself rest against the back of the seat again.

"There's still something I haven't told you, Cassie, but first I have to tell you how I know so much about what happened in Winter Falls fifty and sixty years ago. My grandfather had a mild heart attack when he was only thirty-five. Although my father was little

245

more than a boy at the time, my grandfather told him everything that he knew about Colin McCall and Jeremy Winter. My dad always thought that knowledge of all that evil took my grandfather to an early grave. The second heart attack, a year later, killed him.

"As soon as I finished my internship and returned to Winter Falls, my father passed his knowledge of those events down to me. I think it's possible that talking about it has kept us sane, whereas living with their secrets drove Colin and Connor around the bend."

"What I want to know is why Colin didn't commit suicide," Cassie said seriously. "I think in his case that would have been the easiest way out, if he was too much of a coward to confess to the police."

"Colin's way of atoning for his sins was a simple one, Cassie. He punished himself by staying alive, by living, day after day, week after week, with the crystal-clear knowledge of what he was and what he had done. No wonder your father was a strange man, he came by it naturally."

It was at that moment that Cassie spotted Jess walking on the side of the road, and all thoughts of the "something" Gibby wanted to tell her flew out of her mind.

# Chapter Twenty-nine

Cassie had been watching both sides of the road carefully for the past several miles. She imagined that Jess had hitched a ride with someone driving on the Interstate and gotten out when the Winter Falls exit came up. It was unbelievable that a motorist would stop and pick up a small child walking on a dark road alone clad only in pajamas and not notify the authorities, but people did stranger things every day.

When she saw Jess, her throat constricted and she felt a stab of pain in her chest, in her heart. He was so small, so vulnerable. He looked sick and cold, clad only in his skimpy hospital pajamas. He was trudging along the side of the road, and she could see that each step was painful and took more of his remaining strength than he could afford to give.

"Jess," she yelled, and Gibby applied the brakes before the word was completely out of her mouth. She flung the door open, ran to the child's side, and fell to her knees on the shoulder of the road. She pulled him into her arms, and he fell against her chest, then wrapped his thin arms around her neck. While she held him, she removed her down coat and draped it across his shoulders.

"Oh, Jess, I thought I'd never see you again," she cried, and the boy's tears mingled with her own. Then Gibby was there, lifting Jess into the car, sitting him on Cassie's lap for the last mile of their strange odyssey.

Gibby pulled the Mercedes into the parking lot beside the lake, and Cassie climbed out with Jess in her arms. He wriggled out of her grasp and started to walk toward the lake, but she reached for him and held him back while she watched Gibby take the wheelchair from the trunk and open the back door to extract Jeremy.

"Who's that man?" Jess asked, ceasing his struggles with Cassie long enough to stare at Jeremy for several seconds.

"This man was a friend of your great-grandfather's," the doctor answered.

"What's he doing here?" the boy asked, exchanging glances with the doctor.

"He's going to help you make peace with Wanda, aren't you, Jeremy?"

The old man was sitting up straight in his chair, his head turning rapidly from side to side as he scanned the surface of the lake with his pale blue eyes.

"My God, he remembers," Cassie thought to herself. When her eyes met Gibby's, she knew that he was thinking the same thing.

Gibby gave the chair a push and it moved forward with a lurch before settling into a steady pace. It moved toward the lake as if it knew the way, as if it would have moved in that direction even without Gibby's hands guiding it. Cassie and Jess walked a little behind Gibby, and followed his lead when he wrestled the wheelchair down the steep embankment. As close to the water's edge as he could get, Gibby stopped and applied the brakes to the chair's wheels.

"Call for Wanda, Jess," he ordered, and Cassie protested.

"We have to get her up here to see Jeremy, if we want a reaction from her," Gibby explained. "Call

248

out to her, Jess. If she isn't in there, she'll be around here somewhere. This has been her home for fifty years."

"Out loud," Jess asked, "or in my mind?"

"Out loud."

The boy screamed out the dead girl's name, and Cassie felt chills running down her spine. She was afraid that the girl wouldn't answer, and even more afraid that she would. Nothing happened for several seconds, and Gibby motioned for Jess to call again. He did, and they waited, only Jeremy was squirming impatiently in anticipation of Wanda's appearance.

Gibby raised his hand again, then stopped abruptly. There was a slight movement out in the middle of the lake. Cassie saw it, too: the water looked as if it was being stirred by a giant spoon. Something long and thin protruded from the ice, something white and vaguely familiar. When Cassie realized that it was an arm totally devoid of flesh, she wanted to turn her head away, but she couldn't. She watched in awe as the arm hung there for several minutes before a sudden explosion of water from the hole in the ice brought forth Wanda's head.

Not a head, really, but a skull with empty eye-sockets and streaming dark hair which spread out over the ice like a black shroud. The girl climbed out of the hole and stood on a solid chunk of ice. Putrid sheets of white tissue were flapping around her body. She looked in the direction of the shore, then reached back to help her sisters climb out of their watery home.

They were so tiny, their bones so frail, their hair so lovely that Cassie's eyes welled with tears. For the first time, she was fully aware that her aunts had once been living beings who had had their lives cruelly snatched away from them by the man who sat in the wheelchair beside her.

Although Cassie didn't hear a sound, Jess threw his hands up to cover his ears, and she knew that

Wanda was talking to him in his head.

"Talk out loud," he screamed, "talk out loud."

A loud whining noise issued from the middle of the lake, followed by the metallic sound of Wanda's voice.

"Where were you hiding, Jess McCall? Why didn't you come when I called you? And why have you brought these people who mean nothing to me or my sisters?"

Jess looked at the doctor for instruction, but he got no further. Cassie was so mesmerized by the tableau that was taking place in front of her that she hadn't realized that the girls were moving closer. When she caught on to what they were doing, they were almost to the shore. She reached for Jess's hand, but he eluded her and ran out into the water, as if Wanda were a magnet, pulling him toward her.

Cassie screamed out her son's name, and she thought that she heard her own voice echoing across the lake, her love for Jess giving her voice more power to call him back, a power of good over evil. Gibby took three or four long strides into the water, then dived forward, knocking into the block of ice which held the three girls. They toppled into the cold water, bony arms flailing toward Gibby's head.

Gibby ducked to avoid being struck, and suddenly one of them had Jess. They had climbed onto another chunk of ice and they were moving to another piece, trying to make their way back to the center of the lake. They were dragging Jess along with them.

Just then Jeremy started to move in his chair, to rock it back and forth until it was dangerously close to toppling over. He gurgled and sputtered and made obscene noises until finally Wanda took notice of him. She stared at the old man for a long moment, then turned to her sisters. All three of them turned back to stare at Jeremy. They could have been ice sculptures, they stood so still. Nothing moved, and time itself seemed to wait for them. Gibby stood in the waist-deep water, while Jess sat on the ice, listening for Wanda's next command.

"It's him," the girls screamed out in unison, breaking the silence. "It's the one who did this to us, it's him." Then there was another moment of silence before they shouted again: "Jeremy . . . Jeremy Winter."

Jess was forgotten as they started back to the shore, moving quickly and sure-footedly toward the spot where Jeremy waited, his eyes sparkling with anticipation. When Wanda drew close to him, he threw himself forward and swiped at her body with his thin arms. Wanda brought down her hand and Jeremy's arm snapped in two, the bottom half of it falling into the water, leaving a bloody trail.

Jeremy howled in pain, but it sounded as if he was laughing at the same time. Cassie heaved and tried to avert her eyes from the bloody stump that dangled from the sleeve of Jeremy's bathrobe and dripped bright red blood onto Gibby's expensive Burberry coat. She wanted to help him with what was left of his arm, but she was rooted to the spot. While she was watching Jeremy, Gibby had rescued Jess from the block of ice, and brought him back to the shore. Cassie wrapped her arms around him and held onto him as tightly as she dared. He was shaking with cold, and he had lost the down jacket somewhere, so she rubbed his arms and his cheeks to keep them from freezing. When she looked up, Wanda was staring at Jess.

Then Jeremy grunted and started making obscene noises again, teasing Wanda without the use of words. Before Cassie knew what was happening, Wanda, Helen and Lorraine were all on top of him in the wheelchair, ripping at his flesh, tearing at his hair. They dragged him out of the chair and threw him onto the ground, then jumped on top of him again, beating at his head with their bony hands.

Gibby ran to Jeremy's defense and tried to drag the

three girls off his body. Within seconds, he was on the ground beside Jeremy, with the girls pounding him. Cassie saw blood streaming from a wound in his forehead, and she went crazy.

She sat Jess on the ground and ran to Gibby's side. Shuddering with revulsion, she grabbed Wanda's arm and twisted the girl around so that they were facing each other. When she looked into the girl's empty eye-sockets, she saw them filled with lustrous brown eyes, the eyes of a child who would have grown to be a beautiful woman if Jeremy Winter had not killed her. Then the brown eyes faded away, and the mad, vengeful Wanda was back.

Ignoring Cassie, she and her sisters dragged Jeremy Winter's body, pushed it around the ice, and maneuvered it out to the middle of the lake.

Jess crawled to Cassie's side to watch the sisters drag their prey across the ice. Then suddenly, he was gone from her side, racing into the water, climbing onto the ice, struggling toward the last spot where they had seen Jeremy. It took both Cassie and Gibby to bring him back, and prevent him from following the old man to his grave.

"Stop it," Jess screamed, kicking at his mother and trying to push her away from him, "they're taking my grandpa."

"That's not your grandpa, Jess," Cassie tried to reason with him, "your grandpa died three weeks ago."

"He wasn't my grandpa. Let me go. I want my grandpa Jeremy."

The child was beating on Cassie's chest with almost superhuman strength, and she turned frightened eyes to Gibby.

"Gibby, help me. Tell him—" But what she saw in the young doctor's eyes stopped her cold.

"You're the one who did this," she accused, "you're the one who told him that Jeremy Winter is his grandfather. Why? Why would you do something like that? Something so terrible—"

"Because Jeremy is the boy's great-grandfather. It's the truth, Cassie, I swear it is, and the boy needed to know. Jeremy Winter just gave up his life to save Jess, and your father wouldn't even talk to him. Jess felt as if he had lost everything. He needed to know that there was someone else."

"Not Jeremy Winter. You're lying. I don't believe you."

"Why do you think your father was so hard on you, Cassie? Why do you think he slapped you around when you were a little girl? Maybe it was because he feared that both you and he had inherited a legacy of madness from Jeremy Winter. You weren't supposed to be born, Cassie, you were a mistake. Your father intended to let the Winter lineage end with him. But your mother refused to have an abortion and your father had to face the fact that now there were two descendants of Jeremy Winter. Your every small rebellious act infuriated your father because it reminded him of his biological father. Did he ever tell you how his mother died, did he ever talk to you about that?"

"She died of pneumonia, the year after my father was born. Don't look at me like that, Gibby, he wouldn't lie to me about something like that."

"Your grandmother committed suicide, Cassie, she overdosed on sleeping pills. She didn't want to live anymore after Jeremy Winter raped her and made her pregnant."

"Liar, liar, don't you dare lie to me about my own grandmother." Now it was Cassie who was futilely beating on the doctor's chest with her fists, desperate to make him take back the terrible words that were turning her world upside down.

"It was his last act of violence, Cass, and your grandfather—the man you always thought was your grandfather, Colin McCall—put him in a wheelchair for life for doing it."

"Why didn't you tell me? Why in the hell did you tell Jess and not tell me?"

"I was going to, but you were so vulnerable. I only told Jess because he was suicidal over losing his only grandfather under such dreadful circumstances. I was going to tell you tonight, but I didn't have a chance. Forgive me, Cassie, I was only trying to help you."

"You didn't have any right to keep it from me. How long have you known?"

"A long time," he answered wearily, "too long," and Cassie understood what a heavy burden he had been carrying for her sake.

She turned her attention back to Jess, who had grown quiet in her arms. She looked carefully at his pale little face, and traced the thin white scar on his throat. Then she let herself look deep into his clear blue eyes, his eyes so identical to Jeremy Winter's eyes.

"Let's go home now, champ," Gibby said, lifting the boy out of his mother's arms. Then Cassie could hear him talking softly to the child as he carried him back to the car.

"I'm going to marry your mother, Jess," she heard him say, "and I'll be your daddy then. Is that okay with you?"

By way of answer, Jess lifted his head from the doctor's shoulder just long enough to plant a big smacking kiss on his cheek.